Christmas is irresistible – sparkling,
exciting and so romantic!

There's shopping, decorations, parties, presents,
visiting family and friends; the festive atmosphere
is just laden with love and perfect for

CHRISTMAS
Proposals

Three brand-new stories from top
romantic novelists

"**Carole Mortimer** dishes up outstanding reading
as she blends dynamic characters, volatile scenes,
superb chemistry and a wonderful premise."
—*Romantic Times* on *Married by Christmas*

"**Marion Lennox** pens a truly magnificent tale.
The romance is pure magic and the characters
are vibrant and alive."
—*Romantic Times* on *A Royal Proposition*

"The characters are so rich and in-tune
with one another."
—*Romantic Times* on *The Tycoon's Proposition*
by **Rebecca Winters**

CHRISTMAS
Proposals

CAROLE MORTIMER
REBECCA WINTERS
MARION LENNOX

*M&B™ and M&B™ with the Rose Device
are trademarks of the publisher.*

*First published in Great Britain 2006
by Harlequin Mills & Boon Limited, Eton House,
18-24 Paradise Road, Richmond, Surrey TW9 1SR*

CHRISTMAS PROPOSALS © by Harlequin Books S.A. 2006

The publisher acknowledges the copyright holders of the
individual works as follows:

Her Christmas Romeo © Carole Mortimer 2006
The Tycoon's Christmas Engagement © Rebecca Winters 2006
A Bride For Christmas © Marion Lennox 2006

ISBN 13: 978 0 263 85509 8
ISBN 10: 0 263 85509 0

101-1106

*Printed and bound in Spain
by Litografía Rosés S.A., Barcelona*

Her Christmas Romeo

CAROLE MORTIMER

Carole Mortimer was born in England, the youngest of three children. She began writing in 1978, and has now written over one hundred books for Harlequin Mills & Boon. Carole has four sons, Matthew, Joshua, Timothy and Peter, and a bearded collie called Merlyn. She says, 'I'm happily married to Peter senior; we're best friends as well as lovers, which is probably the best recipe for a successful relationship. We live on the Isle of Man.'

CHAPTER ONE

'HOLD the lift! Shoot, shoot, sh-ooot! *Aargh!*'

Her mad dash to get in the staff lift before the doors closed failing miserably, Juliette came to a frustrated stop. Except that she didn't. Stop, that was.

The three-inch stiletto heels on her knee-high boots, wet from the snow falling heavily outside, found no traction on the marble floor whatsoever, so that instead of stopping Juliette skidded unsteadily along the floor, an expression of complete panic on her face as she slid towards the closing metal doors of the lift, seeming to gain speed as she went.

In those brief few seconds—and she really couldn't have said how many—everything was happening in slow motion, her whole life flashing before her. And what a complete and utter disaster *that* was…

But at the very last second the lift doors miraculously stopped closing and began to open again—slowly, painfully slowly, but enough that she didn't hit solid metal after all, just fell into the lift instead.

Or at least she would have done, if one of the stiletto heels on her boots hadn't caught and stuck in the gap between the lift shaft and the lift itself, holding her foot immobile but hurling her torso forward.

The whole thing might—only might—have been funny.

If she hadn't had an audience to her comic turn.

But the man who seconds ago had stepped into the lift, and had obviously pressed the button to ascend, had unfortunately witnessed the whole incident.

And so it was, as Juliette hurtled into the lift head-first, strong arms reached out to catch her. Which was very unfortunate for the man, because Juliette had instinctively thrust her umbrella out in front of her in an effort to regain her balance as she began to slide. Luckily for him, it had one of those stubby ends, rather than a pointy one, otherwise she would have skewered him with it.

'Are you okay?' he asked with concern, even as he steadied her into an upright position.

Did she *look* okay?

She had just hurtled across ten feet of marble at what had felt like the speed of sound—only to come to a bone-wrenching halt as the heel of her boot became stuck.

To make matters worse, she'd probably ruined her boots, and she'd only had them a week—a present to herself for having successfully completed a month of working at the job from hell. Because the lingerie department in this prestigious store, in the run-up to Christmas, certainly qualified as that! And, with 'just five more shopping days till Christmas', it only promised to get worse...

'Let's have a look at your boot,' the man murmured as he released her and bent down to inspect the damage, giving Juliette an uninterrupted view of the top of his head.

She hadn't been able to look at him before—at first because she'd been travelling too fast to focus on anything, and then because her embarrassment at having literally thrown herself into his arms had been too acute.

She didn't recognise the top of that dark head, the hair thick and ebony, but nevertheless she knew the man had to work at Romeo's, too. Otherwise he wouldn't have been getting into the staff lift in the first place. Probably one of the office bods from the sixth floor; they didn't socialise with the sales staff.

'It—seems—to—be—stuck,' the man muttered, his words interspersed with efforts to release the stiletto heel—and Juliette with it—from the hole it was trapped in.

Well, whoever he was, he certainly wasn't any rocket scientist, Juliette thought disgustedly as she glared down at him. She could have told him that much herself.

This had not been a good day so far, and it certainly wasn't getting any better.

And this man's fingers, as they encircled the slenderness of her ankle, weren't helping, either. His ringless hands were long and tapered, artistically so—not the sort of hands any red-blooded woman could ignore while she still had breath in her body.

He was probably ugly as sin, she decided self-mockingly. With her track record, how could it be any different? A university student who had lied about his age, knowing she didn't go out with younger men. Another man who'd turned out to be married with three young children. And another one who was gay and had just been using her to hide the fact from his family.

The man looked up. 'Perhaps if we were to remove the boot this might be a little easier…?'

No, he wasn't ugly. Sinfully good-looking might be a better way to put it perhaps!

That public-school voice didn't sound in the least foreign, but the man definitely had a Mediterranean look about him. His skin was dark and swarthy—only the deep blue of his eyes at variance with that olive colouring.

He raised dark brows as Juliette continued to stare down at him. 'The boot…?' he prompted.

Idiot, she chided herself ruefully. She had just done a good impression of an elephant trying to perform *Swan Lake*, and now she was caught up in the way he looked! While he probably thought she was a total klutz…

Which she undoubtedly was, Juliette accepted, feeling horribly self-conscious. Could today get any worse? Given the way her luck had going lately, the answer to that was *yes*, it certainly could!

'Of course.' She moved awkwardly to unzip the boot, stepping out of it to move into the lift—her hopalong performance making her look something like Quasimodo, she was sure.

Not that it particularly mattered how she appeared to this man, she decided now that she could get a better look at him. His suit was obviously expensively tailored, the black leather shoes hand-made and the white shirt definitely looked like silk.

One of the executives of Romeo's, then, she acknowledged with disappointment. A man hardly likely to so much as notice that one of the temporary female Christmas staff was even alive! Despite the fact she had just launched herself at him, hitting him solidly in the chest with her umbrella. No doubt he was right now rueing the fact that he had arrived late this morning, because otherwise he wouldn't have met her at all.

'There you go.' He held up her boot triumphantly, then grimaced at the badly grazed heel, at the same time stepping forward into the lift so that the doors were at last able to close.

'It doesn't matter.' Juliette kept her gaze averted from his as she bent to put the boot back on. 'Thanks, anyway,' she added awkwardly, choosing to look down at his expensively shod feet rather than at the man himself.

'At least you weren't hurt,' he said encouragingly.

Her pride was in tatters, but, no, she wasn't physically hurt! Maybe if she had been she could have cried off sick for these last few days before Christmas. She was absolutely—

'Which floor?'

Juliette looked up at him blankly. Only the fact that one of those long, elegant fingers was held poised over the lift buttons made her realise that he was waiting for her to tell him which floor she worked on.

'Four,' she sighed. 'Thank you,' she added with a grimace as the doors closed and the lift began its ascent.

With Juliette's stomach plummeting every foot of the way.

Not a great fan of lifts, or enclosed spaces, she usually chose to walk up the four floors to her department.

'Come and work at Romeo's,' her friend Lisa had prompted her five weeks ago, when Juliette had left her last job.

Left? She had been thrown out through the door so fast her size fours had barely touched the ground! 'It'll be fun,' Lisa had assured her brightly.

Fun? For the first month Juliette had been so bored by the lack of customers that she had been in danger of falling asleep half the time. But the last week had more than made up for that, as hordes of men—old, young, fat, thin, handsome, ugly—had crowded in from morning till night in search of that 'special' piece of underwear for the woman—or in some cases women—in their lives.

Why was it, she had wondered at least a dozen times, that it was only women who worked in the lingerie department? Especially at Christmas. Because some of the conversations she'd had over the last week had been enough to make her blush to the tips of her ears.

Were all men total morons, she had asked Lisa, when it came to buying underwear for the wives, girlfriends, sisters—and in a lot of cases, she was sure, the mistresses—in their lives?

'Totally,' Lisa had answered with a giggle. She was part of the permanent staff at the huge Romeo's store, but in the perfume department.

Lucky her!

Maybe if Juliette's father hadn't died when she was eighteen, or if she'd had brothers, it might not have been so embarrassing for her, but as it was—

'What's happening?' she gasped, her thoughts interrupted as the lift began to make a grating, groaning sound. Her eyes widened and she reached out instinctively to grasp the arm of the man at her side.

'I have no idea, but— ' The man didn't finish what he was saying as the lift came to an abrupt halt. The light flickered on and off, and mere seconds later they were plunged into complete darkness.

CHAPTER TWO

'OH, NO! *Oh, no!*' Juliette's fingers tightened on the muscled arm beneath her hand even as she began to hyperventilate. 'I can't— We're going to—"

'Stay calm,' the man's disembodied voice advised firmly. 'The emergency light will come on in a— There,' he said with satisfaction as a dim red light flickered on over the top of the doors, throwing a dim, eerie red glow over the interior of the lift. Not in the least reassuring!

'I hate lifts.' Juliette heard herself begin to babble. 'I only got in one this morning because I was so late. And I was only late because my alarm didn't go off. And then I missed my bus. And I had to walk. And then you didn't hold the lift for me. And I slid. And my heel got stuck. And my boot's ruined. And—'

'Are you becoming hysterical?' the man asked warily, no more than a blurred outline in the dim red interior.

The lift had stopped somewhere between floors, and

probably no one even knew they were in here. Because this was the staff lift and everyone else had arrived for work on time, instead of late, as they were. And the reason she hated lifts was because small enclosed spaces made her feel claustrophobic. And the lift had stopped *somewhere between floors*!

Juliette took a deep, steadying breath. 'No. I'm…I'm fine.' Perhaps if she said it out loud, it might feel true.

'Good. Hysteria really isn't going to improve our situation.'

She hadn't been trying to 'improve' their situation; she really was terrified.

Although not so much now, she realised begrudgingly.

'Isn't there an emergency button or something we can press?' She groped her way over to where the lift panel had been when she'd last been able to see it—only to find the man had moved in that direction, too, and her hand was making contact with some part of his anatomy rather than the lift buttons.

'Sorry,' she muttered awkwardly. Her cheeks blushed heatedly and she snatched her hand away as she realised exactly which part of his anatomy she had grabbed.

'Perhaps if you just stood still?' His voice was icy with impatience now.

Possibly because he didn't like being groped by a complete stranger in a lift, Juliette acknowledged with a self-conscious wince, as he pressed one of the buttons. A bell could be heard ringing somewhere.

'Er—I'm Juliette, by the way,' she offered, trying to regain her cool and feeling very glad he couldn't see her flaming cheeks.

'Juliette?' he repeated incredulously.

At least she thought he sounded incredulous. Although she couldn't for the life of her imagine why. Except, of course...

'Don't bother. I've already heard all the "Juliette working at Romeo's" jokes that I can stand,' she said brusquely. 'Believe me, with a name like mine, I wouldn't have even considered working here if it weren't for—' She broke off abruptly.

This man was one of the executives, after all. And this job might not be what she really wanted to do, but it was better than being unemployed at Christmas.

'If it weren't for...?' the man prompted interestedly.

'Nothing,' Juliette said with bright dismissiveness. 'And you are...?' It would be nice to put a name to the person she was marooned in this lift with.

'Rob,' he supplied economically. 'Don't you like working at Romeo's?'

'Not when I'm stuck in one of their lifts, no,' she came back evasively.

But it paid the rent, and it also meant that she didn't have to crawl home and admit to her stepmother and stepsister, not to mention her stepsister's boyfriend— the fourth and most recent disaster in Juliette's love-life, David having preferred her stepsister to her!—that her life in London wasn't the success she had assured them it would be.

She shook her head just at the thought of having to do that. 'Do you think that anyone heard—?'

'Hello? Hello, is there anyone in there?' a disembodied voice called out with concern.

'Oh, thank God!' Juliette felt weak at the knees with the relief of knowing that someone was aware they were in there. 'Help!' she cried desperately, even as she moved over to the doors. 'Please help us!' Her voice broke emotionally.

She couldn't help it. She had always had a thing about lifts, and being stuck in the dark wasn't one of her favourite things, either. Even if it was with a man who looked as delicious as Rob.

'Who's "us"?' the voice enquired.

'Does that really matter?' Juliette came back impatiently. 'The lift is stuck. And I want out!' Her voice rose, and she slapped her hand against the closed metal doors as her earlier panic returned with a vengeance.

'Don't do that,' Rob instructed firmly as he grasped both her hands and held them immobile. 'There are two people in here,' he answered the person on the intercom tersely. 'Have you called an engineer?'

'On his way,' the voice reassured them. 'Just try to stay calm, and we'll have you out of there shortly.'

Juliette closed her eyes. Calm? He wanted them to stay calm? When they were stuck in a sealed metal box, suspended God knew how far from the ground floor, with only a couple of wires preventing them from dropping like a stone, to be crushed to death in the fall?

'Okay. Thanks,' Rob told the man, his grasp tightening on Juliette's hands as she fought to be free.

'It is *not* okay!' she gasped breathlessly as she realised they were once again alone. 'I hate lifts! I hate being in the dark! I wish I'd never come here to work in the first— Oh!' Juliette was silenced as Rob muttered something under his breath, pulled her into his arms and kissed her.

She was already disorientated enough without being wrapped in masterfully strong arms and kissed in a way that made her knees weak and her toes curl!

In fact, she had never been kissed like this in her life—crushed against the hard strength of his chest so that she could feel every rigid outline of his body, his mouth exploring hers in a way that made it impossible for her to stand without clinging to him. Or was that just the result of her undeniable fear about being stuck in this lift? Whatever. Her knees were shaking. If it weren't for the fact that Rob was holding her so tightly she knew she really would have collapsed on the floor.

She hadn't had time to reason any of this out when she found herself just as suddenly released, strong hands steadying her as she would have swayed. She was grateful for the gloom in the lift as she felt her cheeks heating furiously again.

She had just been very thoroughly kissed by a complete stranger! Well…not a complete stranger; she did know that his name was Rob, and, although she couldn't remember seeing him before, he obviously worked at Romeo's.

None of which changed the fact that he had just kissed her!

'Opportunist!' she hissed accusingly, stepping back until she felt the lift wall behind her.

He sighed. 'My dear Juliette—'

'I'm not your dear anything!' she cut in indignantly. 'Keep your hands to yourself!' Trust her to get stuck in a lift with someone who wasn't averse to taking advantage of the situation, no matter how gorgeous he was! 'Touch me again at your peril,' she warned, not caring if she sounded like the heroine from a 1930s movie.

White teeth flashed in the darkness. He obviously found her indignation amusing. 'Or else what?' he enquired mildly.

He was laughing at her! First he had kissed her, and now he had the effrontery to laugh at her!

Juliette's anger rose to such a pitch she was actually shaking. 'Oh, yes, that's right—let's laugh at the poor hysterical female! Just because I'm only temporary Christmas staff and you're obviously part of management doesn't mean that I'm not going to report your behaviour to your superior!' As soon as she knew which superior to report him to...

He was leaning back against the opposite wall now, strong arms crossed in front of that broad chest. 'Why am I "obviously part of management"?'

Her eyes widened. She had just told him off for laughing at her, threatened to report his over-familiar behaviour to—well, whoever his superior was, and all he could come back with was to ask how she had known he was one of Romeo's executives!

She gave a scornful snort. 'Probably because I haven't ever seen any of the sales personnel wearing expensive Italian suits and handmade leather shoes!'

'No?' he drawled.

He was still laughing at her, damn it. She didn't care who this man was. Even if he turned out to be the Managing Director himself, she intended—

'You said you're a temporary member of staff for the Christmas period?' he asked with interest.

'And as such expendable?' she challenged him, her voice scathing. 'Well, just try it, that's all. I can assure you, I won't go quietly.' Getting the sack once had been quite enough, thank you very much.

'That hasn't been my experience so far in our acquaintance, so why should I think it will be any different once we're out of this lift?' he came back derisively.

'You—I—' Juliette glared at him. 'It's all right for you. You aren't the one who's got stuck in the lift with a pervert!'

There was a tense silence after her last accusation— long seconds when Juliette could only hold her breath at the enormity of what she had just said. She had really done it now. Not only had she threatened to report one of the management, she had just accused him of being a pervert, too.

What would he do?

She heard a noise. A low, husky-sounding noise that she didn't instantly recognise. And then she did. Rob was no longer inwardly laughing at her, he was actually chuckling out loud now!

It wasn't funny, damn it. She had ruined a pair of new boots, got stuck in a lift, been kissed very thoroughly and all this man could do was laugh at her.

'I wish I had never even heard of Romeo's!' she ground out with frustration. If even one male customer looked her up and down today, and then decided that his girlfriend/wife/mistress was 'probably about the same size as you up top', she would not be responsible for the consequences!

'Why *did* you come to work here?' Rob asked curiously. 'You don't exactly sound as if you're having a good time.'

Oh, she was grateful to have a job at all; although not excessive, the wage did at least pay most of her bills. She just couldn't remember the last time she'd genuinely had a 'good time'...

'In fact,' he continued, 'it doesn't sound to me as if working in any type of store is what you enjoy doing.'

She didn't *not* enjoy it. It was just... There was no way she could even begin to explain to this man how she had moved to London six months ago with such high hopes for her future, her job as a PA to a successful businessman having proved to be every bit as exciting as she had hoped it would. She had travelled with her boss to America, Germany and France, and it had been an amazing experience.

But all of that had ended five weeks ago. And just thinking about that was guaranteed to ensure she didn't have a 'good time' doing anything.

'Beggars can't be choosers,' she responded heavily. 'Although I may not have this job, either, after today,' she added, with sudden depressing realisation. 'I doubt Graham— Graham Taylor—my floor manager,' she explained, just in case this man's executive loftiness meant he wasn't familiar with the floor management, 'will be at all impressed with my reason for being late.' Especially as she had already been late when she'd slid into the lift!

But actually Graham Taylor hadn't seemed impressed by anything she'd done in the last few weeks. The way he had of pouncing on any little mistake she made gave her the distinct impression that he wished Personnel hadn't employed her in the first place. This morning's tardiness might just be the excuse he needed to get rid of her.

'I'll have a word with him—'

'No! No, no—please don't do that,' Juliette pleaded awkwardly. Graham Taylor ran the fourth floor with the precision of a sergeant-major inspecting his troops. He certainly wouldn't welcome the intervention of a member of upper management over how he treated his staff. The man was already sarcastic enough without that!

'Please,' she added cajolingly. 'It's very kind of you to offer—but please don't.'

'But—' Rob broke off as the main light flickered on

overhead, followed seconds later by the lift slowly beginning its ascent. 'At last!' he murmured with satisfaction.

Juliette was too bemused at the thought of being able to escape this metal prison after being stuck with a man who was anything but reassuring to care too much when the lift came to a rather lurching stop at the fourth floor.

The doors opened slowly, to reveal half a dozen or so concerned people, Graham Taylor amongst them, waiting anxiously outside.

Juliette didn't hesitate, stepping straight out onto *terra firma*, her legs shaking with the relief of being rescued. Never again, she vowed. She didn't care how late she was; she was never, *ever*—

'Juliette?' She turned at the sound of that now-familiar voice, so relieved at being out of the lift that she even smiled at Rob as he stepped out beside her. After all, it really wasn't *his* fault that the lift had broken down. She would obviously have preferred it if he hadn't kissed her, but such was her relief at that moment, she could actually have reached up and kissed *him*!

But before she could decide exactly what she should do or say now that they had been rescued, someone else spoke and rendered her—much as Rob might find it hard to believe!—completely speechless.

'Mr Romeo!' Graham Taylor's voice was full of shocked recognition. 'I had no idea! How awful that this should have happened to you, of all people.'

Juliette turned slowly, not even bothered that Graham hadn't shown the slightest concern for her, and looked at the man who had been stuck in the lift with her.

Mr Romeo?

As in Roberto Romeo? Owner of the international chain of prestigious Romeo's stores?

CHAPTER THREE

THIS couldn't be happening to her! Not on top of all the other disasters that had befallen her recently.

'I'm sure, Graham, that Juliette believes being stuck in a lift was an awful thing to happen to her, too,' Rob answered the other man derisively, blue eyes dark with amusement at the look of stunned disbelief on Juliette's face as she stared at him. 'In fact,' he added, stepping forward and taking a firm grasp of her arm, 'I think it might be a good idea if we took Juliette upstairs and gave her a restorative glass of brandy.'

He was Roberto Romeo!

What had she said to him while they were in the lift? Besides calling him an opportunist and a pervert, of course...

Besides calling him those names? Weren't they enough to merit instant dismissal?

God, yes. And he was suggesting giving her a brandy in order to soften the blow.

Her pale cheeks became flushed as she looked at him

with accusing green eyes, her deep red hair loose about her shoulders. 'I'm sure it's very kind of you to suggest it, Mr Romeo—' her tone implied the opposite '—but I—'

'You have no objections to Juliette coming upstairs with me for a while, do you, Graham?' Rob ignored her refusal and spoke to the fourth-floor manager.

Juliette looked at the older man from beneath lowered dark lashes, able to see, even if Roberto Romeo—*Roberto Romeo*, for goodness' sake!—couldn't, that Graham was far from pleased at the idea of one of his temporary Christmas staff being taken upstairs to that holy-of-holies the executive floor. In fact, he didn't seem to like it at all as he shooed his curious staff back to their departments in order to give himself time to formulate an appropriate answer.

Well, he didn't have to worry on her behalf; she wasn't too thrilled at the suggestion herself. Roberto Romeo was giving every appearance of being a concerned employer, but she very much doubted he was the sort of man to make a scene in public, anyway. And the executive suite on the sixth floor, at only nine-thirty in the morning, would be empty of all but the two of them. An ideal time and place to tell her to seek other employment!

'I would really rather just get straight back to work.' She addressed her employer, just wanting to get away. The Christmas music playing over the tannoy system and the extensive Christmas decorations and lights were doing nothing to lighten her heavy mood. But if she could just manage to keep her head down for the rest of the day, perhaps—

Who was she kidding? Roberto Romeo wasn't likely to forget their time in the lift, or their conversation, any more than she was—let alone allow her to continue working in his store.

'That's very commendable of you, Juliette,' he answered dryly, amusement still darkening those incredible blue eyes. 'But I think a visit to the shoe department may be in order first. Your boots *are* ruined,' he added ruefully as Juliette looked totally bewildered by his suggestion. 'And Romeo's owes you a replacement pair.'

Juliette eyed him suspiciously. Was he playing with her? Lulling her into some false sense of security?

The blankness of his expression gave her no insight as to whether that was what he was doing or not. But that didn't change the fact that Romeo's wasn't responsible for the damage to her boot; her own clumsiness was responsible for that.

'Perhaps you could organise that for me with the shoe department, Graham?' Roberto Romeo instructed, before Juliette could assure him that new boots would not be necessary.

Juliette gave a dismayed glance in the manager's direction; Graham was used to giving orders, not receiving them, and, no matter how pleasantly the request might have been made, there had been a steely edge to Roberto Romeo's voice that had let everyone know the suggestion had better be carried out, or Graham would answer to him for the omission.

'Of course, Mr Romeo.' The older man made a quick recovery and answered briskly, but the fact that he didn't even glance in Juliette's direction as he did so told her that she would answer to him later for putting him in such a position in the first place.

Great. She wasn't Graham's favourite person anyway; this could only make that situation worse.

It was okay for Roberto Romeo. From what she'd been able to gather, he usually turned up for a few days—it had to be her luck that he had turned up today—threw his weight around while he was there and then left again, leaving underlings like Juliette to the mercy of floor managers like Graham Taylor. Although, after this morning, that might no longer be any of her concern...

'Good.' Roberto Romeo nodded briskly before turning back to Juliette. 'You're sure you wouldn't like a few minutes to recover from your ordeal?'

That depended on which ordeal he was referring to. Being stuck in the lift in the first place, or discovering that the man who had kissed her was Roberto Romeo himself?

Because she wasn't likely to forget that kiss in a hurry. She had been completely overwhelmed at the time, responding in spite of herself, and she felt even more so now that she knew the man doing the kissing had been Roberto Romeo, the multimillionaire owner of the worldwide Romeo's chain.

Of course, she did have an excuse for her ignorance in that she'd never seen him before—she would definitely have recognised him if she had, and perhaps been a bit more circumspect in her remarks. Perhaps. Because, actually, she really had been too freaked out most of the time to care *who* she'd found herself stuck in the lift with!

But Lisa, the old schoolfriend who was responsible for Juliette getting this job in the first place, had talked of her employer several times since Juliette had moved to London. Consequently, she knew that Mr Romeo was single, aged in his mid-thirties, of Italian descent—obviously, with a name like that!—and that he had started off with one store ten years ago in Milan, and now had one in every major capital city in the western world.

This was the first time, as far as Juliette was aware, that he had visited his London store in some months.

She couldn't help wishing he hadn't decided to pay a visit this time, either!

'I'm fine,' she assured him briskly. 'Absolutely fine.' She flicked the thickness of her hair back over her shoulders and looked up at him.

And instantly wished she hadn't; those intense blue eyes were still laughing at her! Well, at least he found the situation funny—which was more than could be said for her.

'If you'll both excuse me?' she added frostily, not even waiting for a reply before she turned on her damaged heel and strode off towards the staffroom, where she intended leaving her coat and umbrella before starting work.

And trying to regain some of her shaky self-confidence before she had to face the curiosity of the people she worked with. Not to mention the wrath of Graham Taylor...

'So what's he like?' Lisa grinned with unabashed curiosity as she slid her lunch tray onto the table before sitting down opposite Juliette.

Juliette didn't even try to pretend not to know which 'he' her friend was referring to; every member of staff who had spoken to her this morning had asked her the same question. But she doubted that she should tell Lisa, or any of those other people, the terms she had used to describe him this morning—terms like 'opportunist' and 'pervert', let alone the 'arrogantly mocking' she had added to that list.

'Okay, I suppose,' she answered dismissively, her hands cradling the cup of coffee she had opted for instead of lunch. 'If you like the tall, dark and handsome type.'

'Doesn't everyone?' Lisa chuckled. 'Besides, I didn't mean what does he *look* like. I know what he looks like. And don't tell me that you don't like the tall, dark and handsome type, because I know for a fact that you do!'

Of course she did, Juliette acknowledged ruefully; the two of them had been friends since they were eighteen years old. Lisa knew of all her disastrous romantic entanglements—and that, without exception, all of those men had been 'tall, dark and handsome'!

She gave a shrug. 'Being stuck in a lift together isn't particularly conducive to getting to know what a person is like.' Except she knew that Roberto Romeo stayed calm in a crisis. That he was self-confident. Had a wicked sense of humour. And his kisses were bone-melting...

Although she certainly had no intention of sharing that particular fact with Lisa. With anyone, in fact.

Besides, she had spent a very tense morning waiting for someone—probably Graham—to tell her that her employment at Romeo's was at an end. In fact, she had been so preoccupied as she'd waited for that summons that she hadn't even been bothered by some of the more personal remarks made by her male customers. It was also the reason she was only having coffee for her lunch; her normally healthy appetite had completely deserted her.

Lisa shook her head, still grinning. 'It could only happen to you,' she said affectionately.

Yes, it *could* only happen to her! Her adult life so far seemed to have been one disaster after another, so why should she have thought her time working at Romeo's would be any different? She hadn't; not really.

Although being stuck in a broken-down lift with the owner of the company was definitely a first!

'It *did* happen to me.' She grimaced, putting her head in her hands. 'And I'm not sure Graham is going to forgive me for it.' The man had been dogging her footsteps all morning, picking her up on every little thing she did wrong. And as for the replacement boots Roberto Romeo had requested for her—Graham hadn't so much as mentioned the subject.

Lisa wrinkled her nose. 'What *is* that man's problem?' She shook her head, well aware of the manager's sour nature. 'He can hardly blame *you* for a malfunctioning lift.'

Juliette had a feeling that the fourth-floor manager could—and did—do exactly what he pleased. And before the end of the day she was sure it would please him to show her the door!

'He'll find a way.' She nodded, her mood lightening slightly in the face of Lisa's good humour. 'You and I both know that Graham is—' She broke off as she became aware that Lisa was making faces at her across the table, her gaze moving pointedly to the left. What on earth—?

'Graham is *what*, Juliette?' an icy cold voice prompted from behind her.

Graham Taylor's icy cold voice!

That was it, Juliette decided with an inner groan; she was just going to pick up her things from the staffroom, try to make her way home without further incident, take herself to bed and then pull the duvet over her head and stay there until this so-called festive season was well and truly over. Because it was highly unlikely she was going to find anything to feel festive about today!

She swallowed hard, slowly putting her coffee cup down before standing up to face the man who was fast becoming her nemesis. 'Graham,' she greeted him lightly, forcing a bright smile to her lips, putting both hands behind her back and crossing her fingers before making her next remark. 'I was just telling Lisa how much I enjoy working at Romeo's, and what a wonderful manager you are to work for.'

The crossed fingers didn't seem to be working. His expression darkened ominously.

Not that she had thought that it would work. She was sure that Graham was all too aware that she liked him no more than he liked her. She decided to change the subject entirely. 'Were you looking for me?'

Graham continued to stare at her coldly for several long seconds, and then nodded his head abruptly. 'Mr Romeo telephoned down a few minutes ago. He would like you to go upstairs to his office.'

'What? Now?' she gasped, glad she had only had coffee for her lunch; she might actually have been sick otherwise.

The manager gave a humourless smile. 'Well, I hardly think that he meant tomorrow, Juliette.'

Probably because—as they both knew!—she wouldn't even be here tomorrow!

This exchange was typical of Graham's unpleasant manner; 'never be pleasant when you can be sarcastic instead', seemed to be his motto. Although it was a side of himself, Juliette had noticed, that he never showed to the customers or other senior staff.

'I'll go up now.' She nodded awkwardly before moving away.

However, she had no intention of taking the lift up to the top floor. With the way her luck was going today, it would probably break down again.

And, much as she didn't relish this meeting with Roberto Romeo, she didn't wish that on herself, either!

CHAPTER FOUR

'THERE was no need to rush, Juliette.' Roberto eyed her across the width of his desk as she stood facing him, puffing obviously, her face flushed from the effort of running up the stairs.

She really would have to make an effort to join a gym, Juliette told herself as she tried to calm her breathing. She hadn't realised until now just how out of condition she was.

Although the real reason for her being so discomposed, she knew, was seeing Roberto Romeo again—and knowing exactly who he was—rather than having hurried up four flights of stairs.

To make matters worse, he was obviously completely calm and relaxed as he lounged back in a leather seat behind a leather-topped desk, his jacket hanging neatly behind the door, his shoulders very broad in the white silk shirt.

He really was one of the most handsome men she had ever seen—his hair so dark it shone like ebony, his skin healthily Mediterranean, making the blue of his eyes even more startling.

'I didn't rush,' she assured him, still slightly breathless. 'I just preferred to walk up rather than use the lift.'

He grinned in acknowledgement, his teeth very white against his olive-coloured skin. 'I can't say I blame you after this morning,' he commented, his gaze moving down the length of her legs. 'No new boots yet?' He raised dark brows.

Nor ever likely to be, if Graham had his way.

'Not yet,' she evaded, having no desire to get into a negative conversation about one of this man's managers. She was already well aware who was going to come out worst in this conversation!

'Hmm.' Roberto looked at her speculatively over the top of steepled fingers as he rested his elbows on the desk-top. 'Do sit down, Juliette,' he invited her smoothly.

Was that so that there was no danger of her falling down when he sacked her? Probably. Well, he needn't worry. She had no intention of doing that. Anyway, she wasn't altogether sure that what happened in the lift earlier had all been her fault. Most of it, maybe. But if he had just introduced himself properly in the first place, rather than just saying 'Rob', then she would have at least refrained from calling him insulting names. In fact, she didn't think it was fair of him to blame her at all!

She ignored his invitation to sit down; standing only five feet four inches, she was virtually on the same level as him when he sat down, anyway. 'You behaved badly this morning, too, you know.' She launched straight into a pre-emptive defence as she frowned at him. 'For instance,' she continued, before he had time to interrupt, 'if you hadn't kissed me, I wouldn't have needed to call you those names.'

'An opportunist and a pervert,' he silkily reminded her.

Juliette winced. No, he certainly wasn't going to forget any of that in a hurry!

'Well…yes,' she agreed reluctantly. 'But I was upset. And frightened. And, yes, slightly hysterical,' she conceded grudgingly as he gave her a mocking glance from beneath his brows. 'I shouldn't have called you those names, I realise that, but I really don't think that it's fair you should sack me because of it. It isn't as if I was screaming and shouting all over the place. I just panicked for a few minutes, that's all. I don't like lifts. I never have. I'm not too keen on being in the dark, either. But I really think your kissing me was much worse than anything I did to you—'

'Juliette, could you just back up a couple of sentences?' Roberto interrupted softly, those blue eyes no longer full of good humour.

She eyed him warily. 'To the fact that I'm not too keen on being in the dark?'

He gave an impatient shake of his head. 'The part about my sacking you.' He stood up to move around the desk, very tall and powerful in the confines of the office. 'You think I asked you up here in order to *sack* you?' He was frowning darkly.

Juliette felt confused. 'You mean you didn't?'

He leant back against the desk, looking at her bewildered expression. 'As a matter of fact, no,' he told her, sounding slightly bewildered himself. 'I have managers, personnel people, who usually deal with that sort of thing.'

Managers like Graham Taylor, Juliette thought with a mental grimace.

Because even if Roberto didn't intend sacking her, she had a feeling that after her remarks in the staffroom earlier Graham would still find a reason for doing it!

'What is that?' Roberto enquired slowly. 'Every time I mention managers... I noticed a certain...restraint between you and Graham Taylor earlier,' he explained as Juliette eyed him warily.

Restraint? For some reason—and she really didn't have any idea what that reason could be—Graham had taken a dislike to her from the moment the woman from the personnel office had taken Juliette to the fourth floor and introduced the two of them. And it really wasn't anything Juliette had said or done to the manager, because she needed this job too much to be anything but completely compliant and agreeable to anything asked of her.

But she was surprised that Roberto, in the short time he had seen them together, had noticed that restraint.

'And, considering I asked Graham three hours ago to see to a new pair of boots for you...' Roberto continued, before Juliette could come up with a noncommittal answer.

'Oh, that's my fault,' she assured him brightly, very aware that this man was now standing mere inches away from her. And also aware that he had kissed her, and she had accidentally groped him; not exactly a good starting point between the owner of the company and one of his minions. Less than a minion, really! 'I haven't had the time yet.'

'Really?' Roberto murmured.

'Yes—really,' she said firmly. 'We've been very busy this morning. Besides, it's only one boot, and it isn't that damaged, and it was my own fault anyway.' She hoped—really hoped—that he wouldn't give her legs that lingering glance again; she was still shaken from the last time he had done it. Although that steady blue gaze on her face wasn't exactly calming, either…

His mouth quirked humorously. 'We can hardly replace one boot.'

Juliette frowned with frustration at this conversation. 'I'm trying to tell you that I don't need you to replace either or both of them!'

'I know what you're saying, Juliette.' He was no longer smiling. 'I'll phone down to Cathy in the shoe department myself when we've finished here, and you can go and see her during your afternoon break, if that's what you would prefer.'

She would prefer him to just drop the whole subject, and—if he really didn't intend sacking her—let her get back to her work. As far as she was concerned there had already been enough attention drawn to her today, without adding to it.

'Whatever,' she said, anxious to escape before he changed his mind about sacking her for insubordination. 'Can I go now?' she added, after a glance at her wristwatch; her lunch break was going to be over shortly.

'Not yet, no.' Roberto seemed completely unconcerned about the length of time she had already spent up here. 'I've been reading your employment file—'

Juliette's head snapped up. 'You've been doing *what*?'

This man was the owner of a dozen or more stores, with all the many responsibilities that entailed, whereas she was a mere sales assistant—and a temporary one at that. So why on earth was he taking such an interest in her file?

She refused to believe his interest had anything to do with that kiss they had shared in the lift. It might have made her knees shake, and temporarily robbed her of speech, but this man was at least ten years older than her own twenty-three, and had the definite look of a man who had the physical experience to go along with those years.

'I had Personnel send up your employment file for me to look at,' he continued calmly, turning slightly to pick up a folder from the top of his desk, and flicking it open to glance down at its contents. 'According to this, you have A-levels in English, Maths, Economics and German.' He was frowning as he read from the top sheet of paper. 'With a first-class degree in Business Studies. Your last—and apparently first—job was with Barnaby Harris, of Harris International.' He looked up, that blue gaze narrowed on her speculatively.

Juliette had felt herself paling as he'd read from her application form, and her lips were actually feeling numb.

She knew what her qualifications were, and what job she had taken after attaining her degree; she simply didn't understand this man's interest in them.

'Aren't you a little over-qualified to be working as a sales assistant?' Roberto suggested softly.

Well, of *course* she was over-qualified! But it was things that weren't written down on that job application form that had resulted in her taking this job—any job!—at Romeo's.

'The thing is, Juliette…' He stood up, one dark brow rising mockingly as Juliette instinctively took a step away from him. 'The thing is,' he repeated, and moved to sit behind the desk again, 'that I'm without a PA for the next six months or so. And with these qualifications—' he tapped the closed file he had placed back on his desk-top '—you would appear to be more than qualified for the post. So what do you think?' He leant back in his leather chair, blue gaze steadily compelling. 'Would you be willing to give up a job you obviously aren't enjoying—'

'I never said that!' she gasped.

'—in order,' he continued, as if she hadn't interrupted him, 'to become my PA for a minimum of six months?'

Juliette could only stare at him incredulously. He simply couldn't be serious. Could he?

So far in their acquaintance she had attacked him with an umbrella, threatened to report him for his over-familiarity, called him several rude names—it still made her cringe just to think about exactly what she had

called him!—and instead of sacking her, as she had
believed he was about to do, he had turned around and
offered her the sort of job she could only dream about!

A job she couldn't possibly accept.

CHAPTER FIVE

'WOULD you like that brandy now?' he offered dryly as Juliette remained pale and speechless.

'Yes, please,' she replied without hesitation, dropping down into the chair opposite his as she gave up any pretence of appearing calm and composed. Because she wasn't either of those things. Far from it!

Roberto was openly smiling as he moved to the drinks cabinet neatly camouflaged in one of the bookshelves. Juliette was only half paying attention to him as he poured some brandy into what looked like a genuine cut-crystal goblet.

She had come here expecting to be given the sack, and instead this man had offered her the sort of job anyone with her qualifications would grasp eagerly—with both hands. But those deliberate blanks in her file—the reasons she'd had to leave her employ with Harris International—meant that she couldn't even *think* about taking this job with Roberto Romeo.

'There you go.' He placed the brandy glass into her hand, once again standing very close to her.

Too close, with Juliette already feeling so vulnerable. 'Thank you,' she murmured, deciding that perhaps she shouldn't drink the brandy after all—she still had to go back to work this afternoon.

He really was standing very close, she thought agitatedly, deliberately not looking at him, although she was very aware, excruciatingly so, of the quiet strength of that powerful body, of the tangy elusiveness of his aftershave, of the lean strength of those hands she had so admired earlier this morning.

Was it really only three hours since she had first encountered this man? It somehow seemed much longer. Maybe being marooned together in a lift that way had that effect? Or was it something else that made her so aware of him?

'Drink up,' he encouraged huskily. 'I'm sure you'll feel better if you do.'

No, she wouldn't. Because this man had put her in a position where the only way out was to tell him at least some of the truth about why she was no longer working for Barnaby Harris. And just thinking about that was enough to make her feel slightly ill.

'I spoke to Barnaby Harris earlier—'

'You didn't!' Juliette's face paled even more as she looked up at him. What had Barnaby said to the other man? And why, after talking to Barnaby, a man who despised her, was Roberto Romeo still offering her a job? 'You had no right to do that,' she protested weakly, green eyes wide.

Roberto shrugged unrepentantly. 'As your present

employer, I was curious as to why you had left the job after being there only five months.'

Juliette swallowed hard. Perhaps she would have a sip of the brandy, after all; it couldn't possibly make her feel any more light-headed than she already did.

Roberto had actually spoken to Barnaby Harris! How much worse could this get?

Going on past experience, a lot worse.

'Mr Romeo,' she began shakily, and then paused to take a sip of the brandy. The alcohol warmed her inside at least, even if she did feel like ice outside.

'Rob,' he encouraged lightly. 'Or Roberto, if you prefer.' Once again he leant back against the front of his desk. 'I answer to both,' he said with a smile.

'You don't sound Italian,' she came back almost accusingly.

'My English mother insisted I be educated at Eton and then Cambridge,' he explained.

His English mother? That probably explained where he had got those penetrating blue eyes—

What did it matter where he'd got his colouring from? Or where he was educated, for that matter. The less she knew about him, personally or otherwise, the easier it would be to say no to his offer of a job.

Although she still wondered, when he had obviously spoken to Barnaby Harris personally, why Roberto was even making the offer!

She moistened dry lips. 'Didn't Barnaby Harris— didn't he explain that— I don't understand,' Juliette told him irritably, and shook her head in frustration, putting her almost untouched glass of brandy down on the desk next to him before standing up. 'If you've spoken to Barnaby,' she continued, still absolutely dumbfounded that Roberto had gone to the trouble of calling the other man, 'then you must know that— that—'

'That what?' Roberto prompted softly, watching her through narrowed eyes.

That she had been sacked from her last job! That the reason she was working at Romeo's at all was because there was no way, after what had happened, she could ask Barnaby Harris for a reference—or that he would give her one!

Although...

She frowned across at Roberto. 'Exactly what did Barnaby tell you about—about the reason I left his employment?'

He shrugged. 'Something about a clash of personalities.' His gaze sharpened. '*Isn't* that the reason you left Harris International?'

A clash of personalities! That would be laughable— if it were the truth. Which it wasn't. But if Barnaby hadn't told Roberto the real reason she had left his employment so abruptly, then she had no intention of doing so, either. She knew some people would say she was being ridiculous, that she shouldn't let her own career suffer as a result of someone else's actions, but she was not prepared to risk hurting innocent people by talking about the past.

'Never mind.' Juliette dismissed the matter firmly.

'Can I take it from this conversation that I still have employment here as a sales assistant?' She looked at him challengingly; he could hardly say no after offering her the job as his personal assistant.

'The PA job pays more,' he pointed out softly. 'A *lot* more,' he added temptingly.

Juliette eyed him suspiciously. Just because Barnaby Harris had decided not to air his dirty laundry in public and confide the real reason for her dismissal to Roberto, that didn't mean the other man hadn't drawn his own conclusions concerning that 'clash of personalities'. Adding two and two together and coming up with five! He also knew, after their response to each other in the lift earlier, that there was no 'clash of personalities'— at least on a physical level— between the two of *them*…

'Do I still have my job in the lingerie department?' Juliette repeated tightly.

'You do,' he said tautly, losing some of his easy charm in the face of her obstinacy.

She nodded abruptly. 'Then, if you don't mind, I would like to get back to it.'

He sighed with exasperation. 'I really don't think you understand, Juliette. This job as my personal assistant may become permanent. My present PA has taken maternity leave, and I happen to know she's unlikely to come back. Why on earth would you want to continue with a job you're clearly over-qualified for, and which will terminate at the end of the January sale anyway, when you could be in a much higher-paid job that has every possibility of becoming permanent?'

Good question.

But so was the question of why exactly he wanted to employ her.

Because if Roberto Romeo thought 'personal assistant' meant anything more than a working relationship, then he could just think again as far as she was concerned.

She shook her head, her gaze meeting his unflinchingly. 'The only job I'm interested in at Romeo's is the one I already have.'

'Fine,' Roberto snapped icily. 'Then you'd better get back to it, hadn't you?'

She didn't need telling twice, hurrying from his office as if being pursued, once again avoiding the lift to hurry down the two floors to her department.

As it happened, she still had a couple of minutes left of her lunch break, and the repetitive seasonal music was starting to give her a headache. But the alternative of going back to the staffroom and being bombarded with questions from Lisa wasn't really an option.

The main reason for that being she simply didn't have any answers. The opportunity Roberto was offering her appeared too good to pass up—and Lisa wouldn't hesitate to tell her so! But, like Juliette, her friend was sure to question his reason for making it.

And Juliette also questioned Barnaby Harris's surprising response to the other man's telephone call. Barnaby had certainly left her in no doubt, the last time they'd spoken, about his intentions concerning giving her any sort of reference for another job. And yet he obviously hadn't told Roberto the real reason she had left his employment so abruptly—though that was not much of a surprise.

Juliette shook her head, too confused at the moment to make any sense of anything that had happened so far today.

Forget it, Juliette, she instructed herself sternly.

And forget Roberto Romeo.

'Can I offer you a lift home?'

Juliette frowned through the heavily falling snow, easily recognizing Roberto as he sat behind the wheel of the silver sports car that was parked illegally at the bus stop where she stood waiting. Although, considering the foulness of the weather, she doubted any buses were actually going to arrive!

But even if the weather *was* awful, and there was a dearth of buses, did she really want to accept a lift from the man she had only hours ago told herself very firmly to forget?

Especially as she had only just finished answering belated questions from Lisa about her summons up to Roberto's office at lunchtime! The two women had left the store together a short time ago, and Lisa had kept her boyfriend waiting while she questioned Juliette. Extensively.

Consequently, she wasn't feeling kindly disposed towards him at the moment, and would have loved to turn down his offer of a lift home. But, again, she very much doubted, with the weather worsening, that any buses were going to get through…

Juliette's eyes widened as, tired of waiting for her reply, Roberto got out of his car, seemingly unconcerned with the snow falling on the thick darkness of his hair before he joined her beneath the bus shelter.

God, he was gorgeous! It should be illegal for any man to be quite this gorgeous. At the very least he ought to come with a health warning or something.

He smiled down at her, an endearing dimple appearing in one hard cheek. 'It seems to be taking you rather a long time to decide whether you prefer the warmth and comfort of my car to the dubious possibility that the buses are actually still running.'

He didn't bear grudges, either, Juliette acknowledged with dazed appreciation. Did this man have no faults?

Well, of course he did. She instantly answered her own question. He kissed unknown women in lifts, for one thing! And that kiss had definitely had a lasting effect on her...

But ultimately, she had to admit, the promise of a warm and comfortable car, rather than a trudge home through the wet snow, won out over any misgivings she might have about accepting his offer.

'Not at all, Mr Romeo,' she answered stiffly—her teeth were chattering so badly from the cold it was impossible to answer him in any other manner. 'But it's only a mile or so to my flat, and I wouldn't want to take you out of your way.'

Although she had no idea which way *was* his way. It was his first visit to the London store in six months or so, according to what Lisa had told her, so it was unlikely he actually had a home in London. And, as Juliette well knew, there were none of the class of hotels this man would choose to stay at in the direction of her flat.

'It's not a problem,' he told her dismissively, taking the bag out of her hand and walking over to the back of his car. 'New boots?' he added lightly as he moved to open the passenger door for her to get in.

As a matter of fact, they were. He had seemed so determined she should have them, and after the uncomfortable half-hour she had spent in his office she had decided to cheer herself up by choosing some. Unsurprisingly, she'd found that Roberto had indeed telephoned ahead and spoken to Cathy, the shoe department manager.

'Yes. Thank you,' Juliette added awkwardly.

He had been right about the warmth in his car; she was starting to thaw out already. Although she couldn't help a pained wince when, once the engine was turned on, Christmas music instantly filled the close confines of the car.

Roberto eyed her speculatively. 'You don't like Christmas music?'

'I love everything to do with Christmas,' she assured him. 'At least…I did. As a child.' There was a shadow in her eyes now, she knew.

This wouldn't do. She instantly roused herself, not wanting to reveal those feelings of sadness. Roberto Romeo already knew more about her than she was comfortable with.

'But after you've listened to Bing Crosby singing "White Christmas" a dozen times a day for four weeks it starts to wear a little thin!' she continued dryly.

Roberto manoeuvred his car back onto the snow-covered road. There was very little traffic to hinder his way. 'They play the same music at the store all day, every day?' He didn't sound pleased.

Oops. She hadn't meant to get anyone into trouble, only to steer the conversation away from herself. 'Perhaps it just seems that way.' She shrugged ruefully.

And perhaps she should start thinking a little more about what she said around this man. Which shouldn't be too difficult; she already spent eight hours a day doing that with Graham Taylor whenever he was around. Not that it made a great deal of difference; for some reason her manager still didn't like her.

'Hmm. Would you give me directions to your home?' Roberto's concentration was fixed on the road ahead, a small frown creasing his forehead.

If anything, the weather was getting worse. The windscreen wipers were having difficulty dealing with the heavily falling snow. And it didn't look as if the snowploughs and gritting lorries had reached this particular part of London, either, as the snow was settling heavily on the road, too.

Usually dirty, often untidy, the suddenly deserted streets of London had taken on a Dickensian beauty. So much so that Juliette wouldn't have been at all surprised to see Bob Cratchit, with Tiny Tim in his arms, come walking down the street!

She smiled at her fanciful thoughts. She had always loved *A Christmas Carol*, and for many years had read it out loud with her father in the week before Christmas. Before he'd married Sybil. Before Sybil and her daughter Rosemary had moved into the house. After that nothing had ever been quite the same again.

'Juliette, does your flat have a couch?'

She turned blankly to look at Roberto, so lost in memories that she was momentarily disorientated.

Of course she had a couch! What did he think? That she was so hard up she didn't have any furniture? In fact, her flat was more than adequately decorated and furnished, courtesy of the high salary she had earned as Barnaby Harris's personal assistant. And she certainly hadn't got to the stage where she had started selling off her furniture. Yet.

'For me to sleep on,' Roberto explained, when Juliette continued to look at him blankly. His expression was grimmer than ever as he scowled out at the rapidly whitening landscape. 'We may just about make it to your flat,' he added tightly, as he struggled to keep the car from skidding on the slippery road, 'but I'm afraid there's no way I'm going to be able to make it back to my hotel this evening.'

It's not a problem, he had assured her, when she had questioned his offer of a lift home.

Well, it certainly *was* a problem if that offer now meant he had to spend the night sleeping on her couch!

CHAPTER SIX

'YOU'VE got to be joking!' Juliette burst out incredulously, her previous pleasure in the scene around them rapidly dissipating as she realised the weather was making driving hazardous—in fact, downright dangerous, she acknowledged, as Roberto once again fought the pull of the icy conditions to keep the car on the road.

He wasn't joking, she forced herself to accept, feeling numb. The snow was falling so thickly now they would be lucky to make it the short remaining distance to her flat. What was the saying? *I wouldn't send a dog out on a night like this?*

'Take the next left,' she instructed softly. He hadn't even bothered to reply to her previous statement. 'It's the second house on the right,' she added, once he had turned the car onto the right street.

If she had thought the main road was bad, this was even worse. None of the day's snowfall had been cleared from this residential street—a fact made particularly obvious as Roberto's car slowed to a stop several feet past the spot he had intended parking.

But he looked more than relieved to have stopped at all, grinning at her ruefully as he turned in the seat to look at her, the slight pallor of his normally olive-coloured cheeks evidence of the tension he had been under, driving in such conditions.

Juliette grimaced. 'I don't suppose you have too much snow in Italy.'

'In the mountains we do,' he pointed out. 'But I'm usually based in New York.'

She knew she was just delaying the moment they went up to her flat. And Roberto probably knew that was what she was doing, too!

Not because her flat was untidy or anything; she always made her bed and tidied up before she left in the mornings. It was just the thought of Roberto in her home that was so unnerving.

He gave her another smile. 'I don't think the two of us sitting in the car all night is such a good idea.'

No, of course it wasn't. It was just—

'Mr Romeo—'

'I really think you should start calling me Rob,' he cut in. 'And perhaps it might help the situation if I tell you I'm a reasonably good cook?' He quirked his dark brows.

No, that didn't help. Because she thought this was a bad idea. A *very* bad idea.

For one thing, this man had kissed her this morning. For another, he had offered her a job she couldn't possibly accept. And lastly—and most damningly!—

she was aware of this man with every part of her. In fact, certain parts of her were unusually warm...

She swallowed hard. 'I was merely going to warn you that my flat isn't going to be anything like the comfort you're probably used to—Rob,' she said stiltedly, able to see in her mind's eye the sort of luxury this man usually surrounded himself with. For goodness' sake, this Porsche was a prime example of just how wealthy he was!

He continued to look at her wordlessly for several long seconds, and then his left hand reached out to gently smooth a strand of auburn hair from her cheek. It lingered there, his thumb now moving caressingly against her cheek.

Juliette gave an involuntary quiver of awareness, her cheek suddenly feeling burning hot.

'You're cold.' He frowned, evidently misunderstanding the reason for that shiver.

She wasn't in the least cold. In fact, the heat in her cheek seemed to have spread to the rest of her body now. Her gaze was caught and held by those deep, deep blue eyes, her aching breasts rising and falling as she breathed shallowly.

But she stopped breathing altogether when he leaned towards her, his right hand moving across in front of her, his face—those lips!—mere inches away from hers now. What was she going to do if he should—?

'The sooner we get you inside the better,' he announced decisively as he clicked her seatbelt undone—the reason he had been leaning over her!—before moving back into his own seat. 'Having rescued you from the elements, I don't intend letting you freeze to death in my car!'

Not much chance of that, Juliette admitted as she got out of her side of the car. The fact that Rob had only been unbuckling her seatbelt rather than being about to kiss her made absolutely no difference to the heated emotions coursing through her body. Awareness. Anticipation. Desire. Disappointment!

None of which was advisable when it was obvious he was going to have to spend the night in her flat...

As she unlocked the door and let them inside, she tried to see her home through his eyes. The door opened into a small hallway, where she removed her coat and scarf and hung them on a peg before walking through to her sitting room.

She quickly averted her gaze from the three-seater couch where he would have to sleep, instead concentrating her attention on the rest of the furnishings. There was an armchair to match the couch, a television, one wall of shelving that contained her collection of books and several attractive prints on the walls.

Yes, it was small, but cosily so. Too much so, with Rob's powerful presence dwarfing the surroundings.

'No Christmas decorations yet?' Rob asked, looking around.

'No,' she said with a frown. It simply hadn't seemed worth the bother. There was only her here, and she could hardly see herself having a jolly Christmas all on her own.

Lisa had invited her to go home with her and

Jonathan, assuring her that her parents would love to have her there, but Juliette had tactfully declined; it would be even lonelier being somewhere for Christmas where she was basically an interloper.

'Tea? Coffee?' she offered brightly, deliberately not looking at Rob as she moved to switch on the gas fire. 'Or would you prefer something stronger?' She screwed up her face in concentration as she mentally went through her drinks cupboard. 'I have red wine. Or perhaps whisky?' She belatedly remembered she had bought—and already wrapped—a bottle as a Christmas present for her uncle Stephen, and hadn't yet delivered it. She could always replace it tomorrow.

'Red wine will be fine,' Rob said. 'It will go nicely with pasta carbonara—if you have the makings of that, that is?' he offered hopefully.

He really was serious about cooking them dinner, Juliette realised, pleasantly surprised. Amazing. The men she had so far been involved with had all expected her to cook for them, rather than the other way around.

Not that she was *involved* with Rob—or intended being so—but it was still an unexpected treat to have someone offer to cook dinner for her.

She hadn't realised until that moment what a lonely existence she actually led. She didn't go home much since her father had died five years ago—mainly because, with only Sybil and Rosemary living there, it no longer felt like home. Her best friend in London was Lisa, and she lived on the other side of London with her boyfriend Jonathan, so the two of them didn't see each other very often on a social basis.

What was this—self-pity? Was that what she was reduced to? Just because it was only five days to Christmas? She had a gorgeous Italian man in her flat offering to cook her dinner! How sad could she get?

'I'm sure I have,' she answered briskly, moving towards the compact kitchen. The table that stood in the middle of the room doubled as her dining table. She took a bottle of red wine from the rack before handing it to Rob. 'You open that—' she got a corkscrew from the drawer '—I'll check for ingredients.'

And at the same time try to get her marauding senses under some sort of control!

She was twenty-three years old, for goodness' sake, and had had her fair share of boyfriends in the last six or seven years. But she couldn't remember once going to pieces like this just at the thought of spending time alone with one of them.

Except that Roberto was nothing like any of the men she had been out with in the past. Neither was he her boyfriend—even though it looked as if they were going to have to spend the night here alone together—

'Damn!' she muttered, as the bag of pasta she had been taking from the cupboard slipped from her fingers, its contents cascading noisily all over the worktop.

Put all thought of the night ahead from your mind, she ordered herself sternly as she began to gather up uncooked pasta. It wasn't even as if, aside from that job offer, Rob had given her any indication that he even *liked* her. Well…apart from that time in the lift this morning, of course. Juliette somehow doubted he would have chosen that particular method of calming her if she had been sixty and plump!

But he had only been calming her down, she reminded herself firmly.

'Here—let me.' Rob moved close to her in order to help pick up the pasta and put it into the waiting saucepan.

Instantly robbing her of breath. Yet again.

Get a grip, Juliette, she instructed herself impatiently. Yes, the man was gorgeous. Yes, he was too sexy for his own good—or hers. And, yes, it looked as if he was going to have to spend the night in her apartment. But it was only circumstances that had thrown them together like this—both this morning and now. He could hardly have ignored her when she'd come sliding towards him wielding an umbrella. Ordinarily, though, a man like Roberto Romeo wouldn't even have noticed she was alive!

That thought didn't help her right now. Once again her gaze was fixed in fascination on the slender elegance of his hands, and the warmth of his body was only inches away from her own.

'Perhaps you should take your wine and go warm yourself in front of the fire while I start preparing dinner,' he suggested huskily, as she totally missed the saucepan and scattered pasta for a second time.

If she got any warmer she was going to go up in flames!

She dared a glance up at him. And then wished that

she hadn't, instantly feeling as if she were drowning in the depths of those wondrous blue eyes. He had long dark lashes, too, she noticed inconsequentially, even as she felt herself swaying unresistingly towards him. The very air around them seemed to crackle with an awareness that—

Thank goodness the ringing of the telephone in the sitting room shattered the silence—and the moment. Because Juliette had a good idea what would have happened next!

Rob gave a rueful smile. 'You had better get that. It's probably someone checking to make sure you got home okay,' he added softly, when she didn't move.

Juliette couldn't imagine who. Lisa, maybe? Certainly not Sybil. Or Rosemary. And as for David...! One look at the beautiful, blonde and sexy Rosemary, and he had forgotten Juliette ever existed.

'More likely a wrong number,' she said dryly, but went to answer it anyway.

'Juliette?' a voice rasped coldly.

She had been wrong, Juliette realised as she recognised her stepsister's voice. Although she doubted that Rosemary was telephoning to check up on her welfare.

'Yes?' she said guardedly.

'Is he there?' Rosemary snapped without preamble.

That totally threw Juliette. She glanced nervously across at Rob, where he stood in the kitchen doorway, watching her.

'Is who here?' she returned warily. As far as she was

aware her stepsister didn't even know Roberto Romeo, so she would hardly assume that Juliette did.

'Oh, don't act the innocent with me, Juliette,' Rosemary came back nastily. 'You know *exactly* who I'm talking about!'

'If I did, I would hardly be asking, would I?' she replied firmly.

'Don't get clever with me!'

'I can assure you that I'm not.' She sighed, very aware that Rob couldn't help but overhear this conversation. Her side of it anyway! 'Look, I really can't talk just now—'

'I'll just bet you can't!' Rosemary said scornfully. 'And don't tell me again that you haven't seen David, because I don't believe you—'

'But I haven't seen him,' Juliette cut in, confused. *David?* Why on earth would she have seen David— tonight or any other time? 'Not for some time, anyway,' she added heavily. Not since he'd become engaged to this woman, in fact. 'Why on earth would you think that I have?'

'God, you pretend you're so innocent, don't you?' Rosemary sneered. 'Sweet little Juliette. Butter wouldn't melt in your mouth, would it? Well, let me tell you—'

'No, let *me* tell *you*!' Juliette finally found the voice to interrupt, having been momentarily struck dumb by the other woman's vehemence. 'I haven't seen him. I don't want to see him. In fact, after the way he behaved, you're more than welcome to him! Is that clear enough for you? Actually, forget I asked that.' Her voice shook angrily. 'I don't care whether you believe me or not!'

She slammed the telephone down, very aware that Rob was still standing only feet away from her, and that, unless she offered some sort of explanation, he would be drawing his own conclusions concerning the conversation he had just overheard. Conclusions she didn't even want to think about!

Juliette drew in a deep breath before slowly turning to face him.

At the same second all the lights went out!

CHAPTER SEVEN

DÉJÀ VU!

Admittedly this time they weren't stuck in a ten by twelve foot metal box. But, other than that, this situation was very much like the one in the lift this morning.

It was pitch-black outside, the streetlights obviously having gone out, too. The only light in the room was the red glow given off by the gas fire—thank goodness for gas heating! And she was completely alone with Rob. All very reminiscent of earlier today. Except that this time she knew who he was.

Juliette swallowed hard, very aware as, his eyesight clearly having adjusted to the firelight, Rob moved out of the kitchen doorway towards her. It reminded her that there was something else different about their present situation: they were alone together in her flat, with her bedroom—and her bed—only feet away.

'I guess that wasn't one of your parents on the telephone?' he said dryly.

She shook her head. 'Both my parents are dead.' Even saying that still pained her.

Memories of her parents, of her happy childhood when they had both still been alive, especially memories of their Christmases together, were enough to bring choked emotion to her throat.

Although those memories were quickly overshadowed by memories of the sad year following her mother's death, and the even bleaker years following her father's remarriage to Sybil.

Juliette blinked rapidly as she felt the hot sting of tears in her eyes.

It was frustrating, because she wasn't a person who very easily gave in to tears. It hadn't always been that way, but she had quickly found that such emotion would be seen and used as a weakness by her stepmother and stepsister.

God, she sounded like Cinderella now, Juliette realised, with an emotional sniff.

'Juliette, are you crying?' Rob was looking down at her with concern, one hand reaching up to touch the dampness on her cheek. 'I did not mean to make you cry with my thoughtless questions,' he murmured softly, his English more accented with his deepening emotions.

'You didn't,' she hastened to reassure him, at the same time giving a rueful shake of her head. 'Christmases are like that, aren't they? Wonderful family times for some people, and rather lonely for others. For example, I bet you have a huge family back in Italy, just waiting for your return so that the holiday season can begin.'

She spoke lightly for two reasons. One, because she

really didn't want to sound like Orphan Annie. And two, because she had realised that the crackle of awareness that had existed before Rosemary's timely telephone call had just intensified tenfold!

Rob grinned. 'My mother and father, four younger sisters and their husbands, plus numerous nieces and nephews,' he acknowledged affectionately. 'Although I hardly think they will wait for me before beginning their celebrations.'

Juliette was just as sure that they would. She had a feeling that this man, with his warm charm and lively sense of humour, was a pivotal member of his family.

'You grew up with four sisters younger than you?' Juliette could only imagine what it must be like to have so many siblings.

His grin widened. 'It had its moments. Fights over the bathrooms were only the start of it!'

Juliette gave a throaty laugh, every nerve-ending sensitised to his closeness now. A part of her wondered what this wonderful man was doing here, with her, when there must be so many other people he would rather— Oh. Of course. He was stranded here with her—that was the reason he was here, and not with someone of his choice.

Rob frowned as if he sensed her slight withdrawal, taking a step closer, both hands moving up to cup either side of her face as he looked down at her intently.

She was totally mesmerised by the intensity of his gaze as she stared up at him, her breath seeming lodged halfway up her throat.

'But,' he murmured throatily, 'none of my parents' grandchildren are Romeos.'

She blinked, wondering why he had said that. Because the only way for their grandchildren to be Romeos would be if—

'Just in case you were worried that I was a married man with children,' Rob continued huskily.

She swallowed hard before moistening suddenly dry lips. 'And why should I be worried about that?'

'Because of this,' he murmured, before his head lowered and his lips claimed hers.

It was as if the hours since he had held her this morning had never been. Juliette fitted perfectly against the hard contours of his body as he curved her against him, and her arms moved up about his shoulders as she returned the kiss with a response that shook her with its intensity.

Or maybe it was Rob himself who shook her? Whatever it was, her lips opened to his as he deepened the kiss, strong hands moving caressingly down the length of her spine.

Juliette had never felt so alive, so totally attuned to another human being, knowing a feeling of completeness that had hitherto escaped her.

'You are so beautiful, Juliette,' Rob whispered as his lips left hers to follow the sensitive column of her throat, his hands moving to cup the fullness of her breasts, thumb-tips moving lightly over the aroused nipples.

Her legs went weak as pleasure coursed through her body, each caress deepening the emotion. Her neck arched to the marauding sensuality of his lips and tongue—

Juliette blinked, dazed, as the lights came back on as suddenly as they had gone off. Starkly. Soberingly.

What was she doing? she wondered painfully as she stared up at Rob. Accepting a lift from this man had been a mistake. Allowing him to kiss her—and kissing him right back—was pure madness.

Her love-life might have been a disaster so far, but, disastrous as it had been, she had never indulged in going-nowhere physical relationships. As this one would undoubtedly be!

A few days from now Rob would be returning to that huge family in Italy, and she would be left here alone to pick up the pieces of a brief relationship. Sadder, and probably no wiser, either.

The best thing she could do was keep this evening on a light footing. It was circumstances, nothing else, that were pushing the two of them together, and those circumstances—and everything else!—would quickly pass. For Rob, at least.

He was looking down at her searchingly now, eyes very blue. 'What are you thinking?' he enquired softly.

She was thinking that if she didn't soon move away from this man all her resolve of a few seconds ago would count for nothing!

He was just so breathtakingly gorgeous. His shoulders were firmly muscled to her touch, dark hair falling attractively over his brow, those blue eyes dark with arousal and, as for his mouth... Her gaze remained locked on the fullness of his bottom lip, begging to be tasted and—

Stop this right now, she ordered herself firmly. It was one thing knowing how attracted she was to him, something else entirely to act on that attraction!

She stepped back, deliberately ignoring the disappointment that darkened his gaze as she did so. 'I'm thinking that I'm still cold and quite hungry,' she said briskly, knowing she lied about being cold; she was so hot she felt as if she were about to melt. 'And you must be, too. I'm going through to my bedroom to change into a warm jumper and jeans—'

'And I'll continue to cook dinner,' Rob said with rueful acceptance, pushing that dark hair from his brow as he stepped back.

Juliette smiled in relief that he wasn't going to pursue the subject of the second time they had been in each other's arms in twelve hours. 'That sounds like an excellent idea!'

He smiled, shaking his head teasingly. 'I'm more than happy to feed the inner woman.'

As opposed to caressing the outer woman?

No! She really mustn't allow her thoughts to go along those lines. Falling for this man would be her biggest blunder to date!

'I shouldn't be long,' she said lightly.

'I realise this is probably a stupid question—' Rob stopped her as she reached the bedroom door '—but do you happen to have a jumper in there that will fit me?'

As it happened, she did—one of her father's jumpers, rescued from the pile of clothes her stepmother had put out to donate to a charity shop. She wore it herself on occasion when she was at home, not caring that she had to turn the sleeves back several times and that it reached almost to her knees. It would fit Rob perfectly.

She nodded abruptly. 'I'll see what I can do.'

But what she actually did, once she had reached the privacy of her bedroom, was sit down heavily on her bed and think of what had just happened between herself and Rob. She liked him. Really liked him. And, despite her rudeness to him this morning, and her rejection of his job offer, he seemed to be attracted to her, too.

Not a good combination, considering the fact that they were alone here, and he was the rich and powerful Roberto Romeo, and she was his temporary employee, Juliette Standish. Because, whether he was attracted to her or not, she very much doubted that Rob had any intention of presenting his parents with red-haired grandchildren!

Just keep remembering that, Juliette, she told herself firmly as she stood up to change her clothes.

'Here you are.' She handed over the navy blue sweater as she entered the kitchen a couple of minutes later, offering no explanation as to how she happened to have a man's jumper in her possession. They had already been far too familiar for an employer and his employee.

'Thank you.' The scowl between his eyes as he discarded his jacket to pull on the sweater told her that he had noticed her lack of explanation. And that he didn't like it.

Well, that was just too bad. She had no intention of telling this man anything more about herself.

It was better this way, she told herself firmly as she took an appreciative sniff at the sauce he was making. 'That smells wonderful,' she told him as she moved to set the table.

Rob nodded abruptly. 'I hope you like garlic; I very rarely cook without it, even when the recipe doesn't require it.'

'I like it.' Juliette felt a pang of regret as she heard the coolness in his voice.

She had wanted to put some distance between them, and she had obviously succeeded, so it was probably better to leave it that way. Even if she no longer had any appetite for the food he was cooking and her heart felt leaden.

Hadn't she already been hurt enough in the past? Hurt that would be nothing compared to the stupidity of falling in love with a man like Roberto.

'I should have asked, not just assumed, shouldn't I?' Rob rasped a few minutes later as he sat across the table from her, watching as she pushed her food around on the plate without eating any of it.

Juliette looked up at him with a frown. 'Asked about what?' she enquired warily.

He grimaced, sipping his wine before answering. 'You're very beautiful. With a lively sense of humour. You're twenty-one…twenty-two years of age—?'

'Twenty-three,' she corrected, tensing as she wondered where this conversation was going.

He nodded. 'It was arrogant and stupid of me to assume you didn't already have someone in your life.'

Juliette felt her stomach give an uncomfortable

lurch. *Didn't already have someone in your life...* That seemed to imply—

It didn't imply anything, she told herself firmly. Nothing that she was prepared to become involved with, anyway. Nothing that she dared become involved in!

'Don't worry about it.' She gave an unconcerned shrug, deliberately not correcting him. 'This is good, by the way.' She jabbed a fork at the pasta on her plate.

Rob gave a dark frown. 'Then why aren't you eating it?' he demanded.

He was right, of course. She wasn't doing justice to his cooking, felt too agitated about what he might think was going on between them to be able to eat. But her silence just now had taken care of that, hadn't it? Very effectively.

'I'm curious, Juliette,' he continued coldly. 'In the case of you and Barnaby Harris, what does "clash of personalities" mean, exactly? I'm just curious,' he repeated with a grimace, as her fork landed on her plate with a clatter and she stared across at him.

Her mouth tightened, her chin rising defensively. 'I have no intention of answering that.'

His eyes narrowed. 'Why not?'

'Because it's none of your business, that's why!' She glared at him, breathing hard. 'I'm sorry, I really can't eat any more.' She avoided his gaze as she stood up abruptly, taking her glass of wine with her as she went back into the sitting room.

She kept her face averted as she sensed him following her a couple of minutes later, deliberately moving to switch on the television set. That was usually a conversation-killer!

It was this time. Rob moved to sit on the opposite end of the sofa, and the two of them gave every appearance of becoming engrossed in the Christmas film showing—one of Juliette's favourites, *It's a Wonderful Life*, with James Stewart.

Except Juliette was sure that neither of them actually took in much of the film. Rob because he seemed lost in his own angry thoughts, and Juliette because she couldn't stop thinking of the fact that in a couple of hours' time, despite the animosity that now existed between them, Rob would actually be sleeping on this sofa…

CHAPTER EIGHT

'COFFEE!' An annoyingly cheerful voice broke into Juliette's sleep-numbed brain. 'Come on, Juliette,' Rob added cajolingly when she didn't move. 'It's too beautiful a morning to waste lying there. Rise and shine!'

She cracked one eyelid open, instantly closing it again when she found Rob had pulled back her bedroom curtains in order to allow the daylight in.

'Juliette!' Rob chided gently, chuckling softly as she could only groan in response. 'You have to get up and look outside,' he insisted, tilting the bed slightly as he sat on the side of it to shake her gently by the shoulders.

'No, I don't,' she muttered, eyes still tightly closed. Maybe if she didn't look at him he would just go away!

He was surprisingly cheerful for someone who had spent the night on her too-short sofa. Although he had still probably fared better than Juliette. She had tossed and turned until the early hours of the morning, hearing the bells of the church two streets away as they chimed one, two and then three, before finally drifting off into a restless sleep.

And all because she had been so completely aware of Roberto as he slept in the adjoining room, literally only feet away from her!

Somewhere last night, in the middle of *It's a Wonderful Life*, the silence between them had ceased to feel awkward and uncomfortable, becoming companionable instead, and Juliette had felt almost mellow by the time the film had come to its happily tearful end. Until she'd had to make up a bed on the sofa for Rob to sleep in—then it had hit home that he really was spending the night in her apartment. Albeit from force of circumstances...

From his cheerfulness this morning she could only assume that he hadn't been plagued by *any* of the restless longings she had suffered just knowing he was in the next room!

Until last night she really hadn't known what it felt like to be frustrated with desire. Now, the memory of the kisses they had shared earlier only seemed to torment her further. She wanted him. In a way she had never wanted, ached for, any man before. So much so that it had been all she could do to stop herself from getting out of her bed to join him on the sofa in the other room. Madness!

'Sleepyhead,' he murmured huskily now, one of his hands moving to ruffle the softness of her already tangled hair. 'It's so beautiful outside, Juliette,' he added wistfully. 'You really do have to see it.'

'Oh, all right!' She gave in, opening her lids irritably, her breath suddenly catching in her throat as she found Rob mere inches away from her face as he bent over her. 'Would you please move?' she added huskily, memories of last night's wanton desire making her defensive.

Those blue eyes looked down at her reprovingly for several seconds, and then he stood up, shaking his head ruefully. 'You're very "bah, humbug" this morning, Juliette,' he teased.

She was tired from lack of sleep, and still frustrated with desire for this man, totally bewildered by these hitherto unknown emotions—so, yes, she probably *did* sound a little like Scrooge on a bad day!

Which was a little ungrateful of her when Rob was in such a good mood. And he had brought her coffee!

'Sorry,' she sighed, sitting up to push the tangle of hair from her face. 'But what's so interesting outside at—? Oh, no, it's *eight-thirty*!' She wailed her dismay after a glance at her bedside clock. Somehow, in all the churning emotion of last night, she must have forgotten to set her alarm. 'I'm going to be late for work!' she groaned as she threw back the bedclothes and swung her legs to the floor.

Rob grinned down at her, his teeth looking very white against his olive skin. 'Executive order, Juliette. You aren't going into work today. Neither of us is. Take a look outside,' he added, as she opened her mouth to argue with him.

She frowned at him as she stood up, slightly self-conscious in her green nightshirt, even though it more than adequately covered her from her neck to her knees. She simply wasn't used to strolling around in her night-wear in front of any man!

But the beautiful sight that met her gaze after she had walked over to the window more than made up for any embarrassment she might have felt. She gasped her delight as she looked outside.

The snow must have fallen softly all night, coating the streets and houses with a heavy blanket of pristine whiteness. The few people outside, all of them bundled up in heavy woollen coats, scarves and gloves, were walking in snow that came halfway up their calves.

'This is incredible,' Juliette breathed wonderingly, her eyes wide with delight.

'Isn't it?' Rob agreed softly, and he moved to stand beside her, his arm dropping casually about her shoulders as the two of them continued to gaze outside. 'I had no idea until last night that it ever snowed in London,' he murmured with appreciation.

Juliette couldn't answer him, completely aware of that arm draped across her shoulders, of how close Rob was standing to her, of his warmth against her lightly clad body—her body that was even now stirring with desire, with a fiery warmth between her thighs as her nipples became aroused.

Something she knew Rob was becoming aware of, too, as she heard his breath catch in his throat, felt his arm tightening about her shoulders.

This was dangerous. If anything, even more danger-ous than last night had been.

If that were possible.

'Juliette…?' Rob said huskily.

She didn't look at him. Didn't dare look at him. Totally aware that the blanket of snow outside held them cocooned in a world made unreal by its eerie silence. But everything about this situation with Rob was unreal, she acknowledged to herself with a heavy heart. The way they had met. The way they'd continued to meet. The way they seemed to keep being thrown into situations together that were completely beyond their control.

That was it: this whole thing between Rob and herself was beyond her control. His, too, probably…

'I have an idea!' she announced brightly, at the same time moving away from the warmth of Rob's arm, smiling up at him as she ignored the look of disappointment in his eyes. 'As I can't get to work, and you obviously can't get back to your hotel, why don't we go out and shop for a Christmas tree?'

She wasn't one hundred per cent sure about the 'we' part of that suggestion, but it was a way of getting them out of the intimate confines of her apartment. Before they did something they would both regret!

'There's a fruit and vegetable shop in the next street that's selling them, and I'm sure one of the other shops will sell decorations and lights,' she added encouragingly, when Rob didn't respond to her suggestion.

'Okay.' Rob nodded finally, joining in her light-hearted mood as he seemed to shake off his disappointment. 'But I assumed you hadn't bothered with a

Christmas tree because you were going away for the holidays. To family?'

Juliette avoided his searching gaze. 'I told you, I don't have any family as such.' She shrugged, and then felt slightly guilty about dismissing her stepmother in that way. After all, no matter what her own feelings in the matter, her father had cared for Sybil. 'Well, that isn't quite true,' she added with a grimace. 'But what family I do have are going away on Christmas Eve for the holidays. Skiing.'

'You wouldn't like to join them?' Rob queried.

She hadn't been asked!

Not that she would have gone, even if she had been. Ten days in the close confines of a foreign resort, with Sybil, Rosemary and David, had to be her idea of hell!

No, even staying alone in her apartment, watching all the re-runs on television, indulging in Christmas pudding for one, would be preferable to that.

'No, I wouldn't,' she said with a laugh, trying to dismiss the subject.

'You don't ski?'

Actually, she did. One of the last holidays they had taken as a family, before her mother had become ill, had been a skiing holiday in Canada's Whistler resort.

'I just don't like being away from home for Christmas,' she answered evasively.

'But if your family—'

'They aren't close family—okay?' Her voice rose with frustration. She really didn't want to talk about

Sybil and Rosemary—after last night, *especially* Rosemary!—on such a gloriously beautiful morning.

'I see,' Rob murmured slowly. The frown between his eyes said he didn't see at all, but Juliette had no intention of explaining the situation to him.

'I'll go and get showered and dressed, and then we can go out,' she told him briskly. 'Just give me ten minutes.'

She willed him to leave her bedroom. Because that particular danger hadn't completely passed yet. But a Christmas romance had to be even sadder than a holiday one—a clinging on to someone, anyone, in order not to be alone. She was used to being alone, after all.

'Go on, Rob,' she encouraged, when he continued to look at her.

He gave an abrupt nod. 'Don't forget to drink your coffee,' he reminded her before leaving.

It was sweet and milky, just the way she liked her coffee, Juliette discovered as she sat on the bed to drink it. It was so long since anyone had even—*No!* She wasn't a person who felt sorry for herself, and she wasn't going to start now. They had a Christmas tree to buy and decorate, and that was what she would concentrate on.

It was fun choosing the tree with Rob—more fun than she could ever have imagined after his cold withdrawal last night. He went through all the stock the man had in his shop before declaring he had found one the perfect height and shape for her flat.

It looked a little big to her, its six feet in height sure

to dwarf her sitting room, but there was no denying it was a beautiful tree, its branches lush and smelling sweetly of pine.

'We'll come back for it in a little while,' Rob told the shopkeeper after Juliette had paid for it—insisting, much to his chagrin, that she wouldn't let him buy it for her. 'We're just going down the street for some decorations.'

To Juliette's surprise, the shopkeeper meekly accepted the instruction, even offering to secure some string around the tree while they were gone, to make it easier for carrying. When she'd bought fruit and vegetables from this shop in the past, Juliette had always found the man to be taciturn at best. But, for all his inherent politeness, Rob seemed to have a natural air of authority that even the grouchy shopkeeper responded to.

'What?' Rob looked at her quizzically once they were outside the shop, and she continued to stare at him rather than at the slippery pavement.

She averted her gaze, deeply aware that she was starting to like this man a little too much. Oh, she had known she was attracted to him—that was impossible to deny when she melted in his arms every time he kissed her—but liking him as well wasn't a sensible thing for her to do.

'Nothing,' she dismissed with a shake of her head. 'I was just wondering how— Oh!' She didn't manage to finish what she was saying as her feet suddenly slipped from under her. She felt herself falling, grabbing at Rob's arm as she did so, but only succeeded in pulling him down with her.

Rob landed on his back with an *'oof'*, giving a louder *'oomph'* milliseconds later as Juliette landed on top of him, knocking all the air out of his lungs. His arms moved about her instinctively.

'I'm so sorry!' Juliette gasped her dismay. 'I just— My boot slipped on the ice and I—'

'Juliette, will you stop squirming on top of me like that?' Rob bit out through gritted teeth as she struggled to get up from him.

She blinked at the fierceness of his tone, staring down at him with concern. 'Are you hurt? Oh, no—have you injured your spine?' She looked about frantically, searching for help, but the streets were deserted except for a few people across the street, who were all struggling to maintain their own tenuous footing on the slippery pavement. She turned back to Rob, trying as best she could to keep her weight off him. 'Where does it hurt?' She looked him over, as if expecting to find one of his bones sticking out of the flesh.

Rob eyed her ruefully from beneath mockingly raised brows. 'Are you sure you want me to answer that?'

Her concern turned to puzzlement, quickly followed by embarrassed dismay as she felt the hardness of his thighs against hers. He wasn't hurt at all. At least, not physically…!

She frowned down at him reprovingly. 'I thought you were hurt,' she muttered as she moved to get unsteadily back onto her feet. She avoided looking at him as he did the same, concentrating on brushing the snow from her coat and jeans instead.

'I am,' he assured her dryly as he straightened. 'It isn't good for a man my age to keep being aroused and then disappointed in this way. In fact, it's a state I seem to have been in perpetually since you groped me in the lift yesterday.'

'Oh! I didn't— Well, okay, I did,' she conceded, bright wings of colour in her cheeks now. He eyed her mockingly once again. 'But it was an accident,' she added indignantly.

He grinned unabashedly. 'I wasn't complaining,' he drawled. 'Merely stating a fact.'

A fact she had tried not to think about, let alone have a conversation about.

Juliette couldn't even look at him now. Had he really been aroused since that incident in the lift yesterday? She had, just thinking about him, so why shouldn't he feel the same way?

Where was all this going?

Nowhere, came the unequivocal answer. She couldn't allow it to—didn't want to let Rob become the biggest mistake she had made to date.

She looked at him from beneath dark lashes. She could make this more difficult than it already was by taking his remarks seriously. Or she could—

'Maybe this will help cool you down!' she challenged, reaching to grab a handful of snow. She threw it at him, grinning her satisfaction as the soft snow hit him squarely in the face.

'Why, you little—!' He looked momentarily stunned as he wiped the snow from his eyes. But he recovered quickly, bending down to grab his own handful of snow and retaliate in kind.

There followed several frantic minutes of snowball fighting, and both of them were laughing uproariously by the time a shopkeeper came out of his store to tell them to 'mind the winders'.

'Sorry!' Rob called out, before grasping Juliette's hand and running off down the street with her.

'We're going to fall again if we aren't careful,' Juliette warned him. Her footing was precarious, to say the least.

He slowed his pace, but kept a firm hold of her hand as he looked down at her. 'I think it may already be too late to worry about that,' he told her huskily.

Once again Juliette was thrown into confusion. She stared up at him, hardly daring to breathe, her cheeks flushed as she saw the emotion in his eyes. An emotion she was afraid to believe was real!

'Decorations,' she reminded him firmly. 'And lights,' she added. 'Can't have a Christmas tree without coloured lights.'

'We can't?' Rob murmured softly, his eyes still dark with emotion.

Once again, she wasn't too sure about that 'we'. Better not to even start thinking along those lines!

'No, we can't,' she assured him, and she turned into a shop and headed for a display of baubles and beads.

Rob hesitated for a second or two before joining her. Which was all well and good. For now. But what was going to happen when they were once again alone in her flat?

She was so deep in thought on the walk back, totally preoccupied with thoughts of being alone with Rob again, that she didn't notice the man getting out of his Range Rover until he actually spoke to her.

'Juliette? Juliette—I need to speak to you!'

She turned, her eyes widening incredulously as she recognised the man walking down the street towards her.

Barnaby Harris!

CHAPTER NINE

JULIETTE could only stare at Barnaby as if he were the Ghost of Christmas Past—which indeed, to her, he undoubtedly was.

What was her ex-boss doing here? What could possibly be urgent enough to warrant him driving here to see her in weather like this? If he had come here simply to berate her once again for having messed up his life, then he could just— But would he really have made the effort to come here just to do that?

'I telephoned Romeo's and they told me you weren't able to get in to work today.' Barnaby came to a halt in front of her. 'But this couldn't wait, so I drove to see you. I hope you don't mind?' He looked uncertainly at Rob, and then back to Juliette.

That really all depended on why he was here! When she had last seen him, across the width of his desk, he had told her exactly what he thought of her before sacking her. She didn't want a repeat of that conversation in front of Rob, of all people.

And, thinking of Rob…

The mood of camaraderie that had existed between them seemed to have completely dissipated with Barnaby's arrival. Rob was eyeing the other man through narrowed lids, his expression enigmatic and unreadable.

'Juliette, could I please just talk to you for a few minutes?' Barnaby asked hoarsely.

She turned back to him with a frown, wishing him anywhere but here. After their last conversation she would have been happy never to see him again, and with Rob here, too…

She shook her head. 'Barnaby, I don't think—'

'Please, Juliette!' Barnaby urged. 'I really do need to talk to you.'

Juliette looked up at him searchingly. At thirty-two years of age, Barnaby Harris was tall and athletic, with blond, blue-eyed good looks. Before that last scene in his office, his face twisted with fury, Juliette had found him easygoing and pleasant. Today, his expression totally earnest, he looked more like the man she had enjoyed working with for five months.

'Okay,' she agreed reluctantly. 'But you'll have to wait until we've taken these things upstairs—'

'I think I'll get going—if that's okay with you, Juliette.' Rob spoke coolly. 'The roads are obviously passable if Harris managed to get here, so I think I should get back to work.'

'Wait a minute…' Barnaby looked at the other man frowningly. 'I recognise your voice—I spoke to you on the telephone yesterday. You're Roberto Romeo, aren't you?' His voice was suddenly speculative.

'I am.' Rob eyed the other man coolly. 'Perhaps you would like to help Juliette inside with this.' He thrust the Christmas tree into Barnaby's arms before turning to Juliette. 'I will see that this sweater is returned to you,' he added harshly. 'Do not attempt to come into work until the weather clears.'

Juliette could only stare after him, dazed, as he turned on his heel and walked over to his car, getting inside and driving off—slowly, because of the ice—without so much as a second glance in her direction.

Leaving Juliette in a state where she didn't know whether to scream or shout—or just cry!

Okay, so she had accepted that any relationship between Rob and herself would go absolutely nowhere, but that didn't mean she hadn't been enjoying his company—in fact, more than enjoying it.

She was now left with a Christmas tree and assorted decorations that she had absolutely no inclination to put up now that Rob wasn't going to be there to share it with her.

And, of course, she was left with Barnaby Harris, too.

'Hey, I didn't mean to mess things up for you.' Barnaby grimaced in apology as she turned to him accusingly.

He hadn't. Not really. So she and Rob might have dressed the tree together, and he might even have spent the night again—perhaps on the sofa, perhaps not—but tomorrow they would still have returned to Romeo's. Rob as the owner, Juliette as a temporary sales assistant.

She drew in a shaky breath before slowly letting it out again. 'You didn't,' she assured Barnaby flatly, turning towards her door as Rob's car disappeared round the corner at the end of the street.

Barnaby fell into step beside her, staggering a little under the weight of the tree.

Unlike Rob, who had carried the unwieldy thing effortlessly. As he seemed to do most things.

When had she fallen in love with him?

Had it been when he'd taken control of the situation in the lift? When he'd kissed her for the same reason minutes later? When he'd insisted she have a new pair of boots to replace the damaged ones? When, against all logic, he'd offered her the job as his PA? Or had it been when he'd stopped in the snow last night and offered to drive her home? Or perhaps when he'd looked so endearingly familiar wearing her father's sweater? Maybe this morning, when he'd woken her with a cup of coffee in bed? Or when they'd shopped for the tree and decorations, or pelted each other with snowballs like a couple of carefree children?

Did the *when* really matter? The fact of the matter was, she *had* fallen in love with Roberto Romeo. And now that he had left everything had gone even flatter and more colourless than it had been before.

Worse than when she had argued with Sybil and Rosemary? Than when she'd lost her job with Barnaby?

Than working for the manager from hell in a job she absolutely hated?

Yes, Rob leaving was worse than any of those things!

In fact, she really felt as if she were going to burst into tears...

'My arriving like that really did mess things up for you, didn't it?' Barnaby said apologetically as, having let them into her flat, Juliette dropped the decorations onto an armchair and stood forlornly in the middle of her lounge, tears clinging to her lashes. 'I had no idea.' Barnaby put the tree down and turned to her beseechingly. 'I thought when he telephoned yesterday that his interest in you was just as an employee—'

'It was. It *is*!' she corrected herself forcefully, clasping her hands tightly together in front of her as she fought back the tears. 'What can I do for you, Barnaby?' she asked wearily. 'The last time we met I seem to remember you expressing the sentiment that you never wanted to set eyes on me again.'

He looked embarrassed now. 'Things change.'

They might have done for Barnaby, but as far as Juliette was concerned nothing between them had changed...

The first thing Juliette noticed the next morning as she stepped onto the shop floor at Romeo's was that there was different music playing over the tannoy system. Still Christmas music, which was fine with her, but not the same CD that had been playing *ad nauseam* for the last few weeks.

Because she had mentioned the repetition to Rob?

As soon as the thought entered her head she knew how ridiculous it was; as if anything she had said to Rob was of any importance to him! In fact, he hadn't been able to get away fast enough once Barnaby had arrived so unexpectedly.

'Glad you could join us today, Juliette,' Graham greeted her sarcastically as she hurried to the lingerie department.

She felt embarrassed colour warm her cheeks at what she knew Graham wasn't saying.

Rob had insisted on telephoning Romeo's himself yesterday, in order to let them know neither of them would be in to work because of the bad weather conditions.

It was obvious from the scornful expression on Graham's face that he was well aware of the other man's call!

'The snow has all melted.' She shrugged, as usual not responding to his sarcasm; she rarely gave him that satisfaction.

Indeed, apart from a lot of dampness, and the odd patch of snow in sheltered spots, it was hard to believe how bad the weather had been twenty-four hours earlier. The thaw had started yesterday evening, when the temperature had gone up, and by this morning everything had been back to normal. Including the bus service.

'I live out in one of the suburbs, and *I* still managed to get to work yesterday,' the manager snapped.

Bully for you, Juliette felt like coming back, but didn't. There was no point in exacerbating this situation any further. 'That was really dedicated of you,' she said instead.

'Are you by any chance being sarcastic, Juliette?' He glowered at her with narrowed eyes.

'No, of course not.' The man was obviously spoiling for a fight.

Because he knew she had been with Rob yesterday? Probably. But there was nothing she could do to change that. Which meant she would just have to stand here and take it. Whatever 'it' was!

She really didn't need this. Yesterday had been one emotional trauma after another, culminating in that conversation with Barnaby. She had come in to work today hoping to distract herself from all that— as well as perhaps to catch the odd glimpse of Rob— not to get into some strange one-sided conversation with Graham Taylor. And that was before she even started work!

'Hmm.' He snorted sceptically. 'The fact is, Juliette, I feel it would be better for everyone if we were to terminate your contract.'

Did he feel that? Or had Rob put him up to it? It didn't sound like the man she had come to know—and love—but that didn't mean Rob *wasn't* behind this. He hadn't exactly been friendly when he'd left yesterday, and it was anybody's guess what conclusions he had drawn about Barnaby's arrival.

'Immediately,' Graham added forcefully. 'In fact, I suggest you collect your things right now and leave.'

Not again! Her first thought was that they couldn't do this. But her second one was, who were 'they'…? *Was* Rob involved?

'Is there a problem here?'

Juliette turned at the sound of Rob's voice behind her, having read the expression on Graham's face and realised that he hadn't been aware of the other man's presence, either. She also realised, from the frustrated anger on the manager's face, that Rob *wasn't* involved in her dismissal; Graham looked too irritated by the other man's appearance for that to be true.

It was something, at least!

Although that didn't make it any easier to find an answer to Rob's question…

In the event, she wasn't the one who answered Rob at all.

'Juliette has decided she no longer wishes to work for Romeo's,' Graham announced. It was to his employer he spoke, but it was Juliette he looked at as he did so.

Challengingly. Daring her to contradict him.

But was there any point in her doing that? Even if Rob managed to sort this situation out so that she actually kept her job—even if Rob had any interest in doing that—Graham would still find a way of getting rid of her once Rob had returned whence he came. And by the time Rob came back to London again, some time next year, Juliette would be long gone. And long forgotten…

'Is this true, Juliette?' he demanded in a hard voice, those blue eyes icily cold. 'You've decided to leave us?' His tone was accusing.

'Not exactly—' she began sharply, deliberately avoiding so much as glancing at Graham as she heard his sharply indrawn breath.

Rob looked confused now. 'How, "not exactly"?'

Juliette moistened dry lips, choosing her words carefully. 'I'm actually contracted to work until the end of January, but Graham seems to feel that it would be better—for everyone—if I were to leave Romeo's now.'

She knew she was digging her own grave as far as this job was concerned—one way or another she would no longer be working for Romeo's after today—but she was past caring about that. She had had just about as much of Graham Taylor as she could take.

Besides, she didn't think she could bear being this close to Rob over the next few days, feeling about him as she did.

As expected, Graham looked far from pleased, his narrowed gaze fixed on her unblinkingly. Rob's expression was much harder to read. In fact, she had no idea what he was thinking beneath that cold mask. But the fact that she couldn't read his expression was enough for Juliette to know she couldn't stay here any longer—that she had to get away. As far away from Romeo's, and Roberto Romeo, as she could get!

'In fact,' she bit out abruptly, 'I think that's exactly what I'll do. If you will both excuse me?' She didn't wait for a reply from either man before turning on her heel and walking away.

Quickly.

She gave herself no time for second thoughts. Or even third ones. They, no doubt, would come later!

'Do you intend keeping me standing on the doorstep all evening, or are you going to invite me in?'

Juliette couldn't speak at all—could only stare at Rob as he stood in the hallway outside her flat.

She had answered the knock on her door expecting—well, not to find Rob standing outside!

It was eight o'clock in the evening, the end of a day when she hadn't so much as heard a word from him after she had walked out of the store this morning, and now here he was, just casually calling on her as if it were something he did all the time!

'Juliette…?' He frowned. 'Am I interrupting something?'

His English was more accented this evening, she noticed inconsequentially, as though he wasn't quite as sure of himself as he wanted to appear.

Which was ridiculous; she had never seen Rob less than self-assured.

She shook her head. 'I'm just surprised to see you, that's all.' She held the door open for him to enter, taking her time about closing it and following him into the sitting room, frantically trying to think of a reason why he had come here.

'I came to talk to you—and to return this.' Rob held out the bag he had carried into the flat, standing very tall and broad-shouldered in front of the lit fire.

Juliette took the bag and glanced warily inside, the

tension starting to leave her shoulders as she realised it was only her father's jumper that she had lent to him a couple of evenings ago—freshly laundered and ironed, by the clean smell of it.

'Thank you,' she said huskily, unconsciously holding the bag to her chest. She was pleased to have the jumper returned to her; it was one of the few things of her father's that she had managed to salvage when Sybil had cleared out his things from the house only a week after his death.

'Does it have—sentimental value?' Rob was watching her with guarded eyes as she still held on to the bag.

'Yes.' She attempted a smile which didn't quite come off; it was at this time of year she tended to miss her father the most. 'It was my father's,' she explained shakily as Rob continued to look at her.

His eyes widened. 'Your father's? But—' He broke off as the doorbell rang noisily. 'It would seem you're popular this evening,' he said with dry humour.

Juliette had no idea who this second visitor could be. She really didn't know anyone in London apart from Lisa and Rob. Rob was already here, and it was Lisa's night for the gym.

She could only gasp in surprise when she opened the door and saw who stood there.

'Okay, where is he?' Rosemary demanded vehemently, pushing past Juliette as she barged her way into the flat. 'I don't care what you told me the other day. I know that he's here,' she continued, and strode forcefully inside, 'so don't even try to deny it again!'

Juliette could only stare at the other woman with horror.

CHAPTER TEN

'AND who the hell might *you* be?' Rosemary came to an abrupt halt, having entered the sitting room and found Rob there, some of her aggression dissipating in the face of this devastatingly attractive man.

Juliette winced as Rob looked at the other woman coldly, every inch Roberto Romeo at that moment, and obviously not accustomed to being verbally attacked in this unprovoked way. Well…other than by her, Juliette added to herself with a mocking twist.

'This is Roberto Romeo.' Juliette decided she'd at least attempt to take control of this situation.

Blue eyes snapped wide in recognition of the name. *'The* Roberto Romeo?' Rosemary gasped, obviously reassessing Rob now, looking at him from his head to his toes, and then back again. 'Well, of course it is,' she acknowledged sweetly, before turning to Juliette with accusing eyes. 'How on earth do *you* come to know someone like him?'

'Rob, this is Rosemary Carlisle. My stepsister.'

Juliette glared at the other woman, not surprised that the socially aware snob had recognised Rob's name.

'Your stepsister?' Rob repeated, astounded. 'But I thought—' He broke off, staring at the other woman with unreadable eyes.

'Yes?' Juliette prompted, looking at him with a sudden frown. 'What did you think?'

'It doesn't matter.' He dismissed it with an impatient shake of his head. 'Miss Carlisle.' He nodded abruptly. 'Correct me if I'm wrong, but I was under the impression, when you arrived, that you had lost someone…?'

In the surprise of seeing Rosemary here at all—her stepsister had never visited her in London before and then Rosemary's recognition of Rob's name, Juliette had totally forgotten the other woman's initial aggression.

'My fiancé—David.' Anger returned to Rosemary's baby-blue eyes. 'We had a silly argument over—well, it doesn't matter what it was about. I just had the idea that he might have come here to see you.'

Juliette couldn't imagine why. The last time she had seen David had been when he'd told her he preferred her stepsister to her! It had not been a pleasant conversation.

She sighed. 'Look, I told you on the telephone the other night that I haven't so much as seen David for weeks now.'

'Who is this David?' Rob demanded curtly.

Juliette turned uncomfortably to look at him. What on earth must he be thinking of her? First Barnaby had arrived here unexpectedly yesterday, and now Rosemary was accusing her of commandeering her fiancé! Barnaby and David—when the only man she wanted, the only man she loved, was Rob himself.

'As I said, he's my fiancé,' Rosemary answered Rob. 'He and Juliette used to be—well, *friends*, I suppose you would call it,' she said scornfully. 'Before the two of us had met each other, of course.' She laughed. 'Obviously once we had met Juliette didn't stand a chance!' She smiled triumphantly.

Juliette flinched at the purring satisfaction in the other woman's voice. Not because she still cared for David—she didn't. The liking she had felt for him had paled into insignificance compared to the love she now felt for Rob. But because, in the ten years since Rosemary had first come into her life, the other woman had delighted in taking everything from Juliette that she possibly could. Clothes when they were both teenagers, answers to homework for school, friends and even Juliette's father's affection at one stage, when Rosemary had attempted to twist him around her selfish little finger in order to drive a wedge between Juliette and her father.

She hadn't succeeded in the latter; the bond between father and daughter had been far too strong for that. But once Rosemary had realised she couldn't get her own way by that method, she had worked on creating friction between her mother and stepfather, with Juliette as the scapegoat, in order to achieve her goal. The only way to maintain a harmonious existence for her father, it had seemed, had been for Juliette to keep her distance.

It was something Juliette would never forgive the other woman for.

But none of that explained why Rosemary should continue to think, just because the two of them had had an argument, that David had come to *her*. Unless...

'Perhaps your fiancé has changed his mind concerning the choice he made?'

Juliette's head snapped round in Rob's direction as he voiced the thought that had just occurred to her. He was still looking at the other woman with cold eyes, his expression now one of complete contempt.

Did he know? Had he somehow guessed at some of the pain the other woman had deliberately caused her?

But how could he have? She hadn't so much as mentioned her stepmother and stepsister, let alone the misery they had brought into her life.

Rosemary was glaring at Rob now, her beautiful face twisted. 'I told you, we had a silly argument—'

'Over Juliette?' he put in softly.

'Look,' Rosemary snapped, 'I have no idea what your connection is to *her*—' the scorn in her voice implied that she could take a good guess! '—but I can assure you that David has long since got over the silly infatuation he had for her—'

'Her name is Juliette. I suggest you use it!' Rob bit out icily, taking a step towards Juliette, his arm moving protectively about her shoulders. 'And, given a choice between the two of you, I would choose Juliette every time!' He squeezed Juliette's shoulder, as if checking that he was doing the right thing in defending her like this.

In reply, Juliette smiled up at him gratefully. Oh, she knew that this was all for Rosemary's benefit—that once her stepsister had gone Rob would make his own excuses and leave, too. But for the moment it was just so deliciously wonderful to allow herself to feel loved and protected, if only for a matter of minutes.

Rosemary looked as if Rob had actually hit her. Not surprising, really; he was the first person since her father who had championed Juliette over the more beautiful Rosemary. She might almost have felt sorry for her stepsister if she couldn't still feel every barb and hurt the other woman had ever inflicted on her.

Rosemary gave a contemptuous snort as she quickly recovered from the slight Rob had given her. 'And for as long as it takes you to tire of your little game, I'm sure you're welcome to her!' Hard blue eyes raked over them scathingly, coming to rest glitteringly on Juliette. 'It's a pity no one ever told you to hold out for the diamond ring, Juliette,' she added scornfully.

'As you did, Miss Carlisle?' Rob replied chillingly. 'Then might I suggest you look elsewhere for the man who bought you that ring? You have interrupted our evening for quite long enough!'

If he had dismissed her in that icy tone, Juliette knew she would have wanted to curl up in a ball and hide. It didn't have quite the same effect on the more resilient Rosemary, but the other woman did, after one last contemptuous glare in their direction, turn on her heel and flounce out of the room, slamming the door behind her seconds later.

Which was the cue for Juliette's legs to fold neatly beneath her, so that she fell to the carpeted floor.

Or at least she would have done, if Rob hadn't moved his arm from her shoulders down about her waist, easily supporting her weight as he guided her over to the sofa to sit her down on it.

'Brandy, I think,' he announced grimly.

'I don't have any.' Juliette shook her head, slightly dazed. 'But there's still some red wine in the kitchen from the other evening,' she added quickly as his frown deepened at the lack of supplies in her flat.

His disappearance into the kitchen at least gave her a few moments' respite to try and gather her shattered self-confidence. Rosemary had always had the effect of totally disrupting her life. Although this time, with Rob's help, Juliette had to admit that the other woman hadn't succeeded in doing so. It had to be a first!

It also sounded, from what the other woman had said, as if David had come to his senses where Rosemary was concerned. Juliette certainly hoped so. She wasn't in love with him herself, and never would be, but despite what he had done he was a nice man, and certainly deserved better than Rosemary.

'Drink some of that,' Rob encouraged softly as he returned with two glasses of red wine.

She gave him a grateful smile as she took the glass he held out to her and sipped from it. 'You always seem to be offering me alcohol in one form or another!'

Rob didn't return her smile. 'When did your father marry that creature's mother?'

Juliette choked slightly on the wine, swallowing hard before answering him. 'Ten years ago,' she replied huskily.

He nodded grimly. 'And is the mother anything like the daughter?'

She smiled without humour. 'Rosemary is Sybil's clone.' Her eyes widened as Rob instantly launched into rapid Italian—none of it sounding pleasant. 'He was lonely after my mother died,' she added, defending her father. 'We both were. And before the wedding Sybil couldn't have been more wonderful,' she remembered. 'I was just as fooled by her initially as my father was.'

Rob gave a disgusted shake of his head. 'The very thought of you at the mercy of two such women—!' One hand clenched tightly into a fist at his side; the other gripped his wine glass. In fact, his knuckles showed so white Juliette feared for the delicate stem of the glass!

'Hey, I'm not completely defenceless, you know,' she pointed out. 'They didn't have it all their own way.' Although almost, she acknowledged to herself, thinking of the years she'd had to distance herself from her own father in order to make life easier for him with his second wife.

Rob's eyes were narrowed into icy slits. 'You will tell me about it.'

Juliette's eyes widened at this show of indomitable Italian will from a man who had for much of their acquaintance been charmingly easygoing.

'I will?' she echoed softly.

He gave a brief inclination of his head. 'You most certainly will!'

CHAPTER ELEVEN

AND, to Juliette's surprise, she did. She told him of those awful five years until she was eighteen and ready to go off to university, of her father's sudden death before that could happen and of how her stepmother had refused to help with her fees, meaning that Juliette had had to take a job as well as study in order to support herself.

For Juliette's father, as unaware as any of them of his impending death, had left everything he possessed to his wife, except for a trust fund he had set up for Juliette, to be released on her twenty-fifth birthday.

It all sounded so awful when told starkly like that, and yet even as she talked Juliette knew that the last five years on her own had given her a lot of things: self-reliance, for one, and the value of friendship for another. But most of all, she realised, they had made her the sort of person who could love Rob unconditionally.

It was because she loved him, not because he had ordered her to, that she could share these things with him.

'It's their loss, not mine,' she concluded, with a lightness she had never thought she would feel where Sybil and Rosemary were concerned. But talking about those years, sharing them, had somehow released her from the burden of them.

It felt wonderful!

Whereas Rob looked grimmer than ever as he drank the rest of his wine in one swallow before putting the empty glass down on the coffee table.

'I wish I had known of all this before. I would have taken great delight in throttling your stepsister!' he explained harshly, at Juliette's questioning look.

She couldn't help it—she laughed. 'Oh, I think you must have guessed some of it. You ripped Rosemary to shreds at the end there!' she said admiringly.

Rob continued to look down at her with a frown for several seconds, and then he began to smile, too. 'She reminded me of a snake, hissing before it attacks!' He gave a shudder of revulsion. 'Pure venom.'

Juliette could only stare at him in wonder; he was the only man she had ever met who had expressed a preference for her over the sensually beautiful Rosemary.

'What?' he prompted gently as Juliette continued to stare at him.

She broke that gaze and shook her head, looking away self-consciously. She might be grateful to Rob for his championing of her, but she very much doubted she wanted him to realise she was in love with him. And she was. More now than ever.

'You haven't dressed your tree.'

She turned back to find Rob looking at the unadorned tree where it stood in a bucket of earth in the corner of the room. It was as much as she had managed to do after first Rob's and then Barnaby's departure the evening before. She simply hadn't had the heart to do anything more than stop the tree from dying.

She shrugged. 'I haven't had time yet.'

'Of course,' he acknowledged in clipped tones. 'Your visitor last night no doubt prevented it.'

Juliette looked at him with a small frown, not liking the way he'd said that. 'Barnaby? Yes…' she said slowly. 'Rob—'

'Have the two of you made up your quarrel?' Rob demanded, looking grimmer than ever. 'Did he offer you your job back?'

'Yes, and yes.' Juliette answered cautiously, desperately trying to read Rob's expression and failing miserably. 'I've accepted his apology for what happened,' she continued evenly, her gaze not wavering from Rob's rigidly set features, 'but not the job.'

'But I thought this morning when you left—' Something flared in the depths of Rob's eyes—something too fleeting to be analysed. 'Why not?'

Why did it matter to him? Why did anything that happened in her life matter to him? But it did. Juliette knew that it did. And with that knowledge came a hope, a yearning for more. So much more!

'I felt,' she began steadily, 'that it would be better, less awkward for everyone, if I *didn't* go back to work for Barnaby.' She moistened her lips with the tip of her tongue, sure of the emotion she saw in Rob's eyes this time. Relief. 'You see, the truth behind that "clash of personalities"—the real reason I was dismissed—was that I confirmed a hotel booking with Barnaby's wife for a weekend away in Paris.'

Rob looked completely puzzled. 'I don't understand. Did you have the wrong date? The wrong hotel? Although neither of those things sounds serious enough to me to warrant—'

'The wrong woman,' Juliette interrupted huskily, remembering all too well Deborah Harris's stunned silence on the other end of the telephone after Juliette, having failed to reach Barnaby on his mobile, had confirmed the booking with his wife instead.

Juliette raised an eyebrow at Rob's stunned expression. 'I'm sure it can't hurt to tell you any of this now.' She grimaced. 'Barnaby, it seems, had met someone at some business conference or other that we'd both attended in Frankfurt. The two of them kept in touch once Barnaby returned to England, culminating in their deciding to spend the weekend away together in Paris. I thought he was going with his wife, hence my telephone call to her, and Deborah thought he was going away on business with me. When Deborah confronted Barnaby with it, he had to admit he had been going away with another woman. Deborah was devastated. She ended their marriage and began divorce proceedings.'

At which stage, Barnaby had dismissed Juliette.

Oh, he probably wouldn't have got away with it if

she had fought her dismissal—but who wanted to go on working for a man who hated the sight of her? Or watch as Barnaby lost everything in a stupid act of uncompleted adultery? Juliette certainly hadn't!

Rob blinked. 'But I thought—believed…'

'Yes?' She looked at him questioningly.

He gave an impatient shake of his head. 'Why did he come to see you yesterday?'

She gave a rueful smile. 'To tell me that he had finally won Deborah back. He convinced her that nothing really happened with the other woman he was meeting in Paris, that their weekend away would have been their first time together, and that he had actually been thinking of cancelling the whole thing before I telephoned Deborah and it all blew up in his face.' Juliette wasn't completely sure about that last statement herself. But one thing she did know: Barnaby had certainly learnt his lesson!

Rob frowned disapprovingly. 'He should not have behaved in that way to begin with!'

'I think he knows that now.' Juliette smiled. 'Losing Deborah and his two children certainly brought him to his senses in a hurry!'

'Not soon enough,' Rob rasped.

Juliette looked at him searchingly. 'What did you mean just now? What did you believe?'

He made an impatient movement. 'You're not going to like me for this…'

'Tell me anyway,' she invited huskily, still buoyed by the emotion she had seen so briefly in his eyes.

He breathed raggedly before answering. 'I thought perhaps you'd had an affair with Harris, and that he had dismissed you when it ended.' He gave a snort of self-disgust. 'I also thought, until just now, that the person who telephoned you the other evening was in fact Barnaby's wife, accusing you of stealing her husband!'

Juliette stared at him, wondering how on earth—? But she hadn't told him she had a stepsister. Had refused to discuss her dismissal with him. She had a man's jumper in her flat. And then Barnaby had arrived, pleading to talk to her!

Rob couldn't have known that she wouldn't have discussed the reason for her dismissal before now because it would have meant dragging up someone else's very painful past, and quite possibly hurting Deborah and the children all over again. Just as he hadn't known that the jumper had belonged to her father. Or that her telephone conversation the other evening had been with Rosemary, rather than another man's wife. And even *she* hadn't known why Barnaby had needed to talk to her so urgently the night before. He'd explained himself only after Rob had left.

It was hardly surprising, when all of that was taken into consideration, that Rob had drawn the conclusions he had!

Although...

'Why should it matter to you one way or the other?' she demanded. Because it *did* matter to him—she could see that from the pain and self-disgust in those deep blue eyes.

He drew in a ragged breath. 'Will you forgive me? *Can* you forgive me?' he asked heavily. 'You were working at a job you are blatantly over-qualified for, you refused to talk of the reason you left your last employment, you had a man's sweater in your flat and you obviously intended spending Christmas here alone.' He shook his head impatiently. 'The last seemed a classic symptom of mistress syndrome.'

'You *have* been letting your imagination run away with you, haven't you?' Juliette laughed, too happy at knowing the reason for his sudden coolness and departure yesterday to feel offended at the idea of him thinking she was any man's mistress. 'I simply couldn't talk about the reason I'd left Harris International. Angry as I was with Barnaby, I couldn't risk Deborah and the children being hurt. She's a really lovely woman, by the way,' she added teasingly, as Rob still looked decidedly uncomfortable. 'I've already explained about the jumper.' She shrugged. 'And as for my job at Romeo's—I *was* blatantly over-qualified, wasn't I?' She smiled mischievously.

Rob looked relieved to have something other than his exaggerated conclusions to talk about. 'That, and the obvious fact you're a woman, have been more than enough to rankle with Graham since you began working at Romeo's.'

Juliette's eyes widened. 'You aren't telling me *that's* the reason he dislikes me so—?' She broke off awkwardly; after all, the other man was Rob's employee.

'Dislikes you so much he has done everything in his

power to get rid of you?' Rob finished grimly. 'Oh, yes, that is exactly what I am telling you. But now he's the one who has been removed,' he added with satisfaction.

'You haven't sacked him because of me?' Juliette gasped.

'Worse.' Rob grinned. 'I've transferred him to the New York branch.' He chuckled when he saw Juliette's obvious confusion. 'Graham can be a very good manager, but he has one serious failing: he cannot tolerate women who are better-qualified than he is. The overall manager of my New York store is a woman. A fact I forgot to mention to Graham when I gave him two weeks' leave to effect the transfer!'

'That was really mean!' Juliette protested, at the same time unable to repress the laughter that bubbled up inside her. 'God, wouldn't you like to be a fly on the wall when he gets to New York?'

Rob shrugged unrepentantly. 'The lesson will be no more than he deserves. He'll learn it or leave.'

She couldn't exactly disagree with him, knowing that she was far from the only woman at Romeo's that Graham had taken delight in harassing. It helped to know why, and that something had been done.

Although Rob still hadn't given her an explanation as to why any of that—Barnaby, Graham Taylor— should bother *him*. Or why he was really here. He could have just posted the jumper back to her.

'Juliette,' he began softly, his expression intense, 'I have behaved badly. I believed—I have told you what I believed. Really not a very good start to a relationship,' he muttered, sounding disgusted. 'I have no excuse for the things I thought—'

'Don't you?' she cut in huskily, standing up to move towards him, knowing that her earlier instincts hadn't been wrong, that she *had* seen that emotion in Rob's eyes. 'Don't you really?' She stood up, very close to him, reaching out tentatively to place a hand on his chest. His heart was beating very fast beneath her palm.

His expression softened as his gaze moved caressingly over her face. 'Two days ago—only two days? It seems I have always known you!' He groaned, his hands moving up to grasp her arms. 'Two days ago,' he began again, 'a young woman came hurtling towards me, wielding a deadly weapon—'

'It was an *umbrella*!' she corrected with a laugh.

'No matter,' he said, his accent very pronounced. 'As you hurtled towards me, green eyes wide with shock, red hair flying, I knew without a shadow of a doubt that I was looking at the woman of my dreams. Until that moment I had no idea who she would be or what she would look like, but one look at you and I was forever lost. I love you, Juliette, more than words can ever express. My head is full of thoughts about you. I want to be with you constantly, cannot even bear the thought of leaving you here when I go tomorrow.' He gazed down at her with searching eyes. 'Will you try to forgive me, my Juliette? Will you give me the chance to see if you might not grow to love me in return?'

She stared up at him wonderingly, at last having the answer as to why he had offered her the job as his PA:

he wanted her to leave with him when he went tomorrow. He couldn't bear the thought of going without her any more than she could bear the thought of his going!

'You still want me to be your PA?' she breathed softly, knowing she would do it, that she would accept any chance to be with Rob.

'I want you for my *wife*!' he corrected forcefully, his hands tightening on her arms. 'But I will settle for your being my PA if that is all I can have for now,' he added more humbly.

Rob wanted to *marry* her?

It was beyond her wildest imaginings that he should feel the same way about her as she did him!

Except she hadn't *told* him how she felt about him!

She reached up to touch the hardness of his cheek, encouraged by the way his eyes darkened. 'Rob, I love you, too,' she told him with husky emotion. 'I love you, I love you, I love you!' How right, how absolutely perfect it felt to say those words to her own wonderful Romeo. 'Oh, no!' She laughed softly. 'Do you realise that once we're married I shall have to go through life as Juliette Romeo?'

'Does it matter?' Rob asked as he began to rain kisses all over her face and neck, his arms holding her tightly against him.

'No,' she assured him with absolute certainty, knowing that his parents *would* one day have red-haired grandchildren. 'Nothing matters to me as long as we're together.' This man, this wonderful man, this man she loved with all her heart, loved her in exactly the same way!

Rob kissed her slowly and lingeringly on the lips. 'This is going to be a wonderful Christmas, Juliette,' he promised. 'The start of the rest of our lives together...'

And it was. Rob's family welcomed her into their midst with open arms, taking her into their hearts as she had taken Rob into hers and he had taken her into his.

Not just her Christmas Romeo, after all, but her forever Romeo...

The Tycoon's Christmas Engagement

REBECCA WINTERS

Rebecca Winters, who lives in Salt Lake City, has been writing since 1989. Until very recently she also worked full-time as a teacher. She currently writes for Superromance and for Mills & Boon Romance. After an incredible nearly one hundred titles, she's writing more books than ever, travelling, playing the piano, doing genealogy, looking forward to a second grandchild *and* enjoying life to the fullest.

CHAPTER ONE

"THE Roberts residence."

"Ms Roberts? It's Mitch Reynolds."

Immediately Annie's hand tightened on the receiver. She would know his deep, almost grating voice anywhere. It had a sensuous quality that had always unnerved her. Whenever she dropped in to see her mother, who worked at the Hastings Corporation, he inevitably appeared, as if he had radar and knew when she was in the building.

According to her mom, most women thought him the most attractive man alive.

Annie had thought the same thing when she'd first met him at seventeen. There was a dangerous quality about him that had drawn her to him, but of course he'd been too mature and sophisticated for her to even consider getting to know.

David Hastings, on the other hand, was younger and more like the boy next door. He didn't challenge her with every look. He was...safer, and darling.

Six years later, Annie hadn't changed her opinion of either man. Except that now she was a woman she recognized that a type like Mitch Reynolds was more dangerous than ever. Her awareness of him had grown even stronger, if that was at all possible.

Whenever she felt those Arctic blue eyes assessing her, she would tremble for no good reason.

She was trembling now, which was absurd.

Why would the thirty-two-year-old vice president of Hastings be calling here this early in the morning? Surely he knew today was her mother's wedding day?

"I'm sorry, but I'm afraid she and Roger left for San Pedro Port an hour ago."

"Actually, it's you I wanted to reach. Roger told me you would be delivering invitations for the office Christmas party later this morning. I wondered if you needed any help."

A thrill of alarm caused her pulse to race. Why would he be concerned over such a trivial matter?

The temptation to put the receiver back on the hook almost won the day. But out of respect for Roger, who was about to become her new stepfather, she refrained.

Roger, the CEO and owner of Hastings, thought Mitch walked on water, so she didn't dare offend his right arm.

"I appreciate your offer, Mr Reynolds, but I have everything under control."

There was a pregnant pause.

"Obviously I'm keeping you from something pressing."

She tensed. It seemed her response hadn't satisfied him. "If I sound out of breath it's because you caught me as I was walking out the door."

She hated feeling this breathless around him, even over the phone.

"Then I won't delay you any longer. Just remember my door is always open if you need anything."

Annie bit her lip. "Thank you. I'll remember that." But she wouldn't act on his offer. She didn't dare. Instinct told her a man like that could sweep you away until you were no longer in control of anything. Mitch Reynolds was an unknown quantity she knew to avoid at all costs.

Stimulated by anticipation of today's events, Mitchell Reynolds, who preferred to be called Mitch, hung up the phone and levered himself from the bed to get ready for work. The old adage about the early bird getting the worm was definitely in play.

There was nothing Mitch loved more than a presumably impossible challenge. And Annie Roberts rated right up there at the top.

There were reasons why he'd been waiting for the right time to capture her full attention. But, after her cool reaction on the phone, maybe he'd waited too long, and she was too emotionally distanced to respond to him. If he hoped to develop a real relationship with her, then where she was concerned unorthodox measures were called for.

So far their association had been superficial,

because he hadn't wanted to invade David Hastings's space if anything was going to develop between him and Annie. Mitch revered Roger too much to create problems with his son.

But, since he hadn't seen signs of things heating up in that department, Mitch had given himself permission to make her take notice of him.

Not since Hannah had he wanted a woman this badly. In case this was his last chance, he wasn't beyond using everything in his arsenal to win a war she wasn't aware had begun.

A half-hour later he left his Beverly Hills condo, jumped in his car and joined the mainstream of traffic headed into downtown L.A.

The new Hastings complex sat on a prime piece of real estate, well manicured, with leafy ground cover and palm trees. He pulled into his parking space. The white Nissan he was looking for hadn't arrived yet. So far so good.

He left his car and walked into the building, waving to the gardener, who was putting fresh bark under one of the newly planted ornamental trees.

Mitch's office suite was located in the east wing of the ground floor, next to Roger's. Roger's son David's was across the hall.

Since Mitch's secretary hadn't arrived yet, he made coffee for both of them, then planted himself at his desk to read the rest of yesterday's *Wall Street Journal*.

Soon he heard activity in the outer office and buzzed his secretary.

"Mr Reynolds— I didn't realize you were already here. Can I make you some coffee?"

"I already fixed it for us, so come on in and help yourself."

"I will later. Thank you."

He took another sip. "Would you do me a favor and contact Olympia Cruise Lines? I'd like a magnum of champagne sent to the stateroom of Mr and Mrs Roger Hastings aboard the *Olympia Princess*, with my compliments."

"Yes, sir. Anything else?"

"Yes. Let me know as soon as David Hastings comes in."

"He might already be in the building. Hold on and I'll check with Susan."

Mitch drank the rest of his coffee while he waited.

"She says he just walked in."

"Thank you. I'm headed there now. If anything comes up, you know where to find me."

He'd already delivered Christmas presents to the main staff, but still had one more to go. Reaching for David's gift, he exited the private entrance of his suite. David's office was further on down the hall.

"Good morning, Susan."

She lifted her head. "Hi, Mr Reynolds! It *is* a good morning, isn't it?" she exclaimed. "Last day of work until after New Year's."

"Amen," he said, before rapping on David's door.

"Not so loud!" the blond twenty-seven-year-old complained.

Mitch moved inside and closed it.

After assessing the situation, he poured coffee from the cafetière on the sideboard and handed the mug to David. "Too much celebrating with your dad last night?"

"You could say that." He tested the hot liquid, then drank most of it. "What brings you in here? With Dad and Marion off on their honeymoon, nobody's going to get a lick of work done today. I'm calling it quits in about five minutes."

Mitch smiled at the younger man. "Then I'm glad I got here in time to wish you a Merry Christmas." He put the gift on his desk. "You never know what can happen when everyone else starts to let down. Kingdoms can rise or fall in the blink of an eye."

"You sound like Dad," he muttered testily.

"Where do you think I learned that piece of wisdom?"

Roger Hastings was one of Southern California's most renowned and successful commercial developers. Mitch felt privileged to work for him.

David struggled to remove the ribbons from the package. "Golf balls. I can always use these. Thanks, Mitch. I'm afraid I haven't done any shopping yet."

"Don't worry about it."

Just then Susan buzzed David. Mitch could hear her clearly through the speaker.

"Sorry to interrupt, Mr Hastings, but one of Santa's helpers is here, giving out official invitations to the office Christmas party. She has one for you and would like to deliver it in person. Shall I send her in?"

David swore under his breath. "That's all I need. Dad probably told somebody on the committee to make certain I show up."

Mitch could have told him it was a self-appointed committee of one who'd been trying to get David's attention for the last year—without success. Whether it was still a crush on Annie's part, left over from her teenage years, or something more, Mitch was determined to find out.

"Mr Hastings?" Susan called to him again.

"Go ahead and send her in."

As soon as Mitch moved away from the door it opened, and Annie Roberts walked in.

She was a taller, more slender version of her mother, Marion, who was probably Roger's wife by now. Roger had arranged for a minister to marry them aboard ship. Both women were natural dark-haired beauties. But not even Mitch was prepared for the sight of a gorgeous elf in a thigh-length green tunic whose shapely legs went on forever. It was hard to know where to look first.

The second she saw Mitch, the mischievous smile on her face beneath the fetching red elf hat with the bell disappeared, as if she'd just received a shock. At least she wasn't indifferent to him.

Silence filled the room, prompting Mitch to say, "Good morning again, Ms Roberts. May I offer you and David my congratulations on your parents' wedding? That makes you two official stepbrother and sister today."

By her stunned expression, he'd caught her totally

off guard. That was good. It helped him to read between the lines.

"Thank you," she finally said in a tremulous voice. He was curious to understand why she sounded so emotional.

"You make a charming elf, by the way. Doesn't she, David?"

"I hardly recognized you in your costume, Annie."

That didn't surprise Mitch. David could hardly keep his eyes open. Though he was trying hard because Annie was a breathtaking sight. But as far as Mitch was concerned David was a year too late on the uptake. He'd had his chance without encountering any interference. Now Mitch was going to make his move...

"After your parents get back from their cruise, we'll have to arrange a party for them. But one party at a time, right?"

When she didn't say anything, he turned to David. "Did you know Annie's in charge of this year's Christmas party?"

David shook his head. "I had no idea."

"It makes sense, since she has always helped her mother plan it. At least for as long as I've been here anyway."

Mitch's gaze switched back to Annie. "I'm looking forward to seeing the invitation. May I have mine now?"

She was only holding one, of course. He could tell she was upset to find him in here. A flush had seeped into her already colorful cheeks. Was it because she'd been caught red-handed? Or was there some other element at work, too? He'd sell his soul to know.

"Someone else is delivering yours, to your office."

If that was a hint for Mitch to leave, he had news for her.

"I'm sorry to have missed them. Since I'm not in there, do you mind if I look at yours, David?"

"Be my guest. I'm not sure I could read the writing anyway."

Mitch put out his hand, forcing her to give him the scroll tied with red ribbon. If he wasn't mistaken, she trembled at his touch.

He undid it and studied the contents. It was in poetic form. He read it aloud. "'Twas the night before Christmas and all through L.A., the deserving employees at the Hastings Corporation were ready to play. The Roof Garden at the St Regis was decorated with care, in hopes that Mr and Mrs Claus soon would be there. While the children were nestled, all snug in their beds, their parents had visions of a champagne gala running through their heads. With Dasher and Dancer taking a turn around the floor, Santa would give out fabulous surprises galore. So away to the Roof and witness his flight, after he wishes one and all Merry Christmas and goodnight.'"

David squinted at her. "Cute."

It was a lot more than cute. Judging by what Mitch had gleaned from Roger, since working so closely with him, he knew how hard Annie had been hit by the death of her father. All the wonderful memories of her childhood were wrapped up in that poem. His thoughts were verified when their gazes collided. He felt the vulnerability in those troubled gray orbs, and possibly her resentment of him because he'd been the one to read what was in her soul.

"Everyone will love your invitation," he murmured. "Especially Roger. This is the one Christmas Eve party he'll wish he hadn't missed. I know I'm going to enjoy attending. In fact, I can't wait."

He put the scroll on David's desk, then turned to her.

"As long as you have other invitations to deliver, I'll walk out with you. It'll be worth the effort just to see the look on the others' faces when they read your amazing and clever rendering. See you at the party, David," he called over his shoulder.

"I'll make it there at some point."

Noting the deflation on Annie's face, Mitch cupped her elbow and escorted her past Susan's desk. He hadn't wanted to give her time to feel worse over David's less than enthusiastic response.

"It's evident you've outdone yourself on this party. Since I have no more business, let me help you finish delivering the rest of the scrolls."

By the time she'd removed her arm from his grasp, her classic features had closed up.

"Thank you, but I've had other people helping me and it's all done. Now I'm going home."

A home with no one there…

"That's a coincidence. So am I. I'll walk with you to the parking lot."

She shook her head so the little bell tinkled. "You go ahead. I have to change in Mother's office."

"No problem. I'll wait for you."

Her mobile mouth had tightened. "I get the feeling something's wrong, Mr Reynolds."

"Please call me Mitch."

"Mitch, then," she amended, taking an extra breath. "Mother didn't tell me I needed to work with you on this. If I should have done that, then I apologize."

"You've misunderstood, Annie. I only wanted to be of help if you needed a hand. Why don't we talk about it after you remove your very attractive costume?"

CHAPTER TWO

ANNIE locked herself in the bathroom, unable to credit that Mitch Reynolds had been in David's office, standing there larger than life, at the precise moment she'd walked in.

There had been something intimidating about his tall, lean build, and the slightly cruel smile as he'd spoken. A little scar stood out along his hard jaw. Couple that with his unruly black hair and she had hardly been able to think for the adrenaline rush that had assailed her body. She was still shaken remembering how he'd assessed her so intimately with those cobalt blue eyes.

David might as well have not been in the room.

After all the trouble she'd gone to, hoping to garner his interest just this once, it had been Mitch who'd praised her silly poem and offered to walk around distributing the rest of the invitations for her. She didn't want to give him any credit. It was churlish of her, but for some reason she couldn't help it.

Feeling distinctly out of sorts, she changed into designer jeans and a white hooded pullover. After brushing her hair, she put the costume in an old airline bag and left the suite.

The second Mitch saw her, he stopped talking to one of the accountants who'd just received his invitation. In a few swift strides he'd joined her at the main doors to the complex.

She'd never seen him in anything but a suit and tie. Still, that civilized veneer of sophistication couldn't hide his inscrutable side, the one that had made her increasingly aware of him over the last year.

Though he'd never stepped out of line, never said or done anything she could criticize, she couldn't shrug off her uneasy feelings.

Since his early-morning phone call she'd felt a new energy coming from him. Whether it was a comment or a look, he'd managed to set her nerves on edge.

Maybe he didn't think her capable of handling the Christmas party without her mother. Maybe he resented the fact that Roger had given her *carte blanche* now that she was an insider by virtue of his marriage to her mom.

If so, that was too bad, because it was Roger's company, and he was her stepfather now.

As for David, she'd been hoping to have more than a platonic relationship with him one day. The office party had seemed a likely place to make him notice her as an intelligent, desirable woman in her own right. But his half-hearted assurance that he'd "show up at some point" had filled her with yet another disappointment.

David should have been the one to say he couldn't wait for the party.

"Are you all right?" Mitch asked as he held the door open for her.

"Of course."

The cold air felt good against her hot face. Once she'd walked a few yards, she turned to him, brushing some strands of hair off her cheeks. It was time to deal with him head-on.

"I can tell there's something on your mind. If you've any objection to any of my plans for the Christmas party, I'll fix them if I can."

"You seem intent on misunderstanding me, Annie. I only wanted to commend your choice of location for the party."

"Mother reserved it six months ago—"

"On your suggestion," he interjected. "I overheard you talking to her about it at last year's party."

That didn't surprise Annie. Mitch Reynolds had a brilliant mind, and was the eyes and ears of the company.

"It's a wonderful choice of place," he assured her. "You have no idea how much Roger values his employees. A celebration with this kind of elaborate planning and attention to detail reflects his feelings and shows how much he cares. He'll be particularly appreciative of your hard work during this time while he's away with your mother."

"Thank you," she murmured, not knowing what else to say. If David had been saying these things to her, she would have been thrilled. The fact that it was Mitch made her less trusting, which she admitted really wasn't fair to him.

"You're a woman of hidden talents. After you receive your MBA in the spring, I'd like to be the first person you come to see. I know of a position in the corporation that needs a person like you." After a pause he added, "See you at the party."

He headed for his car, which was parked in the VIP section.

Annie stared after him, her feelings ambivalent—because he was so different from the man she'd thought she'd known all these years. To be told she could have a job at Hastings after graduation had been a dream of hers. But she hadn't expected the opening to come through Mitch Reynolds.

Nothing had gone the way she'd planned it this morning. It should have been David who'd walked her out to the car and said all those things to her.

Having been thrown totally off balance, she turned in the opposite direction and rushed to her Nissan. Unable to deal with her conflicting feelings where Mitch was concerned, she was determined to put him out of her mind.

But when he drove by her car and flashed her another penetrating glance, it brought back that moment in David's office, when Mitch's gaze had swept over her, missing virtually nothing. She was still reacting to the weakness that had attacked her.

Maybe this was the way the competition felt when he was about to swoop in for the kill.

Needing to channel her frenzied emotions toward something constructive, Annie took a deep breath and headed for the beauty salon, where she'd made an appointment.

Twenty minutes later she walked in the shop, ready to undergo a drastic change. The receptionist motioned to a guy with spiky blue hair. He examined her with a critical eye.

"Hi, love. What can I do for you today?"

"On Christmas Eve I have to look perfect. I'd like my hair cut short, but not too short, if you know what I mean."

He nodded. "Soft and feminine."

"Exactly."

"Come on back to my chair."

Annie followed the stylist, who was rumored to be one of the best in Hollywood.

Once he'd put the drape around her neck, he said, "I know exactly what you need."

The man was a wizard, and prophetic, too. Within the hour he handed her a mirror. "Long hair is for teenagers. Now you look like a woman."

He was right! His hands had worked magic.

"What color dress are you wearing for the big night?"

"Flaming red chiffon with spaghetti straps."

He winked. "Nice. Whoever you're trying to impress won't be able to look anywhere else."

She shivered, because she was still reeling from Mitch Reynolds's all-encompassing scrutiny. Somehow she had to put the incident behind her and keep her emotions in check.

After paying the stylist a big tip, she left the salon, loving the feel and style of her new cap of soft, gleaming curls. More black than brown, they framed her oval face to her jawline. The change gave her an elegance that had been missing. Surely David would be aware of the difference and find himself intrigued?

Since Mitch had ruined her moment in David's office, she was resolute that nothing would go wrong the night of the party.

Once again she got in her car and headed to her mom's seventies-style home to grab a late lunch. She needed to make a few phone calls to the guys in her study group from UCLA. The presentation for their university marketing class was due after the holidays.

But trying to get four grad students together to divide up the work was difficult, at best. Two of them held jobs, which made it tricky to arrange schedules, but it had to be done.

Annie was thankful for the grant that was allowing her to finish up her MBA without having to deal with a part-time job. The result being that she'd maintained a good grade point average.

The companies that came on campus to recruit new graduates might claim to look at the total student, but it still held true that the top academic achievers got picked first.

She could hardly credit that Mitch had already approached her to come to work at Hastings. His offer would have pleased Annie's father. Before he'd died, he'd made her promise she would distinguish herself in some kind of college pursuit. He hadn't cared which profession she went into. If she so chose, it could even be patent law, the kind he'd practiced. The important thing for her was to focus all her energy on getting that coveted degree. Then her path would be set before her and she would always be able to take care of herself.

Her mom had been in full agreement. She'd pointed out that if she hadn't received her bachelor's degree the Hastings Corporation wouldn't have even considered her application for employment.

As a result, Annie hadn't played as much as she'd studied. While she'd seen friends drop out of college to get married and have babies, she'd avoided heavy romantic involvement to stay the course.

The crush she had on David had helped her remain emotionally unattached from any guys she'd dated. If she went to work for his father's company after graduation they'd see each other on a daily basis. Maybe that was what it would take for him to ask her out. But after today she wasn't sure of anything. Mitch had driven home the point that she and David were now stepbrother and sister. She hoped it wouldn't change David's view of her. It wasn't as if they were related by blood.

As she reached in her purse for her cellphone, it rang. The caller ID said "out of area." Maybe one of the guys in the study group was calling.

"Hello?"

"Annie, honey? I promised I'd call when I became Mrs Roger Hastings."

"Mom—" Tears spurted from Annie's eyes. "I'm so happy for you."

She was, of course. Her mother had been in love with the dynamic owner and head of the Los Angeles–based Hastings Corporation for a long time.

The attractive widower had built a multimillion-dollar business that bought and developed commercial real estate. He'd first hired Marion Roberts as his secretary. In eight years she'd gone from private secretary to being his wife. They were perfect for each other.

Annie could feel her mother's joy. No one deserved it more than she did. After all they'd been through together, after the death of her father, Annie was thrilled her mother had found happiness again.

"To take you on a cruise is so romantic. He loves you, Mom. I'm so excited he finally realized and did something about it."

"Me, too, honey. But I hate leaving you alone at Christmas."

"I won't be alone. Roz and her boyfriend are having me over for dinner. Don't you know your marriage has *made* my Christmas?"

"Annie…"

"It's true, Mom. Some women never get the chance to be married once, let alone twice. Before Daddy died, he begged you to find someone else and be happy. I've always thought Roger was that person."

"He *is* wonderful."

"Then forget everything except making each other happy!"

"God bless you, my darling girl."

Annie clicked off and had a good cry. Afterward she left messages for the guys in her class to phone her.

With that accomplished she ate a sandwich, then left the house to pick up the coupons for the hams they were giving as gifts. She'd already printed off the bonus checks and could start stuffing the Christmas cards. Roz and her boyfriend had agreed to help Annie, and would be coming over for pizza later in the evening.

As long as she kept busy she wouldn't have time to think about the vice president of Hastings, or the way he made her feel no matter how hard she tried to erase all thoughts of him from her consciousness.

CHAPTER THREE

By THREE o'clock Christmas Eve afternoon, Annie had dressed to kill and left for the St Regis Hotel in downtown Los Angeles.

Before this year the party had always been held at the Alhambra House. It was time for a change.

The famous Roof Garden atop the St Regis had a black-and-white-striped canopy fanning out from the ceiling that gave it a garden feel. From the windows you could see all of L.A.

Everyone would love the new, exciting change of venue.

Annie had plans to meet the florist there. Though the hotel had already put up a Christmas tree, and had strung Christmas lights to adorn the canopy, she'd ordered pots of red azaleas and poinsettias for the centerpieces, which would be given away as prizes.

The Roof Garden was circular in design, with four evenly spaced exits.

She'd ordered garlands of evergreens to be draped

in each one, with a large bunch of mistletoe holding up the centers.

When she arrived, she noted with satisfaction that most of the decorating had already been done, right down to the individual colorful elvcs poking their faces out of the flowering plants.

A bank of poinsettia trees had been set in place where the dance band would sit.

She checked in with Mrs Lawson, the hotel restaurant manager, who showed her a back room where she could leave the Santa and Mrs Claus outfits until it was time for the entertainment.

Everyone would be getting a box of chocolate truffles, with a card, a five-hundred-dollar bonus and a gift coupon for a honey-baked ham. Roger was always generous. This year he'd okayed a larger budget than usual to pay for everything.

Annie had decided there would be no head table or placecards. For a change people could sit where they wanted at tables surrounding the dance floor. Better yet, they could order anything they wanted from the menu.

Annie had already worked out a special price with Mrs Lawson to keep the cost of the party down. Buying champagne from a Napa Valley distributor she knew had helped to get a better price in that department as well.

Before she knew it, the hotel dining room staff had started to put condiments on the tables and do the general set-up.

The band arrived with their instruments and settled in. One of them wheeled in a piano and set up the mike.

Hoping David would show up soon, she decided she would ask him to be the master of ceremonies. But deep down she wasn't sure she could count on him. She would have thought he'd phone her, if only to talk about their parents for a few minutes. But no such call had come. Maybe *he* wouldn't come, either.

For the first time since knowing him she wondered if she'd made the mistake of endowing him with qualities he didn't possess. That was the problem with never having gone out with him. They'd flirted a lot, but she was beginning to wonder if she really knew him at all. Odd how her thoughts kept flicking back to Mitch, who'd made all the overtures she would have expected to come from David.

Bemused, she looked around the Roof Garden, knowing all the employees, including David, would be blown away by the setting and decorations.

There was nothing she'd love more than to blow *him* away. But she couldn't do that if he decided to give the party a miss.

Haunted by the fact that Mitch Reynolds *would* come, she started to get nervous and began pacing.

Little by little the guests started to trickle in. While she stood there, wondering what the night would bring, she saw a blond head at the far exit. It was David. He was built like his father. Both of them were six feet with trim builds.

He entered the room from the other side. To her relief

he'd come without a date. Things couldn't be working out better. But with his good-looking face and expressive brown eyes, she wouldn't be the only woman in the room who noticed him.

She knew the moment he saw her, because he paused, then started walking across the dance floor toward her.

Just then the photographer she'd hired appeared out of nowhere. "You look good enough to eat." He grinned, and took her picture. The flash went off, startling her.

"My sentiments exactly." A familiar male voice sounded directly behind her. Suddenly a strong pair of hands grasped her slender waist and spun her around.

She discovered herself staring up into the hot blue eyes of Mitch Reynolds. He was smiling at her with a devilish gleam that set off alarm bells.

"Merry Christmas, Annie. It is you, isn't it? The dress is stunning. So is your new hairstyle. May I be the first at the party to try out the mistletoe? Which I confess is tempting me beyond my power to resist."

Her escape was barred as Mitch lowered that cruel mouth to hers, acting like he'd done this many times before and knew exactly how to satisfy her.

The first touch of his lips wasn't the invasion she'd expected, but rather a persistent coaxing of her own lips to respond. His touch created enough heat to send fingers of awareness through her body. Without knowing how it happened, her mouth opened to the growing pressure of his. Soon they were drinking from each other's mouths as if they were parched and couldn't get enough.

What was supposed to be a holiday kiss, given in fun, had turned out to be something incredibly different. Annie's heart pounded too hard. She could scarcely breathe.

Another flash went off, bringing her out of her dazed state.

She tore her lips from his, trembling so violently it was humiliating.

"Can anyone get in line?" she heard David ask, but by now she'd sneaked into the hall, where she could attempt to recover without an audience.

Both men followed her. Mitch's eyes held an enigmatic glitter.

"That's up to your stepsister."

She was already shaken by what had just happened, and Mitch's needling remark caused her to turn blindly to David. She pressed her lips to his, wanting desperately to wipe out the memory of Mitch's kiss, which had been like an assault on her senses.

David kissed her warmly, the way she'd been dreaming about for years. But something was wrong. And it wasn't because she could smell alcohol on his breath. Though he was putting real feeling into it, she felt…nothing.

Absolutely nothing!

"The band leader is motioning to you, Annie. Shall I see what he wants while you're otherwise occupied?"

Mitch Reynolds was like a specter she couldn't get away from fast enough.

Summoning all the self-control she could muster,

she backed away from David, who seemed reluctant to let her go. The knowledge should have thrilled her.

Practically incoherent, she said, "Excuse me for a minute, David."

"I will—on the condition that you hurry back and sit at my table."

"Let me see what's going on first."

It wasn't until she reached the band that she realized she'd forgotten to ask David to take charge. For those moments in Mitch's arms she'd forgotten everything. It was like she'd always believed. He had the power to sweep you away to a place you'd never been before. That was what had just happened, and she'd gone right along with him—as she'd feared.

Mitch trailed the feminine woman in red who had unconsciously sashayed her way through the tables to talk to the band leader. He couldn't take his eyes off her legs, flirting with him as the red material floated back and forth in a tantalizing rhythm.

While the band leader and Annie had their heads together, discussing the Christmas music repertoire, Mitch took advantage of the time to reach for the mike. Ignoring Annie's vexed expression when she noted his actions, he looked out over the crowd of coworkers and said, "Merry Christmas, everyone! On behalf of Roger Hastings, who's away on his honeymoon with none other than our own Marion, may I welcome you to the Roof Garden for the annual company Christmas party? As you can tell, a certain lovely elf has been busy creating this magical wonderland. Though words can't adequately express our appreciation, let's give Annie Roberts a big round of applause for all her hard work. She's really outdone herself."

The dinner guests burst into enthusiastic applause that lasted such a long time she blushed.

After the din had finally subsided, he grasped her cold hand. She looked so poised, who would have guessed?

"If the band will play their rendition of 'I Saw Mommy Kissing Santa Claus,' Annie and I will start the dancing with the hope that the rest of you will join in."

To anyone else, she looked serene and impossibly beautiful as he pulled her into his arms. But he could feel her bristling from the tips of her toes to the last shiny black curl tumbling over her forehead.

"Relax," he whispered against her warm temple. "The evening has barely begun. Just go with the flow."

CHAPTER FOUR

ANNIE held herself rigid. "There's nothing I'd like more, but I have things to see about, Mr Reynolds."

"After that kiss you gave me a few minutes ago, I think we've graduated permanently to first names, don't you?"

He felt her breath catch. "How much have you had to drink tonight?"

"If you knew me better, you'd know I don't drink alcohol. What else do you want to know about me?"

"Right now, I have this party on my mind. The entertainment needs to happen on time, so those with children can leave and get home to them."

"I'm sure they'll appreciate that. So, what can I do for you?"

After a slight hesitation she said, "Mingle with the crowd and make certain everyone is having a good time."

"We'll do it after a few more dances. I haven't done this for so long I'm rusty."

"In case you hadn't noticed, there are quite a few

female employees here without partners. I'm sure any one of them would be thrilled to dance with you."

He pulled her closer, burying his lips in her glossy hair. She smelled like a field of wildflowers.

"I'd rather be dancing with you. I wanted to dance with you at last year's party, but I thought your card was all filled up. In case you can't tell, you're making me look good out here."

He felt every shocked breath she took. "I can't do this much longer."

"I could do this all night. Just stay with me until the music ends. They're playing 'White Christmas' now. It's my favorite song. Reminds me of Minnesota, where my grandparents raised me. Christmas doesn't seem the same without snow."

"I'm sure it doesn't. Now, if you'll excuse me, there are things to be done."

"I agree. Let's do them together, shall we?" Since that kiss there was no way he was letting her get away from him now.

He swung her around to the edge of the dance floor. Tightening his hold on her hand, so she couldn't run off, he began walking around the tables with her, saying hello to everyone. She tried to pull away from him, then gave up in favor of not creating a scene.

Mitch took a circuitous route, nodding and chatting with people until they'd covered the room. When David saw them coming, he stood up.

"At last! Your dinner's getting cold, Annie."

"There's work to be done, David. She'll have to eat

later," Mitch explained, forestalling anything she'd planned to say to the other man. "If you want to be useful, you could rove for a while, to ensure everything's going smoothly."

Whisking her away once more, Mitch headed for the exit that led to the room where he'd seen the Santa suits.

Once inside, he walked over and held up the Mr Claus outfit. "You picked out the perfect size for me."

Annie glared at him from beneath her lashes.

The fact that it *was* the right size infuriated her. So did his wolfish white smile that had worked its way under her skin.

Hot-faced, she said, "If you had given me time a few minutes ago, you would have heard me ask David if he would play Santa."

Mitch already knew she'd responded to his kiss, but she didn't want him to think she was craving more.

One dark eyebrow quirked. "This costume would drown him. Besides, he's already had a little too much holiday cheer. But if you want me to get him, I will."

Annie averted her eyes. If she hadn't kissed David, and discovered for herself he'd been drinking before the party, she wouldn't have believed Mitch. As it stood, she couldn't allow a flushed Santa with glazed eyes to help hand out the company gifts—especially not when it was Roger's son.

And her stepbrother, as Mitch had reminded her the other day under no uncertain terms.

He flashed her a mysterious glance. "Need help with your Mrs Claus costume?"

She swallowed hard. "No, thank you." Being crushed against his hard body for those few minutes had been all the closeness she could handle.

Right in front of her, he slipped off his shoes. Next he removed his suit jacket. To her shock, he pulled off his trousers before putting on the bottom half of his costume, which was already padded. Then came the red velvet jacket and the big black belt with bells.

Mesmerized by the transformation taking place, she had a hard time believing it was Mitch under the hat and beard.

Realizing she was staring, she slipped the red granny gown over her head, then pulled on the wig with the bedcap. After putting on a large pair of spectacles, she was ready.

Mitch had put on the black Santa boots, making him a good six-four. "Where's my sack, darling?"

Drawing in a fortifying breath, she said, "Behind the Christmas tree, dearest."

He made a "ho-ho" sound, then bent over and kissed her hotly on the mouth. Though his beard scratched her skin, she found herself lost again in the build-up of heat he created with a mere touch.

"That's to keep us warm while we spread Christmas cheer to kith and kin. Then we'll go home for a long winter's nap."

He left the room ahead of her, not giving her time to ponder his remarks, or the way that last kiss had shot through her like wildfire.

He was turning out to be such an unknown quantity,

and she didn't know what he would do next. Anxious and fascinated at the same time, she hurried after him, to tell him what she'd planned for this portion of the program.

But it was too late. He'd already found the big bag that held the gifts, and had dragged it out in front of the tree in plain sight of the crowd, jingling his bells and saying "ho-ho-ho" in a booming voice.

If Annie didn't know better, she would think he played Santa Claus for a living. Mitch could put his mind to anything. It amazed her. A few days ago she couldn't have imagined him in this role, let alone enjoying it. Now that he was performing so brilliantly, she couldn't imagine David carrying it off. In fact, she was beginning to realize it would never have occurred to him to help her.

As Mitch reached in the sack, he lifted his head to their audience. "In case you didn't notice, I brought my bride along tonight to keep me company. It gets mighty cold up there in that sleigh. If truth be known, she gives out more heat than our fireplace at the North Pole."

The crowd roared with laughter, causing Annie's cheeks to burn a fiery red.

"Come closer, darling. I'm going to need your help giving out the gifts our industrious little elves have made."

He filled her arms with as many boxes as she could carry. Then he loaded his own arms and they worked the room while the band played "Santa Claus is Coming to Town."

He'd stepped into the part like he'd been born to it, putting all the dinner guests in the spirit of Christmas.

At every opportunity they whispered to Annie that it was the best party the Hastings Corporation had ever put on.

Annie appreciated the compliments, but she had to admit it wouldn't have been the same without the audacious Mitch Reynolds running away with the show.

He'd told her she was a woman of many talents, but she couldn't hold a candle to *his* performance—on or off the stage.

When she'd delivered the last gift, she joined him at the bandstand and took over the mike.

"An elf has put a Christmas sticker on the back of one of the chairs at each table. Whoever is sitting there can take home the centerpiece."

There were more cheers before everyone checked their chairs.

Mitch took the mike back. All she could see of his face were his dark blue eyes, studying her with a look that made her panic. He was going to do something outrageous again, and there was no place to hide.

Once more he turned to the crowd. "My bride has worn herself out, working so hard. Her poor little feet need a rest, don't you think?"

Their captivated audience responded with a resounding, "Yes!" and started clapping.

"No, Mitch— Please—" she cried. It did no good. He picked her up in his strong arms without missing a breath.

Carrying her toward the nearest exit, he called out, "Merry Christmas to all, and to all a goodnight."

When he paused beneath the mistletoe, she had an idea what was going to happen. Before her groan could escape his mouth had descended on hers once more, blocking out the light, the noise, the music—everything except the frantic pounding of her heart.

Furious with herself, because she'd discovered she wanted the kiss to go on and on, she found the strength to break it. On a burst of inspiration she turned her head toward the audience and called out, "Can't you at least wait until we're back in the sleigh, Mr Claus?"

The room exploded with laughter. The applause seemed to crescendo.

Chuckling out loud, Mitch carried her all the way to the back room. He slowly let her down until her high heels touched the floor.

"That was the perfect exit line, Mrs Claus. Remind me to do this with you again next year."

The moment made her feel close to him in a way she would never have dreamed. Weaving in place from the contact, she pulled off her spectacles. "Next year Mother will be back in charge."

She removed the wig and her granny gown, taking as much time as possible in an effort to recover.

"I had a lot of fun tonight, Annie."

"So did I," she answered honestly, and kept busy putting everything in the garment bag.

"But—?" he prodded.

In order to let him finish getting changed, she kept her back turned to him.

"No buts. With your help, it was a smashing success.

I can understand what my mother meant when she said Roger stole you away from the competition. No one can match you at what you do best. It's no wonder he has already made you vice president."

"Rather than David, you mean?"

Annie wheeled around angrily, noting that Mitch was back in his formal navy suit jacket and striped tie, looking dark and aloof and…undeniably gorgeous.

"I didn't say that."

"You didn't have to. You forget I've seen you coming and going from the office for years now. Not much escapes you when you're a bystander there, or at other company parties."

The mention of other parties caused Annie to shudder. Last year she'd tried so hard to get David's exclusive attention when they'd been seated at the head table. But he'd only stayed by her side for a little while before excusing himself to go to another party. Crushed by his departure, she'd been left to face her nemesis, Mitch Reynolds, who had been seated across from her, evidently observing her pain through those all-seeing eyes.

"If you want to join David now, feel free. I'll take care of the costumes." He plucked the garment bag from her arm. "The shop's address is right here on the label. I'll make certain they're returned after Christmas."

Her lips tightened. "The clean-up is part of my job."

"Nevertheless, after everything you've put in to this party, it's the least I can do."

The *least* he could do?

On the verge of hysteria, she muttered a thank you, reached for her purse and rushed toward the dining room, almost colliding with David in the hall.

"There you are." But when he put his hands on her arms, she felt she should be the one steadying him.

"How about I take you home in a cab and we'll celebrate our parents' marriage over a bottle of champagne?"

This was exactly how she'd hoped the evening would end.

"I have a few more things to do here. Why don't you meet me at Mom's in a half-hour."

"She lives on Canyon Drive, right?"

"Yes. 1094."

"I'll be there, waiting for you."

He brushed his lips against her cheek just as Mrs Lawson came to find her.

After signing for the party, Annie hurried into the dining room to pay the band.

All the guests had left. The only people who remained were the dining room staff, quietly going about straightening the room.

The second Mitch emerged from the hall, carrying the garment bags, she noticed a waitress approach him with a poinsettia and an azalea. He managed to juggle everything without problem.

Annie couldn't help but wonder if the flowers were for a woman he was planning to meet now that the party was over. It was Christmas Eve, after all, and the night was still young. He'd had his fun with Annie to ratchet up the excitement for their guests. But now he was going home to some woman who no doubt couldn't wait to be in his arms.

Until tonight she'd never given a thought to his personal life, beyond the probability that he had some beautiful woman in tow all the time. She could tell herself she wasn't really interested in what he did outside of office hours, but that would be a lie. She'd had a taste of him tonight. In her heart of hearts she knew she wanted more…

The photographer waved and let her know he'd send the bill and the prints to the office.

After one last walk around, Annie realized her job was done. With a curious mixture of satisfaction and let-down, because Mitch had gone, she left through the far exit and hurried to catch the next elevator going down.

Tonight she wouldn't have to go home to an empty house. David was going to be there. Her plan to spend Christmas Eve with him had actually worked. Yet the thought of being alone with him at last didn't make her heart race, or anything close to it.

"You," she gasped quietly, when she saw that Mitch was already inside the elevator.

He lounged against the wall, watching her through hooded eyes.

"You were expecting David?"

"I—I wasn't expecting anyone," she muttered crossly. "David has already gone ahead."

The door closed and the elevator began its descent to the lobby, fourteen stories below. Halfway down, it came to a stop without fanfare. At the same time the light went out, entombing them in total darkness.

She bit her lip. "The show is over, Mitch. We don't have an audience to play to right now."

She heard a strange sound come from his throat.

"You're the one standing next to the control panel, not me. If I didn't know better, I would think *you'd* staged this to get me alone," he murmured, in that wry, mocking tone of his.

She blinked. "You mean we're really stuck in here?"

CHAPTER FIVE

"SO IT seems. Don't worry. Some transformer probably overloaded because of all the Christmas lights. The power company will get it fixed before we know it."

She fought to control her panic. "I don't believe it." She moaned the words.

"Things could be worse. It might have happened during dinner. I'd say it's a good thing you got everybody out in time. Thanks to your party going off with precision, only you and I have to go down with the ship."

"That's a horrible thing to say!"

"I'm sorry, Annie. I didn't mean to upset you." His apology sounded genuine.

"I know, and I didn't mean to snap. It's just that I don't do well in enclosed spaces."

"Few people do."

"You seem to be handling it."

"That's because I have Mrs Claus with me. She keeps me steadied."

"Is everything a game to you?" She hated his con-descension.

"Sometimes real life can be too painful."

His admission stunned her. "I'm sorry I said anything. Don't mind me. I'm not at my best right now. If we don't get out of here soon, you're going to find yourself locked up with a raving lunatic."

"In that case, I believe in making the most of a situation. If we're stuck here for the night, indulge me while I pad the floor with our costumes. Then we can sit or lie down and be comfortable."

She could hardly swallow. "Do you really think we could be in here till morning?"

"Maybe."

"I'm supposed to be home by now!"

"I know. I heard you making plans with David. When he learns the power is out, he'll realize you got caught somewhere and come to rescue you."

She sucked in her breath. "That was an unkind thing to say."

"What do you mean?"

She expelled a tortured sigh. "We both know he's had too much to drink. He'll probably fall asleep waiting for me."

"All's not lost. When we're freed from our prison, you'll be able to drive home and wake him up."

She hugged her arms to her waist.

"I've never seen him like that before."

"Neither have I. But, given the fact that his father just got married, and his own engagement didn't work out, he's probably feeling a little isolated right now. Probably the same way you're feeling, with your mother gone."

"You certainly assume a lot."

"Roger has confided in me from time to time. He told me how much you loved your father, how hard it's been to lose him. Maybe it's because I've known loss, too, that I can relate. When my fiancée got killed in a skiing accident in college, I think I drowned my sorrows for a solid month. After I finally pulled out of the worst of it, I vowed never to drink again. It didn't solve anything—only displaced the pain which came anyway."

Maybe it was the darkness, but she could feel his remembered pain. To know he'd loved a special woman gave her new insight into his psyche.

"What was her name?"

"Hannah."

"I'm so sorry, Mitch." Her voice shook. "Were you skiing with her? Is that how you got that scar?"

"No to both questions. She was on the ski team. There was an icy track. She skidded off course into a tree. I was at the library, studying."

Annie closed her eyes tightly, but tears trickled out between the lashes anyway. She knew what it felt like to lose someone you loved.

"It's history, Annie. Don't waste any tears on me."

She wiped the moisture off her cheeks. "I'm not."

"And I got the scar in high school, playing basketball. Some spectator threw a beer bottle on the floor, and

I fell on a jagged piece of it. Right. I've got everything ready now. If l sit first, then I can help you down."

"Thank you, but I'll stand for a little while longer."

After a silence, he said, "In order to avoid a fate worse than death, I make it a rule never to take advantage of a woman in a dark elevator."

She laughed gently, helpless to do otherwise. How could she ever have thought she couldn't trust him?

"I'm not worried about that."

Annie knew a lot of things about him she hadn't known before. And when you knew certain things about a person you started to care.

The last thing she wanted to do was care about Mitch Reynolds.

"Well, at least let me help you stay warm. It may not be a white Christmas in L.A., but it's cold out."

In the next instant she felt him put his suit jacket around her shoulders.

Her body immediately absorbed the warmth from his.

"Thank you."

"You're welcome."

"Now you're going to freeze to death."

"Not after those kisses you gave me." He squeezed her arms before letting her go.

It was a good thing, or he would have known she was trembling for another reason than the cold.

He sat down next to her legs. "You don't seem as frightened as before."

"That's because you've helped me get my mind off myself. In fact, without your assistance tonight, the party wouldn't have been such a huge hit with everyone. I owe you a lot."

"Don't give me any credit, Ms Roberts. It had your signature written all over it. Whatever part I played, my motives were strictly dishonorable."

"You mean Roger decided I couldn't be trusted to handle the party on my own, so he put you in charge of me?"

"Roger had nothing to do with my involvement," he bit out.

Like quicksilver he'd changed into the man who could be uncomfortably remote on occasion. But at least now she thought she knew some of the reasons why.

"Are you going to leave me hanging?"

"That's right. You're an intelligent woman. Maybe one day you'll figure it out."

She blinked. "Did you think I was going to fall apart because my mother got married, and so you decided to be there to pick up the pieces?"

"Well, you must admit the two of you are exceptionally close."

"Of course we are. After Daddy died of heart failure we had to pull together. But it doesn't mean we haven't lived our own lives since then. To be honest, I was hoping Roger would propose to Mother last year, but it didn't happen."

"That's because he knew you worshipped your father and might not be able to accept him in your lives."

"Not accept Roger?" she cried out, aghast. "I'm crazy about him! I always have been."

"Then he's a lucky man, in more ways than one."

Still trembling, she said, "If anything it was Mom who was worried David might not be able to accept her. Before Mrs Hastings died of cancer I understand their family was very close-knit, too. Mom thought maybe that was the reason it took Roger so long to get around to proposing."

"Well, with David waiting for you at your house, it looks like everyone's been worrying for absolutely nothing."

It was shocking how they could be talking seriously for a few minutes—really communicating—then suddenly she heard that mocking tone in his voice once more.

"You still haven't told me why you volunteered yourself as co-chairman of the Christmas party. The truth now."

"Have you considered I might not have had anyone to take to the party with me, and didn't want to sit there alone?"

"No," she blurted. "That possibility would never have occurred to me."

"Why not? David came by himself."

"Because you're nothing like David."

Not anything like him...

Disturbed by her train of thought, she pulled the edges of his suit jacket closer together to keep out the cold.

"You mean I'm not confident enough to show up on my own the way David did?" he drawled.

She rested her head against the wall. "There's no one with more confidence than you on this planet."

"Is that so?"

She shifted her weight, getting tired of standing. But she couldn't bring herself to sit down next to him, never mind the reason why.

"I meant it as a compliment."

"I took it as one."

Before she could say something she might regret, there was a strange whirring sound, then the light came back on. Once again they were continuing their downward journey.

Oddly enough, Annie wasn't quite ready for the experience to be over. Mitch still needed to explain himself.

With unconscious male agility, he got to his feet and checked his watch.

"It's five after midnight. The magic hour. Merry Christmas, Annie."

Impaling her with his dark blue gaze, he placed his hands on the wall, trapping her between them.

"You wouldn't begrudge a lonely man one last Christmas kiss before we part company, would you?"

Beneath the banter she sensed a hunger in him that matched her own. His lips brushed provocatively against her neck and throat, producing a moan from her before he did a takeover of her mouth. The sensuality of his deep kiss was so erotic she molded herself to him without being aware of it.

They kissed many times. Each one brought greater pleasure, until she thought she couldn't contain all her feelings.

"Mitch," she cried helplessly, before he devoured her mouth once more.

In the morning she knew she would regret her loss of control, but for the life of her she could deny him nothing tonight. His mouth had become the center of her universe. She wanted this conflagration to go on and on.

Out of her mind with desire, she slid her arms around his neck, making it easier to kiss every part of his masculine face. What a gorgeous man he was...

"Annie?" Mitch whispered against her swollen lips. His breathing sounded ragged.

"What?" she asked, close to being delirious. She'd lost track of time and place.

"We've reached the underground car park. People are waiting to get in the elevator."

She was dazed by sensations she'd never experienced in her life, and her eyelids were slow to flutter open.

Over Mitch's broad shoulder she saw two couples, watching them with amused interest.

She let out a cry of embarrassment before disentangling herself from his arms.

Her cheeks had to be as flaming red as her dress.

She helped him gather up the costumes and the flowers.

On their way out she heard Mitch wish their small audience a Merry Christmas.

The whole situation was humiliating, but she had to tough it out in front of this man who'd taught her what could happen when desire went unleashed.

"Annie?"

To her surprise, David came running up to them.

She groaned in displeasure. Her first thought was, *Not here, not now, David.*

How incredibly ironic it was to think there'd been a time when she'd *wanted* David to be there.

"When I heard there was a power outage downtown I came here by taxi and waited by your car. Are you all right?"

"I—we're fine."

She didn't dare look at Mitch.

David's brown gaze eyed her with concern. "Thank heaven they got the main transformer repaired. Where were you when the lights went out?"

"In the elevator," Mitch declared. "I'm happy to say Ms Roberts was able to calm my hysteria while we were trapped in there. She's worth her weight in gold."

With that remark, Annie's legs almost buckled. She could feel David's curious gaze studying both of them. He seemed to have sobered up some.

Her hands shaking, she rummaged in her purse for the remote to unlock her car. The two men took charge. Between them they put the costumes inside.

"Not the flowers," she cautioned, when Mitch started to place them on the back seat.

"Why not? They're yours."

She darted him a searching glance. "But I thought you were tak—"

"I asked the waitress to save them for you," he interrupted her. "A souvenir of the most fabulous party the Hastings Corporation has ever seen." He shut the back door and opened the driver's door for her.

"I'll second that," David said. "It *was* terrific. Everyone raved to me about it."

"Thank you."

"I'll follow you in a taxi. You don't want me to sit on the costumes," David murmured.

Mitch must have heard him, because he said, "Merry Christmas, you two. Drive safely, Annie."

After what had transpired in the elevator, it came as a shock to watch his tall, lean physique walk away from them. A hollow feeling enveloped her as she realized Mitch was actually leaving her there so David could see her home.

For him to leave her this bereft, she could hardly stand it.

"Annie? Are you okay? Would you rather I got a lift with you?"

Once, not too long ago—like as recently as the day her mother had left with Roger—Annie would have been euphoric to hear David say something like that to her.

"No— I—I mean, I'm fine," she stammered.

She hurriedly got in behind the wheel. "I'll see you at the house."

Then she backed out of her parking spot and headed for the exit. Without giving David another thought, she looked for Mitch's car. But it seemed he'd disappeared already.

Now that he'd given her the thrill of her life, along with helping Marion's twenty-three-year-old daughter with the party, it appeared he couldn't wait to spend Christmas with a woman of his own age and taste.

Annie might be young and inexperienced where intimacy was concerned, but even she recognized that Mitch was too virile a man to lead a monk's life. But for the tragic accident that had killed his fiancée he'd be married by now, and would probably have several children.

While she drove, reliving those moments of ecstasy in his arms, she heard a honk. It jerked her back to reality.

Looking around, she realized David was letting her know she'd driven past her mom's house.

Dismayed by her emotions, which were in utter chaos and had caused her mind to blank out for the twenty-minute drive, she made a U-turn and barreled into the driveway. She left the garment bags in the back, but reached for the flowers.

David paid the cab driver and joined her at the front door of the house.

"Let me help you with those." He took the plants from her so she could let them inside.

She walked through the foyer to the living room and turned on the Christmas tree lights.

"Just put the flowers on the coffee table. I'll make us some coffee. I'm afraid it will have to be instant."

"Sounds good to me." In the kitchen, he said, "It's nice and warm in here. Don't you want to take off Mitch's jacket?"

"Oh— I forgot I was wearing it."

She'd grown accustomed to its warmth. Mitch

should have said something, instead of striding away without looking back. How could he have just left like that?

"A minute ago you almost forgot where your mom lived. What's going on, Annie?"

CHAPTER SIX

DAVID watched as she removed the coat and hung it over the back of one of the kitchen chairs.

"I guess I'm tired."

"It's no wonder. You knocked yourself out for the party. Dad's going to be doubly grateful to you."

"Doubly?"

He nodded. "For your hard work, and for letting him marry your mom. He's been in love with her for a long time."

She filled mugs with hot water and added the coffee granules.

"Don't tell anyone, but Mom wanted to marry him last year. Mitch said it was because of me that he didn't propose sooner."

David's eyes grew serious. "Mitch has a point. From the beginning it was your father this, and your father that. Dad didn't think he could win either of you over."

Annie smiled. "Mom had the same problem where you were concerned. Everyone in the company knew you and your father worshipped your mother. My mom wouldn't have dared try to compete, but somehow love won out in the end."

He grinned. "It sure did."

She passed him his coffee. They both started to sip the hot liquid.

"So, what's up with you and Mitch? He's a dark horse if ever there was one."

His comment startled her. "I'm sure I don't know what you mean."

"Come on, Annie. Except for one other time, I've never known the great Mitch Reynolds to act so out of character."

She put down her mug. "In what way? What other time?"

He cocked his head. "The weekend after I broke up with Barb, he cornered me in the parking lot and told me to leave you alone because Dad was ready to propose to your mom and didn't need that complication to foul things up."

Her pulse quickened. "I don't know why he'd say something like that when you've never even asked me out."

He eyed her speculatively. "Barb accused me of always flirting with you when you came around the office. I couldn't deny it. Mitch's lecture was considerably stronger. He told me I was a bastard for toying with your emotions when I wasn't ready for a serious relationship with anybody. He managed to make me feel selfish and guilty as hell for even thinking of it when you were about to become my stepsister."

An explosion of excitement filled Annie's body.

She averted her eyes. "I had no idea. How embarrassing—for you and for me."

"Mitch has this sixth sense about things. I think he's suspicious by nature. It's no secret my father brought him into the company because Mitch's powers of observation are uncanny. He's aware of everything going on, and can troubleshoot any problems—and that makes him an invaluable asset. Since then he's been protective of Dad, and he came on so heavy with me I knew I'd have to watch myself when you came into the building. For the last few months he's been like my personal watchdog. The second you show up, it's as if he's fine tuned, or something."

A shiver ran through her, because she knew what he meant.

"Take, for instance, the other morning when you arrived with the party invitations."

She darted David a questioning glance. "I have to admit I was surprised to see Mitch in your office that early."

"You weren't the only one. In the first place he barged in without asking me if I was busy. He's never done that before. I thought I'd made a mistake on one of my reports and he'd come in to ream me out. To my surprise he wished me Merry Christmas and gave me a present. Then you made your entrance.

"For a minute I thought he was going to give me another lecture about you. But for once I wasn't worried, because I figured there'd be no reason for you to be at the office party—not when the folks were away on their honeymoon and you don't even work there. For all I knew you had a heavy Christmas Eve date with some lucky college guy. But from the moment you walked in I felt like I was at a play where you and Mitch were the actors and I was the spectator. Under other circumstances I would be jealous."

"Jealous of what?" she cried.

"Of the way you two feel about each other."

"You're crazy, David Hastings! Mitch doesn't feel *anything* for me."

What had gone on between them was a purely physical thing on his part.

"He doesn't even know me."

Correction. He now knew she melted whenever he touched her. It was the most dangerous piece of knowledge for him to have.

"I'm sure your father asked him to make certain the party didn't fall flat. As you said, he was acting a part to put some pizzazz into the festivities. Don't take anything he said or did seriously."

Annie needed to listen to her own advice or she was in terrible trouble.

"You mean you weren't affected when he kissed you?"

"Of course I was. What woman doesn't like a surprise kiss under the mistletoe?"

"So my kiss left you in that same breathless condition, too?"

She eyed him curiously. It was truth time. But she

didn't want to hurt his feelings, or at least not hurt his masculine pride, so she said, "You couldn't tell?"

His brows lifted. "I wasn't sure if it was your reaction to Mitch or not. I'd been drinking beforehand, and I'm no expert on the subject of his effect on women. He keeps his private life to himself. Still, something has been going on inside him over the last few days. The crowd at my table kept asking me if the two of you had a thing going."

"That's preposterous," she exclaimed. "I'm afraid the only woman he ever loved was his fiancée, Hannah. She was killed while they were in college."

David looked taken back. "I never knew about that. When did he tell you?"

"In the elevator."

"How did she die?"

After she'd related the details, he shook his head. "That's tough. I had no idea."

"I guess no one did."

"If you're convinced his strange behavior has nothing to do with you, then I have to believe you. I guess it doesn't really matter. It isn't as if you're an employee and have to work with him on a day-to-day basis."

"Heavens, no."

"Well, enough said about him, then. Why don't we go in the living room? If you'd like to start planning the party for our parents, we could do that."

Annie could hear everything he was saying, but her mind was fixated on something Mitch had said to her a few days ago.

*After you receive your MBA in the spring, I'd like to
be the first person you come to see. I know of a position
in the corporation that needs a person like you.*

"Y-You know what, David? It's late, and I'm too
exhausted to think clearly. Would you like to come
over some time during the holidays and we'll put our
heads together?"

"Sure. I'm not good for much right now, either. I'll
call you in a day or two and we'll go from there." He
kissed her forehead. "Merry Christmas, Annie. I never
had a sibling and I love the idea. Welcome to the family."

Tears smarted in her eyes. "I like the idea of a
brother, too. Merry Christmas, David."

She walked him to the front door and watched him
walk away and hail a cab home.

The kiss he'd just given her felt the way she imagined
a brother's kiss would feel if she'd grown up with one.
That had to be the reason she'd felt nothing when he'd
kissed her beneath the mistletoe.

You could try to make something happen. You could
want it with all your heart. But if it wasn't meant to be,
all the planning in the world couldn't change the outcome.

But another person could…

Annie suddenly had a suffocating feeling in her
chest, because she was very much afraid that person's
suit jacket was hanging on the kitchen chair.

What was it Mitch had said to her about being an
intelligent woman?

Maybe one day you'll figure it out.

Had it been the alcohol talking, or had David hit

upon something Annie wouldn't have guessed in a thousand years?

Filled with a different kind of energy, she walked back in the kitchen. Without conscious thought she slid her arms into the jacket and pressed the lapels to her chin. A faint trace of the soap Mitch used in the shower assailed her.

She drew in a shaky breath, recalling the different ways his mouth had seduced her throughout the evening. Every time he came near or touched her, her body turned to liquid. Whatever else might be imagined, the chemistry between them was explosive.

Something told her that the strange vibes she'd sensed around him all year long were the other side of the most primitive emotion known to man. It was called desire. Something you never got over once you felt it.

Filled with questions only he could answer, she strolled into the living room and lay down on the couch to look at the Christmas tree.

She and her mom had decorated it the other day—their private ritual in remembrance of Michael Roberts, beloved husband and father.

Her thoughts drifted to Mitch. Were his grandparents still alive? Did he have brothers and sisters to share Christmas with?

He'd been right about the snow. She was a Californian through and through, but how she'd love to wake up to a white Christmas.

Why had he moved here if he missed Minnesota so much?

When she couldn't stand not having answers to any of her questions, she went to bed. Tomorrow she would open the few presents sitting under the tree, then go into the office and do the paperwork she'd put off in order to plan the party.

When she got to the end of her mother's list of things to do, she'd get busy reading ahead for next semester's coursework.

After that, Roz and Larry were expecting her for a cheese fondue dinner at their apartment.

It was a far cry from the Christmas she'd planned when David had still been the object of her desire.

Her desire...

Until the Christmas party she hadn't known its true meaning. Thanks to Mitch Reynolds, she'd come alive and would never be the same again.

Mitch had barely entered his condo when his cellphone rang. Who in the hell was calling him at one-thirty Christmas morning?

His mood already black at the thought of Annie and David alone in her house, where more experimenting was probably going on, he checked the caller ID. When he saw who it was, his mind leaped to several conclusions—all of which filled him with dread. The last time he'd had such an unorthodox call, it had been the police, giving him news no one should ever have to hear.

He clicked on. "David?" His body broke out in a cold sweat while he held his breath, waiting to hear that he or Annie had been in an accident.

"Sorry, Mitch, but I figured you weren't asleep yet."

David's voice didn't sound like this was an emergency. Mitch exhaled in exquisite relief.

"I just got in. Are you and Annie all right?"

"She's fine, but I'm not. If Dad were available, I'd talk to him. But since he isn't, and this concerns Annie, I hope you don't mind if I dump this on you for a minute?"

Mitch stopped pacing. "Dump away. I'm not going to bed yet."

"Thanks. Let me explain first that you've been right all along about me. I've treated Annie like a jerk. To be honest, I never thought Dad would actually marry Marion. Now that he has, and Annie and I are related, I really feel like a louse for leading her on. It's weird, you know?"

Mitch relaxed. "I can only imagine."

"After I helped her into the house, I decided to take your advice and just be honest with her. The way I did it was to welcome her to the family and tell her it was nice to finally have a sister."

Mitch rubbed his scar, which was throbbing. "How did she take it?"

"On the surface she seemed okay. But I felt like a worse heel just leaving after that, when I knew she was alone. Here's my dilemma. It isn't as if she's someone I'll never see again. We're going to be part of each other's lives from here on out."

Mitch sucked in his breath. "If you called to ask me if you did the right thing, the answer is yes. You handled it with as much finesse as anyone could have."

"Thanks. Coming from you, that means a lot. But it doesn't take away the bad taste in my mouth for not having dealt with her sooner. And here's my other problem. She wants to plan a party for the folks. I told her I'd call her in a few days and we'd talk about it, but—"

"Not a good idea," Mitch broke in.

"I agree. That's why I'm calling you—to get advice from someone outside the problem. Sorry you have to be the one I picked on, but since you know the whole situation, I trust your judgment."

At this point Mitch's brain switched to overdrive. "Since the three of us were in your office when I offered to help plan a party for them, let *me* run with the ball. That leaves you free to fly to Sacramento this week and get a head start on the bidding for that property we were talking about."

"You'd do that?"

David sounded relieved. Mitch had the grace to feel ashamed for some of the thoughts he'd harbored about him over the past year.

"You're not in an enviable position at the moment. Not with Annie needing a cooling-off period. I'll be glad to help out."

Annie's breathtaking response earlier tonight had started a fire he intended to make hotter.

"I owe you, Mitch. Would you believe there was a time a few months ago when I wanted to punch you out for interfering?"

David didn't know the half of it. But Mitch kept his thoughts to himself.

"But that's water under the bridge now." David went on talking. "I'm sure Annie will work with you. She knows how close you are to Dad. And she respects you—otherwise she wouldn't have asked you to take charge at the party tonight."

Mitch let that false assumption pass. All was fair in love and war.

"For what it's worth, Mitch, you're a good man to have around. Even though Dad's been saying that about you for years, I want you to know those are *my* words. I think maybe I can get some sleep now. Merry Christmas."

"The same to you, David." He hung up the phone. *"The same to you,"* he whispered.

For the first time in ages he felt like he had when he'd been a boy, on the verge of opening the one Christmas present he'd been dying for.

CHAPTER SEVEN

Since Roger had moved the company into the new facility, he'd added more security. Annie's mother had had to get Annie her own security pass so she could come and go from the building.

Once she'd flashed it to the security guard at the main doors, she entered the complex.

It seemed a shame the security men had to work on Christmas Day, but then that was the whole point.

It didn't matter about her, of course. She didn't have anyone at home. But those men had families.

Oh, well, Roger probably paid them time and a half and gave them extra perks for protecting the premises.

When the night watchman saw her through the window, he came out of his cubicle.

"Merry Christmas, Annie. What are you doing over here, today of all days?"

She smiled. "I have some work to do, and I wanted to return this suit coat to Mr Reynolds. He lent it to me after the party last night. Would you mind opening his office so I can leave it for him?"

"I'll do it right now."

They walked down the hall together. He undid the lock and waited while she put it over the chair in his secretary's office. As soon as she came out and shut the door he asked if she wanted her mother's door opened.

"No. I have her key. Thanks, Mel."

He nodded. "Have a good one."

"You, too."

Once seated at her mom's desk, she opened the pile of mail that had accrued over the last few days. A lot of it was Christmas cards sent to the firm. Some of them had personal messages intended for Roger. One in particular was Mitch's.

Helplessly fascinated by anything to do with him, she undid the envelope. He'd sent a large card with a beautiful picture. Inside, Mitch had written in his own dynamic cursive, "Do you have any idea how great it is to work for a boss who's the kindest man I've ever known? All the best to you, Roger."

He'd signed it with a simple "M."

Annie unconsciously pressed the card to her chest.

Where Roger was concerned, it was as if Mitch had taken the words out of her mouth.

Before the office party she would never have guessed he could have written something so heartfelt. In fact at times his slightly forbidding vice presidential persona ruled out the possibility that he even had a heart. Now she knew differently.

But that first kiss under the mistletoe had proved he was all too human. From that point on he'd methodically exposed the woman in her until she'd been a pulsating mass of need. As for the wicked, outrageous antics he'd pulled all evening—they'd revealed the type of man he really was. A remarkable man, when she gave herself permission to admit it.

"I thought I might find you here."

Annie's head flew back in shock, while her insides vibrated at the sound of his male voice.

Except for his eyes, that burned like blue flames, she almost didn't recognize him in jeans and a well-worn leather bomber jacket.

Good heavens...

He moved closer. "What's got you so interested you didn't even hear me knock?"

She slid his card back in the opened stack, but it didn't prevent him from picking up the envelope he'd stamped and sealed a few days earlier.

His compelling mouth curved at one end. How had she ever thought it had a cruel twist?

"Mom asked me to open the mail for her."

"Did you like my card?"

Since she'd been caught in the act anyway, she said, "As a matter of fact I loved it."

His eyes narrowed on her upturned features. "I just opened *my* mail, but I didn't get what I was hoping for."

She'd give anything to know what he'd been looking for.

"Maybe next year," he murmured. "Thanks for returning my suit coat." It dangled from his hand. "The second I saw it, I knew that a certain charming elf was in the building somewhere."

She lowered her eyes to the desk. "I'm afraid that elf has retreated to the North Pole, never to be seen or heard of again."

"What a shame. I took a fancy to her."

Afraid to take him seriously, because she wanted to believe it too much, she said, "The latest company gossip says that you took a fancy to Mrs Claus, too."

He grinned, causing her heart to slam against her ribs. "That same rumor mill is spreading fiction that you and I are a couple. And though *we* know it isn't true, it might be wise to perpetuate the myth for a while."

The word "myth" shattered her fragile heart to tiny shards.

"Why would we want to do that?" She congratulated herself for keeping her voice steady.

He pursed his lips. "So David will get the message that you're over him. After all the years that you had a crush on him, it's hard for him to realize you've outgrown it. He's a little confused at the moment."

Annie's hand tightened around the letter opener. "What do you mean?"

"Your breathless response to my kiss, when you and I have only been acquaintances up to now, has done some damage to him. It's just as well that he'd had too much to drink and only got a vague impression that he might not be the only man in your life."

"But you're *not* in my life."

"For his sake let's be glad that for the moment he

believes I am. The problem is, he could be hurt if this isn't handled carefully. Take it from me, a man is vulnerable after a broken engagement. In your case it's more complicated, because he's your stepbrother now."

She froze. "So what is it you're trying to say?"

"Maybe the best way to handle it would be for him to think you're interested in me—or at least open to the possibility. For the rest of the holiday you're welcome to use me."

The knife just kept driving deeper. "To do what?"

"To help you plan the party for your parents. I'd already decided to give them one. Under the circumstances we might as well do it together."

She clutched the sides of her chair so hard it cut off the circulation. "David said he was going to call me about it."

"I know. He just phoned me to talk shop and mentioned it in passing. That's because he's unsure of what to do about you now that he assumes you and I are an item."

After last night, everyone at the party would be assuming the same thing. She needed to fight her way through this so Mitch would never know how devastated she was. She'd actually begun to believe he wanted to get to know her better. Not just on a physical level, but in other ways. The job offer—the revelations about his fiancée—it had all been a starting point. Or so she'd fantasized.

"I thought it the perfect opportunity to tell him *I* would help you take care of the party if he wanted to leave on business in the morning."

"What business?"

"He's bidding on a project for us in Sacramento. By the time he gets back on New Year's and discovers we're together, he'll accept the fact that you've moved on and will only ever be his stepsister. Then, after you go back to school, it will have all blown over and he'll settle down to find the right woman. That will relieve Roger more than you know."

She gritted her teeth so tightly it was a miracle they didn't all crack.

Finally she'd figured out what secret mission had brought Mitch into the office.

He'd lost his true love, but he wasn't above using David as an excuse to have a little fun with her. And why not? She'd lit up like spontaneous fire with every kiss and caress he'd given her, and it was the holiday after all.

So what was to prevent her from giving him what he wanted for a little while longer? Slowly lead him on, then break it off as brutally as he'd just broken her heart.

All she really had to do was continue on the way things had been going. Let him keep coming on to her. Let him keep taking over. Never realizing she was on to him big-time until it was too late.

Her first impression of him hadn't been wrong after all. He was a dangerous man. But she could be dangerous, too. Just how dangerous he was about to find out.

"I—I'm not sure if your idea will work, but the last thing either David or I want is to create problems for Mom and Roger. They've suffered enough pain and deserve some joy."

She eyed him solemnly. "I've already made plans

with friends for this evening, but if you want to talk ideas tomorrow, we can."

"Good. I'll come by your house at noon. We can go to lunch and decide where to have the party."

"I have a better idea," she reasoned. "Why don't you come to the house at two and I'll treat you to the Christmas meal Mom always made for our family? If I don't fix it, it won't seem like Christmas even came this year. I didn't feel like making it for one person— but, since you're offering to help smooth the waters with David, it'll be worth the trouble."

For once he didn't have an instant comeback. She waited until he finally said, "Do you want any help?"

"Not this time. I'm not the greatest cook in the world and I need the practice without anyone looking over my shoulder."

"Understood. I'll be there at two."

She didn't miss the glimmer of satisfaction in his eyes before he left the office, closing the door quietly behind him.

This is all-out war, Mitchell Reynolds. I've let you win the first few rounds. But the mother of battles is coming. Then the tide is going to turn, and I can't wait...

Mitch let out a groan of pleasure and put down his fork. "That was the best Christmas feast I've had in years."

"Thank my mom. They're her recipes, but I must admit it tasted better than I thought it was going to."

"When Roger finds out she's a marvel in the kitchen, he'll probably want her to stay home."

"If he takes early retirement, that's exactly what she'll do. Deep down she's a homebody."

His intelligent eyes assessed her from his place across the dining room table. "What about you?"

"I'm not sure what I am yet. As you reminded me yesterday, I've just started to spread my wings—and I like the feeling."

Her remark could be taken several ways. She wondered which way he'd chosen to take it.

He sat back in the chair, drinking the rest of his coffee. "Speaking of homes, how would you feel if we give the party at my beach house?"

She stirred in her chair. "I didn't know you had one."

He put down his cup. "It's in San Clemente. I bought it six months ago and have been remodeling it in my spare time."

Hmm. A condo in Beverly Hills and a house on the ocean. That had to be the best-kept secret at the Hastings Corporation.

There was no question Mitch was a millionaire in his own right. It proved what hard work and brains could do when your heart had died.

Annie was impressed. And she'd bet he knew she was so impressed she would agree to drive down and see it with him.

He'd be right. She was going to fall in with all his wishes…except for the one she planned to refuse him at the last minute.

"I would imagine Mom and Roger will love it."

"Good. Tomorrow I'll drive us down during the day, so you can get an idea of the layout for yourself."

He was as transparent as the crystal she'd put on the table.

"In that case I'll have to get an early start at Mom's office in the morning."

He nodded. "I have business, too, so I'll pick you up at eight-thirty and we'll go in together before we leave for the beach."

She lowered her eyes, afraid he would read the excitement in them and figure out she had an agenda of her own.

"Let me help you with the dishes." He got up from the table and started clearing it.

She knew exactly what was going to happen. Once they were at the kitchen sink he'd slip his arms around her waist, kiss her neck and continue the softening-up process until he had her where he wanted her. The way she'd been last night—biddable in his arms.

Deciding to let him suffer a little longer, she remained seated. He was going to have to work harder than that for what he had in mind.

When he came back in the dining room for more dishes she said, "I make it a rule never to allow a dinner guest to slave in my kitchen."

He put his hands on the back of one of the chairs. "You sound like you mean that."

She smiled up at him. "It's called saving you from a fate worse than death."

His lips twitched. "I like the way your mind thinks, Ms Roberts."

He stretched, drawing her gaze to the play of muscle across his back and shoulders beneath his green polo shirt.

"Under the circumstances, I take it you won't mind if I go back to the office now. I'm in the middle of some delicate negotiations that could take me into the night to work out. With a turkey dinner like the one you've just fed me I'm good for hours, and I'll be able to concentrate with no one else around."

Her heart lurched, but she managed to keep munching on the last of her pumpkin pie. How could she have forgotten for one second that she was dealing with a pro who didn't follow the normal rules of engagement?

"You have an amazing work ethic, Mitch. The guys I date could learn a lot from a successful man like yourself. I'll walk you to the door."

His eyes were shuttered. "Don't bother to get up. I know my way out. I'll see you in the morning. Be sure to bring a parka and a pair of good walking shoes."

So he was planning to take her for a romantic walk along the surf? She wouldn't disappoint him.

"I won't forget. At least let me thank you again for the Christmas present. I'm sorry I didn't have one for you."

"What do you call the superb meal you went to all the trouble to fix me?" With those words, he disappeared.

Clever as a fox. That was Mitch Reynolds.

She wandered into the living room to inspect the little Christmas ornaments he'd given her.

After she'd opened her package, he'd hung them on the tree. Mr and Mrs Claus.

If she weren't on to him, she would have been completely taken in by his ruse.

She flicked Mr Claus with her finger. He swung back and forth, catching the light. Her eyelids squeezed tightly together as she remembered the thrilling taste and feel of his mouth beneath his Santa beard.

Years from now, if she was lucky enough to be married to the right man and had a daughter, she'd warn her about tall, dark, gorgeous men with piercing navy blue eyes and a scar on their jaw. They could tempt a saint, but could never be tamed by one.

Except that Hannah had brought him to his knees.

Annie felt shame for envying the dead woman who'd stolen his heart to the point that he'd wanted her for his wife.

CHAPTER EIGHT

SAN CLEMENTE was a Spanish-styled coastal town south of L.A. It had been founded in a romantic setting where there was some of the best surfing in Southern California. Inside and out, Mitch's home reflected the local flavor, preserving the integrity of the original architecture. It was a jewel of a find only someone in his exclusive circle of friends would have known had come on the market.

No doubt he'd brought other women down here, but all that had been kept secret. He was a dark horse, all right.

After he'd given Annie a tour, they'd walked along the surf for several hours.

He'd found them a charming spot overlooking the ocean to eat crab legs. For once they'd just made conversation, which had almost convinced her they were a normal couple out on a date. But nothing could be further from the truth.

Finally they returned to his beautiful beach house.

"What do you think?" he asked, as she looked up at the windows from the sand.

"You already know what I think. It's fabulous. The perfect place for a party."

"What about a place to live in year-round?"

She put her hands in her coat pockets, wondering what he was driving at. "If you're talking about yourself, I can see it would require a lot of driving back and forth from L.A. But it would be worth it to come home to this every night."

She turned her head in his direction. "Are you planning to sell your condo?"

His eyes held a faraway look. "Not until my grandparents have passed away. I'm thinking of moving them out here. They're already old, and getting older by the minute. Would you believe they've never seen the Pacific Ocean?"

Just when Annie thought she had him all figured out, he said or did something to change her perspective in a totally different way.

"Have you told them you'd like them to come?"

"Yes. But they don't want to be a burden and are fighting me. You don't know stubborn until you've met them. If I can't get them to consider it, then I'll have to tell Roger I'm moving back to Minnesota. They need me, even if they pretend they don't."

She tried to breathe normally but couldn't. The thought of him moving so far away was anathema to her.

"You don't have brothers or sisters to help share in their care?"

Though she'd promised herself she wouldn't get

more involved with him, she couldn't help wanting to know anything and everything about his life.

"No. My parents died in a freak car accident when I was three."

"How awful," she murmured.

"I don't remember it. My grandparents raised me with high expectations. When I got a scholarship to Stanford they insisted I go and make them proud. But it's a pretty empty world without them in it—except for the times when I fly back to see them, of course. I went to see them just before the Christmas break."

Every revelation caused her to rethink her assessment of him. "Can't you get them to come for a visit, if nothing else?"

"With the right incentive it might be possible," he murmured.

"I should think a party at your own home to celebrate your boss's marriage would be a good enough reason. I would imagine they'd love to meet the man whose faith in you has been repaid a hundred fold."

"A hundred fold?" he queried, with a heavy dash of irony.

"Those are my mother's words. She was just repeating to me what Roger said about you."

"That's very gratifying to hear, but I'm afraid it's a big exaggeration."

No. If anything it was an understatement.

"If you'd like, I'll extend the invitation myself," she offered. His grandparents probably didn't know how important a man Mitch was. "When I let them know how much it will mean to my new stepfather to meet them, maybe they'll think twice before saying no."

His gaze trapped hers. If she wasn't mistaken, she thought she saw something flicker in those dark blue depths.

"You'd do that for me?"

If he only knew...

"Of course. The trick is to get them here. Once they arrive in San Clemente, and see what a heavenly spot this is, maybe they'll consider moving here. It's certainly worth a try. Otherwise—" Her voice trembled.

"Otherwise what?" he prodded, as if he really wanted to know.

"I'm afraid Roger's going to be in for a horrible shock when you tell him you have to leave the company. It won't be the same without you."

I won't be the same. There was no kidding herself about that.

"You're forgetting David."

She shook her head. "He could never take your place. In fact I have a hunch he'll end up doing something else one day. He isn't like you."

Mitch eyed her so intently she was afraid he could see through to her soul.

"You mean he doesn't have fire in his belly?"

It was unnerving the way he could read her mind.

"He has other fine qualities."

"I agree. He's a much nicer person than I am."

At one time Annie might have thought that, but no longer. She'd learned too much about him over the last few days. But she needed to keep her thoughts to herself—unless she wanted him to know how she really felt about him.

She pulled her hands back out of her pockets. "Since we've set a date for the party, why don't we go up to the house and phone your grandparents right now?"

She heard him take a deep breath. "I was just going to suggest it."

He cupped her elbow and they began climbing the stairs from the beach. It was the first time since the night of the office party that he'd touched her.

She hoped he couldn't tell how sensitive she was to the contact, how much she craved it.

In the face of his concern over his grandparents, she dismissed the idea that he'd brought her here because he'd been playing a game of seduction.

Judging from the tone in his voice, it was vital to him that his family be taken care of—if not here, then back in Minnesota.

Should that happen, he would disappear from her life. She was starting to panic over the possibility.

Crazy as it sounded, she knew she'd fallen in love with him. For a year or more she'd been intensely aware of him. In fact she had to admit to the strange thrill she'd always felt when she had visited her mother and found him following her with his searching gaze.

Roger had sung his praises for so long, she'd known he was a different breed of man—one who commanded the respect of other men. And he was a man her own mother admitted was so attractive that he drew women without even trying.

For a long time Annie had feared her adult feelings for him, not recognizing what was going on inside her. Now she knew why. Her newly awakened heart was quaking with the knowledge that she'd met the man she wanted to marry.

But, much as she ached for his love in return, she refused to be his plaything.

He'd said something about coming to see him in the spring after she graduated. But that would be pure torture if he only wanted her around for professional reasons.

How her mom had continued to work for Roger when she'd had little hope he would ever love her was beyond Annie's comprehension. She could never handle that kind of pain.

To be in the same building with Mitch and never be able to express her love would be tantamount to being handed a sentence of perpetual agony.

Already feeling the pain, she raced up the last few stairs ahead of him.

The sooner Mitch made this phone call, the sooner she could ask him to take her home. It was time to get out of the fire.

When they reached the house and went inside, she'd already removed her parka, afraid he would help and she would let him. That would lead to more temptation, and ultimately more regrets.

While she found a seat on the couch facing the ocean,

Mitch put another log on the fire, then pulled out his cellphone to ring the people who'd raised him.

Once he began to talk, she heard a tenderness in his tone that bespoke a lifetime of loving.

The more she listened, the more critical it became that she get them to say yes.

"Annie?" he whispered.

She jerked around and took the phone from him. The look in his eyes told her he didn't hold out much hope.

Crossing her fingers figuratively, she said, "Hello? Mr and Mrs Reynolds?"

"We're on the line." His grandfather spoke up.

"Good. It's Annie Roberts. I just wanted to urge you to come out for this party Mitch and I are planning. Your grandson is like a son to Roger Hastings, and I know Roger has wanted to meet you for a long time. It would mean the world to my mother, too. She's worked at the Hastings Corporation even longer than Mitch, and is very fond of him. Please say you'll think about it."

The silence on the other end prompted her to get up from the couch and walk to the other side of the living room, out of earshot.

"I can't tell you how much it would mean to everyone. Your grandson is a legend around here." Her voice shook. "You'd be so proud of him. He's a credit to the way you raised him." They had to be remarkable people.

She heard someone clear their throat before Mitch's grandfather said, "What do you think, Martha?"

"I'd like to go, if you would."

"Well, then, young woman, I guess it's settled."

Annie had to hold back her tears. "That's wonderful. Why don't you tell Mitch? Here he is."

She found him over by the fireplace and handed him the phone without looking at him. If he could see her eyes, he'd divine her deepest feelings.

She moved over to the windows, waiting for him to finish talking to them. Soon the room grew quiet. She sensed his presence behind her.

"I thought you told me a certain Christmas elf had retreated to the North Pole." He sounded happy.

"I guess she made a small detour on the way."

"I guess she did. Do you have a suggestion how I can thank this elf?"

"Elves don't want or need thanks."

She heard his sharp intake of breath. "Why is that?"

"Because they're not human," she teased, and slowly turned to face him with a smile. "The important thing is that your grandparents said they'd come. I'm thrilled for you. Now, if you don't mind, it's getting late and I need to go home."

He studied her for a moment. "What's your hurry? We still have to decide on a caterer and work on a menu."

Maybe they'd get around to that, but the way she was feeling right now she would crawl into his lap at the slightest invitation. Then heaven help her.

"Could we discuss it on the way home? I'm meeting with my study group later tonight. We've got to finish a project and turn it in after the holidays."

It was a half-truth. Her group *had* decided to get

together one night this week, but they hadn't finalized which night. Of course Mitch didn't know that—which was for the best, because she was in a precarious emotional state right now. Since the conversation with his grandparents, the situation had changed. She no longer trusted herself to be around him.

He flashed her an enigmatic glance. "I'll get your coat."

In a few minutes they were traveling back to L.A. on I-5. It had already grown dark and felt like ten at night instead of six-thirty.

By the time they reached her mom's house, all the party details had been worked out.

"Tell me about your project," he said, after shutting off the motor.

She'd been afraid he'd bring that up.

"It's for a marketing class."

"What's the precise assignment?"

He *knew* she'd lied to him about the group coming over.

"We have to plan an ad campaign for a fake product," she said, before bolting from his car.

He was right behind her when she reached her front door. "Have you thought of one yet?"

"Yes, but nothing's been decided."

Wishing he would leave, she pulled out her keys and unlocked the front door. "Thank you for lunch, and the tour of your beautiful home." She was praying he wouldn't touch her or she'd be lost.

"Thank *you* for talking to my grandparents. It made all the difference."

"I'm glad, Mitch. It will be wonderful to meet them." She had to clear her throat. "Well, goodnight…"

He didn't budge. "Before I go anywhere, I'll see you inside to make sure you're safe."

She panicked. "Of course I'm safe."

"Humor me," he said, in an authoritative voice. "A woman on her own, coming home to an empty house in the dark, is taking a risk."

Annie moaned. Letting him come inside would be a much bigger risk, but he'd left her no choice.

With her heart thumping in her chest, they entered the house. She ran ahead to turn on lights, then returned to the living room.

"As you can see, you worried for nothing. But I appreciate your concern." She took the lid off a box of chocolate orange sticks sitting on the coffee table. "Please take as many as you like before you go."

After a day of wind and salt spray, most women Mitch knew would have excused themselves to freshen up. Not Annie, who didn't need any artifice. He loved her disheveled hair. He loved the curve of her mouth that hadn't seen a coat of lipstick for hours. The lights from the tree illuminated the sheen of her dark curls. He had an overpowering desire to run his fingers through them.

His gaze took in her khakis and the black cashmere sweater she wore, providing a perfect foil for those luminescent gray eyes fringed with sooty lashes. They lightened or darkened according to her emotions.

His eyes didn't miss the curious throb at the base

of her throat. Its incessant movement revealed a heightened state of nervousness that meant she was frightened.

Of him? Or herself? It was time to find out.

"What is it about me that threatens you so much you had to pretend to get home to study?"

Even with the few feet separating them he felt her body tauten.

"I admit I used that as an excuse to come home, but it isn't because I feel threatened. If that were true I wouldn't have driven to San Clemente with you in the first place."

"So why are you poised like a deer in the forest, sensing a hunter close by?"

She put the candy back on the coffee table. "I don't think of you as a hunter."

"Then why is your heart racing? I can hear it from here."

"David isn't the only one confused," she admitted.

"Meaning?"

She tossed her head back. "Meaning I got the shock of my life Christmas Eve, and I'm not proud of it. You would think that a woman almost twenty-four years old would have the emotional maturity to recognize a one-sided crush for what it was. The kiss you gave me was like a glass of ice water thrown in my face to wake me up."

"Didn't you like it?"

She stared at him with accusing eyes. "You know I did. My problem is, I was so fixated on capturing

David's interest I didn't do enough experimenting over the years. Then an experienced man several years my senior comes along and opens up a whole new world of enjoyment to me."

Mitch would take that for openers. "I'll admit I enjoyed kissing you, too."

"But that's the problem, isn't it? I've discovered how easily I could be swept away by sheer physical pleasure. I don't know whether to thank you or curse you. Under the circumstances, I'm going to chalk it up to my coming of age and leave it at that."

She could leave it at that all she wanted. *He* intended to deal with the rest on his own terms.

"Thank you for your honesty, Annie. It's another of your qualities I admire. I'll see you in the morning. Goodnight."

CHAPTER NINE

ANNIE tried not to think too much about it when she didn't see Mitch in the building the next day. After two days with no sign of him, she decided he must have flown out to Minnesota.

At the end of the third day she left the building to get together with her study group. On the way to the parking lot she happened to see Elaine, getting into her car. Her husband and children were with her.

Mitch's secretary wouldn't have come by unless there was an important reason.

"Hi, Elaine!"

The other woman turned around. She held a stack of files in her arms.

"Annie! How are you?"

Since Mitch's departure from Annie's mom's house earlier in the week, she'd been suffering withdrawal. But that wasn't news she wanted anyone to know, least of all Elaine.

"I'm well. How are you?"

"Terrific. That was the best office party I've ever been to in my life. You and Mitch brought the house down."

Her hands formed fists in reaction. He'd done a lot more than that to Annie.

"Chuck couldn't believe the bonus. It made our Christmas."

"Roger will be glad to hear it." She took another breath before asking, "What are you doing here? This is supposed to be your vacation."

"I know, but Mitch is sick and asked if I'd bring a couple of files to him. He says he needs to go over some figures that weren't scanned into the computer."

It had been so unlike Mitch not to make an appearance at the office, Annie had driven herself crazy wondering what was going on with him. Of all the reasons she'd considered, illness hadn't been one of them. The knowledge was almost as unsettling as the fact that he hadn't called Annie for help. He knew she was working at the office all week, to cover for her mother, yet he'd phoned Elaine and forced *her* to come in.

Apparently Annie's honesty the other night had produced the desired effect, because he'd left her strictly alone.

It appeared Mitch didn't need her help, or David's, until the night of the party. The invitations had already gone out.

It proved Annie's theory about men and their pleasure. They took it where and when they could find it. Now that she was out of sight, she was no longer on his mind.

How unfair that he filled her thoughts until she couldn't eat or sleep anymore.

Elaine's children called out the window for her to hurry.

"I'm sorry, Annie. We're taking the kids to a movie, and they're not happy that we have to drive to San Clemente first."

After a slight hesitation, Annie said, "I'm headed in that direction for a study group session. I'll take those for you if you want."

"You're not making that up just to help me out? It's something you would do."

Annie crossed her heart. "We're meeting at one of the guys' houses at Dana Point. My backpack's in the car. I know where Mitch lives. It won't be more than five minutes out of my way."

"You're an angel." Elaine handed the files to her.

Annie waved the family off, then hurried over to her car and got in to start up the motor.

On the way to San Clemente she rehearsed what she would say when Mitch opened the door, but nothing sounded right.

Maybe a better idea would be to phone him and tell him she was leaving the files between the screen and his front door. That way she and Mitch wouldn't have to see each other.

Before long she arrived in his neighborhood and pulled out her cell to call him. Unfortunately she was told to leave a message.

She could do that. But if by a horrible stroke of fate

something happened to the files before he knew they were outside, she might live to regret it.

The only thing to do was ring his doorbell.

She pulled into the latticework carport covered in bougainvillea and shut off the motor.

Grabbing the files, she got out and rushed to the door.

Her whole body tensed as she pushed the button. It took a while before she heard a click. Then the door opened and she discovered Mitch, standing there in a white T-shirt and gray sweats. He was in his stocking feet, and his hair looked more disheveled than usual. With a five o'clock shadow, he had a raw male appeal that kindled the ache inside her.

"Hello," he said, in that low, husky voice she'd been missing.

"Hi, Mitch. Elaine came by the office as I was leaving. Since I was on my way to Dana Point anyway, I told her I'd drop these off."

He took them from her. "What's in Dana Point?"

"Mike Teale lives there. The study group is getting together at his house tonight. In case you were wondering, that's the truth."

"I'm sure it is," came the bleak response.

Somehow it made her feel guilty rather than defensive.

He gazed at her through veiled eyes. "Elaine must have been relieved."

"I believe so. They were leaving to go to a movie." Feeling more awkward and uncertain by the minute, she turned to leave, then paused. "She said you'd been ill. Are you all right?"

"I haven't been sick in the way you mean. I was up on the roof the other day and hurt my Achilles' tendon, so I've been nursing it."

"What were you doing up there?"

"Checking a vent, but the tiles were slippery."

"Why didn't you get a roofer to come out?"

A half-smile broke the corner of his sensuous mouth.

"My grandfather was a building contractor. By the time I graduated from high school I'd learned the business from him, and I never once hurt myself until now."

"That's why this house is so beautiful! You've been remodeling it yourself! Now I'm *really* impressed."

But a band had constricted her lungs. For someone as strong and tough as Mitch to stay home, his injury had to be more serious than he was letting on.

"I'm sure it's painful. Don't let me keep you."

She had the impression he was so miserable he couldn't wait for her to leave.

"Mitch? As long as I'm here, is there anything I can do for you?"

He rubbed the back of his neck. "I was going to ask Elaine if she had any painkillers with her. Is it possible you carry a bottle around?"

"No, but I'll run to the store for you right now."

"That isn't necessary. I don't need any more until I go to bed. If you wouldn't mind, maybe you could stop by with some after your study session and just leave it in that potted plant?" He motioned to the large terracotta jar by the door.

He didn't want to see her again. She reeled, before recovering enough to say, "I'd be happy to do that for you."

"Then this old man thanks you."

He slowly shut the door in her face.

Message received, Mr Reynolds.

By the time she'd backed out of his driveway she had dissolved into tears. No way would she make it through the study session.

The drive to Mike's house didn't take long. After giving him the ad campaign she'd printed out she begged off, saying something important had come up. If the guys needed to talk, they could call her on her cell.

With that accomplished, she went to the nearest store for medicine. She also picked up a can of soda and two gel-packs, already chilled, so he could ice his injury.

A few minutes later she drove back to his house and marched straight to the door. This time she had to ring twice before he answered.

The second the door opened she said, "Don't you think asking me to leave your medicine in a plant outside your house in the dark is a little absurd?"

A stillness surrounded him. "I was only attempting to obey your rules, so you wouldn't think I'm out for what you hold most dear."

She swept past him, red-faced, and went into the kitchen to put the sack on the counter. He came in, limping.

While she opened the soda she said, "I'm breaking the rules this once in the hope that you'll still be able to host the party."

She undid the cap on the pills. "Here. Take some."

He did her bidding without remonstration.

"I brought you some ice packs. The pharmacist said to apply for twenty minutes, then wait twenty and apply again." She put one of them in the fridge.

"Let's get you in bed with this one, then I'll leave."

He followed her down the hall. "What happened to your study group session?"

His bedroom was a mess. Evidently he'd been living in it for the last three days.

She set out to make his bed with clean sheets and made sure he could get in it without lying on a magazine or newspaper.

"I dropped off my proposal. They'll get back to me later."

He lay down like an obedient child.

Avoiding his eyes, she said, "Which leg is it?"

"My right one."

She propped it with pillows, then he told her where to put the ice pack.

"That's cold."

"It's supposed to be."

He darted her a searching glance. "Are you sure you're not a nursing student?"

"Positive. So don't get any ideas that I'm going to give you round-the-clock care."

"You made that clear the other night."

"Then we understand each other." She got up from the bed.

"Could I ask you one more favor?"

"What is it?"

"Will you look for the remote to the TV? I think it fell under the bed."

Annie got down on the floor. "Found it." She stood up and handed it to him. "Anything else before I go?"

"Can you put those files where I can reach them?"

She placed them next to the pillow he was lying on. As she stood up, their eyes met. Something flickered in the recesses of his. She almost stopped breathing.

"Do you know what?" he whispered in a husky tone.

"No, and I don't want to know."

"I'm going to say it anyway. I'm glad you're not an elf."

For no good reason her heart began to thud. "Why is that?"

"As you reminded me the other day, they're not human—but you are." He pulled her down so she was half lying on top of him. "I don't give a damn if there's no mistletoe. I need to kiss you again whether you come willing or not."

"No—" she begged. But her cry for mercy went unheeded. He buried his mouth in hers and began kissing her. Over and over again. Long, hungry kisses that called up her desire until she matched him kiss for soul-destroying kiss.

With a groan he rolled her over, crushing her so close against his hard frame it felt like they were one pulsating body of need.

"You were right to be frightened of me, Annie. I want you so badly I'm losing control." He pressed his face to her curls. "It's the reason I told you to leave the medicine outside. I knew that if I got you in my arms again I'd never want to let you go. Do you hear what I'm saying?"

He kissed her with increasing passion, stirring up flames that licked through her body. The pleasure-pain he created was so intoxicating she was in danger of losing every inhibition.

"You're a beautiful woman. I want to hold you, look at you. I want to make love to you for hours. But if you're not prepared to stay the night with me, then you need to leave now."

His powerful body trembled, communicating the strength of his desire for her, but he was giving her a choice.

She could stay with him and experience a night of ecstasy. He would be her first lover. But she wouldn't be his.

Naturally there'd been other women who'd known rapture with him, including his fiancée. How did they stand it when he grew tired of them and moved on?

How would *she* stand it?

After covering his face and mouth with kisses one more time, because she couldn't help herself, she found the strength to ease away from him and get to her feet.

While she swayed in place, he lay there, looking up at her through smoldering eyes.

"This isn't a game we're playing now, so you'll have to let me think about it. To go to bed with you would be the biggest step I've ever taken in my life—"

"Take all the time you need," his gravelly voice

broke in. "But a word of caution. Don't come near me again unless you mean it."

His warning succeeded as nothing else could have to make her face reality.

"In other words, it's up to me whether we have a relationship or not?"

"That's right. Except for the night of the party, I'll be leaving you strictly alone."

When it came to the bottom line, he gave no quarter.

She shivered, because the corporate side of him had taken over.

All she had to do was get into bed with him and he'd know she meant it.

And because she was in love with him, nothing would be easier. *Until one day it wasn't.*

Annie might not have many answers to life's questions yet, but there was one thing she did know. She didn't want a future with him or any man that had an "until" in it...unless it was "until death and beyond."

To love a man like him would bring suffering and joy in unequal measure.

Annie wasn't willing to endure a lifetime of one for a fleeting moment of the other.

"Stay where you are, Mitch. I'll let myself out."

She left the room before racing through the house to her car.

CHAPTER TEN

ONCE Roger had left the house, Annie followed her mother into the bedroom. It was so good to have her home. She hugged her again before letting her go.

"I don't have to ask how the honeymoon went."

Her mom blushed—something she didn't do very often. "I'm so happy, Annie, and I want you to be happy, too. I have a present for you."

"I already opened it, on Christmas morning."

"Yes, well, this one's a little different."

She walked over to her dresser and drew an eight-by-ten envelope from the drawer.

Annie took it from her. "You've got me curious." She opened the flap and pulled out a deed to the house made out in her name.

Tears welled in her eyes. She stared at her mother through the blur. "I can't take this, Mom."

"It's yours now, rather than having to wait to inherit it. For the time being Roger and I will stay at his house. But we're planning to buy one we can make our own."

"That's the way it should be. Two newlyweds starting out fresh."

Her mom put an arm around her. "Roger won't come by for me until tonight. Let's go in the living room and talk. I want to hear about what you've been doing, and how the office party went."

"Everything was great. When you go back to work you'll discover a ton of thank-you cards for Roger. He's the most generous man I've ever known."

"It's certainly one of the reasons I love him so much. Did David help you?"

"Yes." Thanks to Mitch's goading. "He floated around to make sure everyone was enjoying themselves."

"Did he bring someone with him?"

"No. As a matter of fact he came back to the house after. We've planned a party for you the day after tomorrow."

"I know! Since David's still in Sacramento, Mitch Reynolds met us at the ship to welcome us back. I understand it's going to be held at his beach house?"

Mitch had met them at the dock? Her heartbeat sped up.

"Was he limping?"

"A little. I understand he hurt his foot while he was up on his roof, but he still took care of everything and wouldn't let me carry my bag. Why do you ask?"

Annie patted one of the sofa pillows. "I took him some files right after he hurt himself. I'm glad to hear he's doing well enough to be up and around."

"Me, too. He raved about you, honey. Apparently he's had a flood of e-mails telling him it was the best party the company has ever had, bar none. Mitch also added that you made a very fetching elf who delighted everyone. He gave us one of the invitations you created. After Roger read it he was all choked up, and he said, 'That's our Annie.' Roger has grown to really love you."

"I love him, too."

Her mom reached out to squeeze her hand.

"I knew you'd do a wonderful job. I'm so proud of you, honey."

"Thanks," Annie whispered.

She could feel her mother's eyes studying her. "What's wrong? And I'm not talking about the fact that my marriage to Roger has changed things for all of us. You're not yourself. Did David say or do something to hurt you?"

She shook her head. "This has nothing to do with David. It's true I had a crush on him for years. I guess everyone in the office knew it. But, believe me, that's all over. We're both very happy to be stepbrother and sister."

"Roger will be relieved to hear it. He wants so much for the four of us to be a family."

"That's no problem, Mom. David's easy to love."

"Then let's talk about Mitch Reynolds."

She felt a stab of pain. "Why would you bring *him* up?"

Unable to sit still, Annie slid off the couch and reached for an orange stick.

"According to Mitch, you spent every second of your spare time working on the party or at the office. Since the two of you have had to be closely associated throughout this whole holiday, I have to conclude your weight loss has something to do with him."

Marion Roberts hadn't made it to be Roger's private secretary for nothing.

"My diet must be working."

Her mother continued to look at her speculatively. "All right. I'll leave it alone. But if you ever want to get something off your chest, I'm here."

"I know you are, and I appreciate the offer, but there's nothing to discuss."

Her mom stood up and wandered over to the tree. "These little Santa ornaments are darling. Did Roz give them to you?"

Her first instinct was to lie. But she couldn't do that to her mother.

"No. They're from Mitch. He helped me pass out the party gifts in the Santa costume I rented."

Her mother winked. "I'd have almost missed my wedding to see that."

"He really was something."

Her mom nodded. "He really *is* something. Speaking of presents, Mitch asked me to give you this when I got home." She reached for her purse, lying on the coffee table.

Annie's adrenaline kicked in. "What is it?"

"Photos from the office Christmas party." She put the packet in Annie's hands. "He's had several sets of prints made up, so you can keep yours as a souvenir."

Annie frowned. "But the photographer was supposed to send the bill and the pictures to *your* office. I've been watching for them so I could mail the pertinent ones out to employees."

Her mother hunched her slender shoulders. "Mitch said you'd done enough work for ten people, so he was happy to take care of it. They're wonderful pictures!"

"You've seen them already?" Her overworked heart plunged to her feet.

"He gave Roger and me a similar packet. We looked at them on our way home in the limo. Your new haircut suits you. It's gorgeous. As for the party, it looked sensational. Roger couldn't believe all the trouble you went to. It erased the guilt he's been feeling for deserting everyo— Oh!" she cried, mid-sentence. "There's the phone! It might be Roger. Excuse me for a minute, honey."

Her mother ran to the kitchen as if she were a teenager who'd been waiting for her boyfriend to call.

Annie looked down at the packet. Her hands shook as she reached inside.

The first one showed her staring wide-eyed into the camera.

The second one was so shocking she almost fainted.

The photographer had caught her and Mitch in a clinch not meant for anyone else's eyes.

They looked like two people madly, desperately in love.

Not by any stretch of the imagination could she pretend to her mother that it had been a simple kiss beneath the mistletoe, meant in fun and nothing more.

And that had been *before* she'd known she was in love with him.

If the photographer had been in Mitch's bedroom last week—

Afraid to look at any more pieces of incriminating evidence, she rushed through the house to her bedroom and shoved the packet in a drawer, out of sight.

The photos would give Mitch every reason to believe she'd meant it at the time.

They would certainly have convinced her mother and Roger that she was over David. If ever they'd needed proof, then the way she was hungrily kissing Mitch would have removed all doubt.

"Annie?"

She swung around to see compassion in her mother's eyes.

"As you've found out, Mitch is nothing like David. Just be careful."

"It's too late for that warning. I'm in love with him. But you don't have to worry, Mom. Once the party for you is over I'll be back in school. I'm thinking of going on to law school. An MBA will be an asset if I specialize in contract law."

A pained expression crossed her mother's face. "Roger and I shouldn't have gone away to get married."

"Please don't say that!" Annie cried. "I'm glad you did. Coming up against a man like Mitch was a lesson I've been needing for a long time. So let's not talk about him ever again. I'd rather take you to lunch and hear all about the wedding ceremony and your trip."

The party was in full swing, but Mitch didn't know how long his grandparents would be able to stay awake.

While Marion and Annie circulated with David, he decided now was the time to take Roger aside.

"Could I talk with you alone for a minute?"

"Of course."

Roger followed him into the study. "Marion and I are crazy about your house, Mitch. It's the kind of place we'd like—right on the beach, and a moderate size."

Mitch leaned against the closed door. "How would you like to buy it from me at a reduced price?"

Roger did a double-take. The two men had been in business too long not to read between the lines.

"What's going on?"

"My grandparents arrived yesterday. As you can see, even with their canes they're both too feeble to have made the trip. I bought this place with the idea that they would live here, where I could take care of them. But it's not going to work. They're happy to be here for this occasion, but they want to go home. They want to die there, and I can't blame them. It's too late for such a big change in their lives. Under the circumstances, I'm afraid I'm going to have to resign."

The word hung heavy between them.

Roger grimaced. "I understand. But I have to admit I'm staggered by your news."

"I'm sorry. If there were any other way... But there isn't."

Roger pursed his lips. "Maybe this would be the best time for me to sell the company. Marion and I have been talking about spending more time together."

"Do it while you have your lives and your health!" Mitch said fiercely.

Roger eyed him with concern. "After losing Hannah when you did, it's a damn shame you wasted all these years working with no woman to go home to."

"Many times I've thought the same thing about you and Marion."

"You know why I didn't propose sooner?"

"I do."

The other man's brows lifted. "So what's this move going to do to you and the woman you've had your eye on?"

Roger knew damn well it was Annie.

"I don't know yet."

"You sound like me, while I was wondering whether it was too soon to propose to Marion or not. Under the circumstances you'd better hurry up and figure it out. On this trip I discovered all over again that when you've got love, nothing else matters. Pull out that picture of the two of you and take one more good long look."

Mitch had already done that—more times than he was willing to admit.

"Where's the man known to be so decisive he pulls the rug out from under everybody before they know what's happening?"

Mitch made a sound in his throat.

"When it comes to Annie—"

"I know. Believe me, I know. But now I'm kicking myself for the years I denied Marion because I was worried I'd be proposing too soon. Don't repeat history, Mitch."

Annie wasn't Marion. She hadn't been married before. This was all too new to her. Mitch was terrified he'd frightened her off.

"What about my house, Roger?"

"Let me discuss it with Marion. When are your grandparents going back?"

"They want me to take them tomorrow."

"Then go ahead and do whatever you have to. But I'd like one more favor from you."

"Name it."

"Stay on in an advisory capacity until I decide what I'm going to do?"

Mitch nodded. "I already planned on it. I'm keeping the condo. That way I can fly out once a month."

"Thank you, Mitch. Now, I think we'd better join the party. We'll keep this quiet for the time being."

"I'd appreciate that, Roger."

Relieved to have dropped that bomb, Mitch headed for the kitchen, where he'd seen Annie dart seconds ago on those long, gorgeous legs of hers. She looked stunning tonight, in a creamy two-piece suit with a strand of pearls the same color.

She'd been waiting on his grandparents all evening. They weren't the type to warm to other people in a hurry, but he could tell they were charmed by her.

While she was looking in the fridge, Mitch said, "Can I help?"

She pulled out a quart of milk. "Your grandmother wants to go to bed, but first she needs warm milk to take her pills."

He reached in the cupboard for a mug and handed it to her.

She thanked him and heated it in the microwave. So far she'd avoided looking at him directly. All he needed was a sign.

Dammit, Annie. Give me one.

"I think everyone's having a good time. Don't you?"

"How could they not, in a house this beautiful and with food so fabulous?" She retrieved the mug and hurried past one of the caterers to the living room.

She was treating him in that offish way she had once before. But in this case he was gratified by her behavior—because he knew what was driving it.

The physical side of their relationship was not the problem. What if she wasn't ready for a big commitment with him? Several times she'd talked about his being older.

An older man with old grandparents. She probably found the whole thing a turnoff.

He watched from a distance as she helped his grandparents down the hall to the master bedroom. He enjoyed the fact that they'd allowed her to help them. She had a way…

Was it because she was an innately kind person? Or was it wishful thinking that she truly cared for them because she was beginning to care for *him*?

CHAPTER ELEVEN

ANNIE took the empty mug and put it on the bedside table. "Is there anything else I can do for you?"

Mitch's grandmother was tucked in the king-sized bed. His grandfather Donald had just come out of the bathroom, dressed in pajamas and a robe.

"You're spoiling us." Martha laughed quietly.

"That's what Mitch is going to do to you when you move here to live," Annie said, unaware that Mitch had come into the room until he walked over to kiss his grandmother.

"I'm afraid I can't talk them into it, Annie. I'll be taking them back home tomorrow."

Pain spiked through her body, almost incapacitating her.

"If we were younger…" Martha whispered, looking up at her grandson through watery eyes.

Donald nodded. "We've lived in one place all our lives."

Annie moved to the end of the bed, struggling to maintain her composure.

"Then I'll say goodnight, so you can get a good night's sleep before your long flight tomorrow. It's been wonderful to meet you."

Donald stared at her. "Have you ever been to Minnesota?"

"No."

"It's different than here."

Annie forced a smile. "I bet you had a white Christmas."

He nodded. "That, and blizzards, and below-zero temperatures. But we love it."

"There's only one thing missing..." Martha murmured.

"Not anymore," Mitch declared.

His grandparents looked at him in surprise.

"Tonight I told Roger I'm leaving Hastings and coming back home to live with you."

So he'd really done it... Annie grasped the footboard for support.

Donald shook his head. "You can't do that, son."

"I already have. Everything's settled."

"You're not thinking clearly," his grandfather argued.

Even in his late eighties, he could be intimidating. It helped Annie understand Mitch as never before.

She paused at the door. "Even before you came Mitch told me that if you couldn't move here, he was going home. If there's one thing I know about your grandson, it's that he never backs down."

That cruel smile was in evidence once more. "Annie knows me well."

Yes. She did. Too well.

"Are you coming with him?" his grandfather asked unexpectedly.

Her face prickled with heat. She made the mistake of looking at Mitch. His gaze was enigmatic as he said, "I told them we wouldn't be seeing each other again unless you wanted to."

While she reeled from a surfeit of pain, his grandfather said, "What's the problem, young woman?"

"Donald!" his wife cried. "For heaven's sake! What goes on between these two is none of our business."

Annie was sobbing inside. *Nothing* was going on between them. Mitch only wanted a physical relationship.

"Have a safe flight, all of you."

Without looking at Mitch, she stole from the bedroom and ran into the next one to get her purse.

She saw David at the front door, playing host to the last guest. He took one look at Annie and said, "What's wrong? You look ill."

"Where's Mom?"

"She left with Dad. He said he had something important to talk over with her and wanted to leave. They asked me to drive you home."

"Could we go now?"

"Sure."

She dashed past him and hurried out to the street, where David's car was parked.

He was right behind her, and used the remote before helping her inside. In a few minutes they'd reached the freeway. He looked over at her. "How about telling me what's going on? That's what a brother is for, you know."

"You're very sweet, but there's nothing to tell. I'm in love with Mitch, and he's not in love with me. He's going home with his grandparents for good."

"I heard. Dad told me before he and your mom left the house. Have you told Mitch how you feel?"

"He knows without my having to say anything." Her voice wobbled. "After seeing that picture taken at the party, *everyone* has to know."

"You were certainly caught out, all right. Just remember there were two people in that picture. An objective observer would say you weren't the only one swept away."

She groaned. "So swept away he's leaving and never coming back."

"We're talking about Mitch, remember? As long as I've known him, he's liked all his 'i's dotted and his 't's crossed. He never goes for the clinch until he knows the competition's bottom line."

"A woman shouldn't have to say it first."

"Where did you get a strange idea like that? I have a hunch he's afraid you're using him to get over me. Since our folks left on the cruise, he's been sabotaging me right and left. He needs to know you mean it."

Mitch's words came back to haunt her. *Don't come near me again unless you mean it.* But he'd been talking about something else.

"Mitch knows I had a crush on you. Nothing more."

"Knowing Mitch as I do, he's not going to be convinced until he hears the words he's waiting for."

"You honestly think he's waiting for a declaration of love?" she scathed.

"What do you think's the reason he called Elaine instead of you to help him out when he got hurt? He was terrified to call you, only to find you came to him out of pity."

Her head jerked around. "Pity? But he couldn't possibly think that! Not after— Well, not after we got stuck in the elevator."

"Well, well, well… Now it all comes out. Don't you know you've tied the great Mitch Reynolds into knots? Give the poor guy a break and let him know how you feel!"

A feeling like an electrical current charged through her body. She could hear Mitch's words. *You're an intelligent woman. One day you'll figure it out.*

Was that what Mitch had meant?

"Still want to go home?" David prodded. "Or shall I turn the car around?"

Maybe she'd be making the biggest mistake of her life, but she had to find out.

"Do you mind? Turning the car around, I mean?"

"What do *you* think?"

He pulled off at the next exit and they got back on the freeway once again, headed for San Clemente.

"Got your excuse all figured out?"

"Yes. I was in such a hurry to get out of there, I ran off without my coat."

"You mean the way Mitch left you when you were still wearing his? That excuse works every time. Mel told me you returned it to Elaine's office—and then who should show up in your mom's office but the big man himself, carrying it with him?"

Annie made a face. "Is there nothing sacred at the office?"

"No." He took the exit and headed for Mitch's street. "Isn't that Mitch's car, screeching around the corner toward us?"

Annie's heart leaped. It *was* Mitch.

Oh, please let it mean he was coming for her because he couldn't help himself!

David started to slow down. Mitch pulled up right next to him. Both men lowered their windows.

Annie didn't dare look at Mitch.

"Where were you going like a bat out of you-know-where?" David spoke first.

"Annie left her coat," came Mitch's deep voice.

"Hear that, Annie? We were just coming back for it. Want to hand it through the window?"

"Not unless you two have other plans for the rest of the night." Mitch's voice sounded so fierce it was almost frightening.

"No, Mitch. Dad asked me to drive her home."

Before getting out of the car, Annie squeezed David's arm to thank him. Then she hurried around to the passenger side of Mitch's car. He'd already opened the door for her.

The warm interior felt good. He reached in front of her to close it, brushing her midriff in the process. Any time he touched her, she trembled with desire.

When she dared a glance at him, his profile looked

chiseled. "If you don't mind, I don't want to go home yet. Could we park down on the beach for a while?"

The tension was palpable. "I don't think that would be a good idea." His voice rasped.

"I do. Otherwise I won't have your full attention."

She felt the shudder than ran through his body. "Annie—"

"I know—" She broke in on him. "You told me not to seek you out again unless I meant it."

"Is that why you asked David to bring you back?"

She sucked in her breath. The time for honesty had come. "Yes. I used my coat for an excuse."

His hands had tightened on the steering wheel until she could see the whites of his knuckles.

"You still need an excuse to let him down gently?"

"No. It was the excuse I was going to use on you, so you'd let me in the house. Luckily for me I didn't have to ring the bell and wake up your grandparents. Please could we just drive down to the beach to talk?"

She heard a sharp intake of breath before he turned the car around, causing his tires to screech once more.

It didn't take more than two minutes to find a spot near the surf. He stopped the car, but kept the motor running for warmth.

"Your grandfather said something that made me realize how hard it's going to be when you leave."

"Hard on whom?"

She moistened her lips nervously. "Me, of course."

"Really? I wouldn't have guessed."

"You didn't know my father, but I'm like him in

temperament. He took a long time before making a decision, even a small one. But once he did, he never looked back. I've been thinking about you and me."

"And?" he fired.

"I've decided I want to be with you if *you* really mean it."

His chest heaved. "You think I don't?"

"I'm not talking about just going to bed together. Here's my proposition. We get married in Minnesota. The family will come out for it. We'll live with your grandparents. I'll finish up school there. By late spring I hope to be pregnant. Your grandparents are waiting for at least one great-grandchild. There's no time to waste.

"Think of all the time Mom and Roger wasted when they could have been happily married for the last two or three years. Instead they tiptoed around each other, afraid to speak their minds because of David and me. It's made us both feel terrible. And another terrible thing—you're going to be thirty-three pretty soon. It's long past time you settled down, with a wife who loves you more than life itself. What I can't figure out is why you didn't kiss me under the mistletoe at the company party *last* year, after David left? Instead you sat there fuming at me. Surely you realized I'd have been putty in your hands? We'd be married by now.

"And when I think how honorable you were in the elevator. After you put your coat around me I kept waiting for you to kiss me again. I never wanted you to stop. And the afternoon I made dinner just for you. I wanted to show you I could cook. Of course I thought you'd start kissing me in the kitchen while we did the dishes. Then you took off and it killed me. If your leg hadn't been hurt, I probably would have crawled into bed with you that day, too.

"What I'm trying to say is that I want to be near you forever. But, since you haven't said a single word this whole time, I guess our ideas of 'meaning it' are two different things. You can drive me home now."

She was in so much pain she couldn't bear it.

"Would you like to put your coat on before we go?"

"No." Her voice shook, because David had been wrong and she wanted to die. "It's plenty warm in here."

"Suit yourself, but there's something in the right pocket you might want to see."

"If it's a gift for helping you with the party, I'd rather not accept it. Under the circumstances, I'm sure you understand."

"Then I'll get it out for you." He reached in back and pulled out a scroll tied with red ribbon.

The pain was excruciating. "I already have one for a souvenir."

"This one's a little different," he explained. "I'll do the honors."

He slid the ribbon off and opened the parchment.

Clearing his throat, he said, "'Twas the night after New Year's and all through Santa's house, not a creature was stirring, not even a mouse. Mr and Mrs Claus were all snug in their bed. With their arms wrapped around each other, they had nothing to dread.' Darling?" he whispered, "you know how much I've loved you all these years."

"I do, dearest," she answered, her voice full of tears.

"Will you agree to marry me and become my true wife?"

"You're asking me to marry you *now*, when I've been waiting all my life?"

"'I know I'm not perfect, even if children think it's true. Will you forgive this one flaw and just say I do?'"

"Oh, Mitch—" Moved deeper than tears, Annie pulled the paper away from his hands. Wrapping her arms around his neck, she pressed her lips to his and told him the words he needed to hear. "I love you, my darling, darling Mitch. Let me tell you the ways."

Her words went on for a very long time.

"Annie," he cried exultantly, crushing her so tight she couldn't breathe. "Where have you been all my life?"

"Right where I was supposed to be, until you found me waiting for you. I want to marry you, Mitch Reynolds. I adore you. You don't even begin to know how much."

"That'll do for starters," he said, before sliding a diamond ring on her finger. "Before you ran out I had big plans to give this to you tonight. But I was afraid you'd think it was too soon."

She cupped his handsome face in her hands. His eyes blazed with blue fire. "Now you know otherwise. Let's get this sleigh back to the house, Mr Claus. There's a lot of work to be done before morning."

He gave her a hard, hungry kiss. "I think we'd better have a definition of terms first."

"Well—" She smiled provocatively. "With the negotiations over, I'm in your hands now. It's all up to you. Didn't you say something at the office party about going home for a long winter's nap?"

A Bride for Christmas

MARION LENNOX

Marion Lennox is a country girl, born on a south-east Australian dairy farm. She moved on – mostly because the cows just weren't interested in her stories! Married to a 'very special doctor', Marion writes for Medical Romance™ as well as Romance where she used to write as Trisha David for a while.

In her non-writing life, Marion cares for kids, cats, dogs, chooks and goldfish. She travels, she fights her rampant garden (she's losing) and her house dust (she's lost). After an early bout with breast cancer she's also reprioritised her life, figured out what's important and discovered the joys of deep baths, romance and chocolate. Preferably all at the same time!

CHAPTER ONE

'TELL me again why I've bought this wedding salon.' Guy Carver was approaching Sandpiper Bay with dismay. 'You didn't say this place was a hundred miles from nowhere.'

'You want to expand.' On the line from Manhattan, Guy's partner sounded unperturbed. 'Sandpiper Bay makes more sense than any other place in Australia. I told you...'

'You told me what?'

'It has the world's best surf,' Malcolm said patiently. 'It's surrounded by arguably the world's loveliest National Park, and half Hollywood owns property at Sandpiper Bay. Where are you now?'

'On the outskirts. It looks...'

'Don't judge until you see the town. Even my wife thinks Sandpiper Bay is great. She's furious you're doing the planning and not me.'

'As if *you* could plan a Carver Salon.'

'What's there to plan?' Malcolm demanded. 'Order

a lake of ice-grey paint, give the widow a paintbrush and take a few days off.'

'I don't have time for a few days off,' Guy snapped, irritated by his partner's cheerfulness. 'I need to be back in New York on the twenty-sixth for the Film Conglomerate do.'

'We can handle Conglomerate with our hands tied. Spend Christmas on the beach.'

'Or not.' Christmas was a wasted day as far as Guy was concerned, and he had better things to do than surf. This year he'd timed this trip deliberately so he'd be flying home on Christmas Day. Christmas mid-air would get him as far away as was possible from useless sentiment.

He'd joined the coast road now, and he had to admit the place did look spectacular. Sandpiper Bay appeared to be a tiny coastal village bordering a shimmering sapphire sea, with rolling mountains beyond.

'So what am I looking for?' he demanded of Malcolm.

'A shopfront on the beachfront shopping strip. It's called Bridal Fluff.'

'Bridal Fluff?' He didn't explode. His voice just grew very calm. 'Did I hear right?'

'Sure did. The ex-owner's one Jenny Westmere. Widow. Apart from her dubious taste in naming her salon, she sounds competent. We've offered her twelve months' salary to make the transition easier.'

'There can't be a transition from Fluff to a Carver Bridal Salon,' he said grimly. 'I'll gut the place.'

He was turning into the main street now, and what he saw made him blanch. Bridal Fluff was indeed...

fluff. The shopfront was pastel pink. The curtains in the windows looked like billowing white clouds, held back with pink and silver tassels. A Christmas tree stood in the window, festooned with pink and silver baubles, and a white fluffy angel smiling seraphically down on passers-by. The name of the shop was picked out in deeper pink, gold and silver. 'What the…?'

'Don't judge a book by its cover,' Malcolm said hastily, guessing what he was seeing. 'We don't need to give this woman any organisational role. We're just keeping her on the payroll to keep the locals happy. Every other salon we've acquired, the previous owner has been so chuffed to be associated with the Carver salon that the takeover's been a piece of cake. The bottom line is money. I've checked the books. I said it was a good buy and I meant it.'

'And if it's not…?'

'If it's not we'll just have to wear it.'

Malcolm had worked with Guy for years. Guy's reputation for dazzling event management left everyone he worked with stunned, but his personal reputation was for being aloof. Malcolm's cheerful nature, combined with a brash business acumen that matched Guy's, made them a formidable team. Together they'd built the Carver empire into the most lucrative events management chain in the world.

'No need to fret,' Malcolm was saying now, all breezy certainty. 'You and Mrs Westmere will get on like a house on fire.'

'Mrs Westmere?'

'Jennifer Westmere. I told you. The widow.'

'Great,' Guy muttered, pulling into a parking lot by the pink door. 'Middle-aged, frumpy and dressed in pink?'

'Nah,' Malcolm said, though he was starting to sound uneasy. 'The reports I have say she's young. Twenty-eight.'

'And I'm stuck with her?'

'The contract stipulates twelve months' employment.'

'I'll buy her out,' Guy said grimly. 'I should have stuck to Manhattan and Paris and London. I understand weddings there.'

'Then we'd miss out.' Malcolm cheered up again. 'Now you're expanding the Carver Salons worldwide, it's time we moved into Australia. Sandpiper Bay's more hip than Sydney or Melbourne. There's a huge buzz about the Carver Salons expanding. So go meet the lady with the pink fuzz. Make friends.'

'Not even close,' Guy muttered as pulled his car to a halt and finished the conversation. 'Friends? As if.'

Jenny was kneeling on the floor and tackling about a hundred yards of hemline when he walked in. It was the fourth time she'd been around this hem. The dressmaker had thrown her hands up in horror, and now Jenny was left holding the baby. So to speak.

'I know it's not right,' the bride's mother was saying. 'We practised last night, and as she swept up the aisle I was sure the left side was longer than the right. Or was it the right longer than the left? Anyway, I knew you'd want to check. It has to be perfect.'

'Mmphf,' Jenny mumbled through pins, and then the door swung open.

Guy Carver.

This man's weddings were known throughout the world. *He* was known throughout the world. The phone call to Jenny offering to buy her premises had left her poleaxed.

'But why?' she'd stammered, and the man handling the deal for Guy had given her an honest answer.

'Eight of the ten most prestigious weddings in Australia have been held within ten miles of Sandpiper Bay in the last two years,' Malcolm had told her bluntly. 'There's a caveat on new businesses in what's essentially a historic commercial district. Setting up a business from scratch would be complex. Our people have checked your premises. Your building is big enough for us, and you already have a reputation for providing service. We'll do the rest. If you're at all interested, then we just need to settle on a price.'

She'd named a figure that had seemed crazy. Ten minutes later the deal had been sealed.

Jenny had replaced the receiver, stunned.

'It's more money than I ever dreamed possible,' she'd told her mother-in-law, and when Lorna had heard how much she'd gasped.

'That's wonderful. You'll be able to buy Henry whatever he needs.'

'I will.' Jenny smiled her delight. Even Lorna didn't know the depths of her despair at not being able to provide Henry with optimal medical treatment.

'But what will you do with yourself?'

'That's just it. They're offering me a job, doing what I'm doing now, only on a salary. Twelve months' paid work, with the possibility of extending it. Holidays,' she said dreamily. 'Sick pay. Regular income with no bad debts.'

'And Guy Carver as your boss? Working with someone the glossies describe as one of the world's sexiest men?'

They'd grinned at each other like fools at that—a twenty-eight-year-old widow and her sixty-year-old mother-in-law letting their hormones have their head for one wonderful moment—and then they'd put their hormones away and thought seriously about what it entailed.

'Does he have any idea what he's letting himself in for?' Lorna had demanded. 'A country wedding salon...'

'It won't be a country salon for long. Currently the international jet-setters and the rich locals bring their own planners. Carver wants that business. I'm guessing most locals will stop being able to afford him.'

'Just like the rest of the businesses in this town,' Lorna said, grimacing.

'Sandpiper Bay's changing.'

'It's being taken over by the jet-set,' Lorna agreed. 'Every property within a twenty-mile radius is being snapped up at extraordinary prices by millionaires who spend two weeks of every year here.'

'We can't stop it.' Like Lorna, Jenny was ambivalent about the changes to their rural backwater, but there was little choice. 'The guy acting for Carver said if I didn't agree then they'd buy out the old haberdashery and set up in opposition. We'd be left with the brides that couldn't afford Guy.'

'Which would be most of our brides.'

'Right. I'd go under. As it is, my wealthy brides subsidise my poorer ones.'

'Which is why you're a lousy businesswoman.' Lorna gave her daughter-in-law a subdued smile. 'Like me.'

'Which is why I'm selling,' Jenny said firmly. 'We have no choice.'

So the arrangements had been fine. Sort of. Up until now it had been phone calls and official letters, with the business operating as normal. Only there was suddenly a lot more business, as people heard the news. Jenny was fielding phone calls now from as far away as California, from brides thrilled with the prospect of a Guy Carver wedding. She'd put them off, not clear when she'd officially be running Carver weddings, not really believing in the transition herself. But now the man himself was standing in the doorway.

'I'm looking for Jennifer Westmere,' he said, in a rich, gravelly voice, and Jenny's current bride gasped and pointed down.

'She's here.'

Jenny pushed aside a few acres of tulle and gave Guy a wave. 'Mmphf,' she said, and gestured to the pins in her mouth.

'I'm here on business,' he said enigmatically, and

Shirley, the mother of the bride she was looking after, gave a sound that resembled a choking hen.

'You're Guy Carver. You're taking over this salon. Ooh, we're so excited.'

Guy stilled. Uh-oh, Jenny thought. One of the stipulations in the contract was that this takeover be kept quiet until the salon had been transformed to Carver requirements. But that hadn't been stipulated until the third phone call, and in the interim Lorna had managed to spread the news across Sandpiper Bay.

There was nothing she could do about that now. She watched as Guy sat, crossing one elegantly shod foot over the other. 'Carry on. I'll watch,' he said, his voice expressionless.

Great. Jenny went back to pinning, her mind whirling.

The man was seriously...wow! He was tall and dark, almost Mediterranean-looking, she thought, with the sleekly handsome demeanour of a European playboy. Not that she knew many European playboys—to be honest, she didn't know a single one—but she imagined the species to have just those dark and brooding good looks. He looked almost hawk-like, she decided, and she also decided that the photographs she'd seen in celebrity magazines didn't do him justice. His magnificently cut suit and his gorgeous silk tie screamed serious money.

Actually, everything about him screamed serious money.

There was a Ferrari parked outside her front window.

Guy Carver was sitting in her salon.

Was he annoyed about the lack of confidentiality? Was he annoyed enough to call the deal off?

'What's the problem with the dress?' Guy asked in a conversational tone, and she mmphfed again and waved a hand apologetically to the bride's mother.

'The hem's crooked,' Shirley Grubb told him, beaming and preparing to be voluble. 'Kylie's not getting married in a crooked dress.'

'When's the wedding?'

'Next Thursday.' Shirley looked smug. 'I know two days before Christmas is cutting it fine. We were so lucky to get the church. It's just this dratted dress that's holding us up.'

'When was the dress ordered?'

'Oh, she's had it for years,' Shirley told him, ready to be friendly. 'When Kylie turned sixteen I said we'll buy your wedding dress now, while your father's still working and while Jenny's here to organise it. No matter that you don't have a fella yet. Just don't put on too much weight. That was four years ago, and now we can finally use it.'

'Um…right,' Guy said mildly. 'When's the baby due?'

'Mid-January,' Shirley said, and beamed some more. 'Aren't we lucky we got the dress made? When we ordered it I told Jenny to leave heaps to spare at the hem. I was six months gone with Kylie before my old man did the right thing, and here's Kylie got her fella the same way. Hot-blooded, we are,' she said, preening. 'It's in the genes.'

Guy appeared to be focussing on the tip of one of his

glossy shoes. Wow, Jenny thought. Guy Carver chatting to Mrs Grubb. Has he any idea what he's getting into?

She went on pinning. It gave her breathing space, she thought. So much tulle...

'Why did you choose Bridal Fluff to organise your wedding?' Guy asked conversationally, and Jenny winced. She just knew what Shirley would say, and here it came.

'Lorna—that's Jenny's mother-in-law—and me went to school together. Lorna won't charge me.'

Ouch. This technically wasn't her salon any more, Jenny thought. Nor was it Lorna's. It belonged to Guy.

'So this arrangement was made a long time ago?'

'When we were girls. Lorna always said she'd plan my wedding, and any of my kids' weddings and any grandkids' weddings, and when I rang up last month she said sure.'

'Lorna isn't planning your wedding,' Guy said mildly. 'It seems Jenny is. And Jenny works for me.'

For the first time Shirley seemed unsure. Her mouth opened, and failed to shut again.

'You mean,' she said at last, 'that we have to pay?'

It was time to enter this conversation. Jenny carefully removed the remaining pins and set them into her pin box.

'Any arrangements I made before Mr Carver purchased the business will be honoured,' she said. 'I'll take care of Kylie's wedding.'

'And the rest of them?' Shirley looked affronted.

'Maybe in my own time,' Jenny said. 'Not from this salon.'

'Well…' Shirley was about to start a war, Jenny thought, and Shirley's wars were legion.

'Leave it, Ma.' For the first time Kylie spoke up. She was a pale, timid young bride, and only the fact that her prospective husband was even more timid than his fiancée—and totally besotted—made Jenny feel okay about the wedding. But now Kylie had a flush to her cheeks, and she turned to Guy as if she was trying to dredge up the courage to ask him something important. 'Mr Carver…?'

'Yes?' Guy was staring down at Jenny—who was meeting his look and holding it with a hint of defiance. Things were about to change in her life because of this man, and she wasn't sure that she liked it.

'When did you buy Bridal Fluff?' Kylie asked, and Guy turned and gazed at the bride.

It wasn't a great look, Jenny thought ruefully. The first of her brides that Guy was seeing was a waif of a bride in a vast sea of tulle. Her dress had been made when she'd had a size eight waist. It had been close fitting then. Now two strips of satin had been sewn into the waist to accommodate her advanced pregnancy. Jenny had attached a loose-fitting lace camisole to disguise the bulge a little, but it was no small bulge. The fact that the bulge kept changing meant that the hemline kept changing as well.

As well as that, Kylie's mother had definite ideas on what a bride should look like—which was a vision in every decorative piece of lacework she could think of. The veil even had tiny cupid motifs hand-sewn onto the netting. Seeing the veil turned into a train, Jenny estimated Guy was looking at approximately eight hundred cupids.

This was not one of her most elegant brides.

'Do you officially own this place yet?' Kylie asked, and Guy nodded, with what appeared to be reluctance. 'Yes.'

'Then I'm a Carver Bride,' Kylie said, suddenly ecstatic. She held her hands together in reverence. 'Like in those glossy magazines we buy, Ma. I'm the first Australian Carver bride. I reckon we ought to phone some reporters.'

'No,' Guy snapped, rising and looking at Kylie in distaste. 'You're not a Carver Bride. You are Mrs Westmere's responsibility. My takeover was supposed to be confidential, and the name-change won't happen yet. There'll be no Carver Brides until my people are here and we can get rid of this…' he gazed around the salon with distaste '…this fluff.'

Had he made a mistake? Guy watched as the hemmarking continued. 'It's a small place,' Malcolm had told him. 'The council has the power to make all sorts of complications, like refusing our requests to expand the building. We need to keep the locals on our side. Make an effort, Guy.'

Maybe he hadn't made an effort. But really… Kylie, a Carver Bride? Some things were unthinkable. And what had happened to the confidentiality clause? It could be a disaster.

He waited on, ignored by the Grubbs, which suited him. Finally the hem was finished, and Kylie and her mother sailed off down the street to spread the news. Indignation was oozing from every pore.

They might be indignant, but so was he.

'I understood this takeover was to be kept quiet,' he said, in a voice that would have had his secretary shaking. Cool, low and carefully neutral.

It didn't have Jenny quaking. 'Your accountant, or whoever he is, should have said that earlier. My mother-in-law had ten minutes between offer and acceptance where that stipulation wasn't known. Ten minutes can mean a lot of gossip in Sandpiper Bay.'

'It means I can call the contract off.'

'Fine,' she said and tilted her chin. 'Go ahead.'

He was taken aback. She should be apologising. He'd come all the way here to find the terms of the contract had been breached, and all she was saying was take it or leave it.

He'd come a long way. Maybe it didn't matter so much. If he worked hard to get the place sleek before anyone important saw it…

That meant he also had to get rid of unsuitable clients. Fast. Clients like the Grubbs had no place in a salon such as this.

'Why the hell did you take that pair on?' he demanded of Jenny, watching through the pink-tinged window as Shirley tugged her daughter into the butcher shop next door.

Jenny was still on the floor, gathering pins. When

she answered, her voice was carefully dispassionate. 'It's obvious, isn't it? They're local, and I'm the local bridal salon.'

'They'll do your reputation no good at all. And as for you being the local bridal salon… We have a contract. Unless I walk away, you're no longer in charge. And you won't be doing weddings like this.'

'Right.' Jenny sat back on her heels and eyed him with disfavour. 'So the Pregnant-with-Tulle-and-Cupids isn't a Carver look?'

He choked. She eyed him with suspicion, and then decided to smile. 'Great,' she said. 'That's the first positive I've seen. I hoped you'd have a sense of humour.'

He collected himself. 'I haven't.'

'Yes, you have. I can see it. It's a pity it seems the *only* good thing I've seen.' She went back to gathering pins.

His jaw dropped. She was criticising him, he thought, astonished. She was on his staff. Criticism was unthinkable.

He tried to remember when he'd last heard criticism from his staff—and couldn't.

'You realise things are going to have to change around here?' he said cautiously. 'There'll be less fluff, for a start.'

She thought about that as she kept sorting pins, and suddenly she smiled. Which threw him all over again. It was an amazing smile, he decided, feeling more than a little confounded. Somewhere his vision of the Widow Westmere was being supplanted by this girl called

Jenny. This woman? Okay, a woman. Her body was slim and lithe. Her glossy brown curls were cut in a pert, elfin haircut, which, combined with her informal jeans, her T-shirt and the smattering of freckles on her nose, made her look about fourteen.

But she wasn't fourteen. There were lines around her eyes, soft lines of laughter—but more. There was that look at the back of her eyes that said she'd seen a lot. There was not a trace of fluff about her.

This woman was a widow. There had to be some tragedy...

He didn't need to know, he told himself. She was here for twelve months to smooth the transition. Her leaving after that would be marked with a card of personal regret. When his secretary put those cards before him to sign he could hardly ever put a face to the name.

He liked it like that. He'd gone to a lot of trouble so it was like that.

He gazed around the shop, searching for something to distract him. Luckily there was plenty of distraction on offer.

'Three Christmas trees?' he said cautiously, and Jenny nodded, whatever had amused her obviously disappearing, the edge of anger creeping back.

'Lorna put up the big one in the window. She organises it halfway through November and it drives me nuts. Pine needles everywhere. The one in the entrance is a gift from Kylie's fiancé—he works in a timber yard and came in with it over his shoulder, looking really pleased with himself. Then the guys at Ben's work brought me one. How could I refuse any of them?'

'Ben?'

'My husband,' she said, and there was that in her voice that precluded questions.

'So…' he said, moving on, as she clearly intended him to do. 'We have three fully decorated Christmas trees, two mannequins in full bridal regalia and one groom in what looks a pretty down-at-heel dinner suit. Plus Christmas decorations.'

'They're not Christmas decorations,' she said tightly as he gestured with distaste to the harlequin light-ball hanging in the centre of the room and the silver and gold streamers running from the ball to the outer walls. 'The ball and streamers are here all year round.'

'You're kidding?'

'Nope,' she said, with a hint of defiance. 'We run the most garishly decorated bridal salon in the southern hemisphere. Our brides love it.'

'Carver Brides won't.'

She nodded. 'You've made that plain. It wasn't kind—to swat Kylie and Shirley like that.'

'If anyone publishes pictures of Kylie as a Carver Bride…'

'They won't. They might be provincial, but they're not stupid.'

'They sound stupid. What the hell was Malcolm about, buying this place?' Guy demanded, and Jenny's face stilled.

'You don't like it?'

'It's a backwater. Sure, it's scenic...'

'Do you know the average income of our locals?'

'What has that to do with it?'

'A lot, I imagine,' she said. 'There's two types of business in this town. First there are the businesses that provide for the original inhabitants. The likes of Shirley and Kylie. Those who you consider stupid. Then there are those that cater for the elite. We have no less than twenty helicopter pads in the shire. Millionaires, billionaires—we have them all. In your terms, not a stupid person in sight. The town has a historic overlay and a twenty-acre subdivision limit, so development is just about non-existent. In the last ten years every place coming onto the market has been snapped up by squillionaires. You know that, or you wouldn't have bought here.' She hesitated. 'You really want to get rid of the likes of Kylie?'

'I didn't want to imply all the locals are stupid. But if Kylie can't afford me...'

'She won't be able to afford you. None of the real locals will. Why do you want me to stay on?'

'To ease the transition.'

'There won't *be* a transition. You've just told Kylie there won't be Carver Brides until your people are here. I thought...according to the contract...I'd be one of *your* people.'

He might as well say it like it was. 'You won't have any authority.'

Any last hint of a smile completely disappeared at that. 'So the offer to employ me for a year was window-dressing to make me feel good about you guys taking over?'

'I can't employ you if you seriously like…' he stared around him in distaste '…fluff.'

'The fluff's Lorna's'

'Lorna?'

'Lorna's my mother-in-law,' she said. She was speaking calmly, but he could see she was holding herself tightly on rein. 'Lorna set this salon up forty years ago. She had a stroke eight years ago, and advertised for an assistant. I got the job and met Ben. Now it's my business, but Lorna still puts in her oar. Lorna's been incredibly good to me. If she wants pink, and the locals like pink, I don't see why she can't have it.'

'Carver Salons are sleek and minimalist.'

'Of course they are. So you're here to toss the fluff?'

'I'll do the preliminaries,' he told her. 'That's why I've come—to decide what needs to be done. By the look of it, we'll start from scratch. We'll gut the place. My staff will take over the rebuilding, and everything that comes after.'

'But you'll still employee me?'

'We envisage a smooth transition.'

'You're employing me for local colour?'

'I didn't say that.'

'You didn't have to. I can't see me fitting the image of a Carver Salon consultant.'

'Have you ever met a Carver Salon consultant?'

'As it happens, I have,' she said, almost defiantly. 'A year ago I had a…well, I needed a holiday, and my parents-in-law sent me to Paris. I wandered through your salon, just to see how the other half live. Only of course I wasn't up to standard. I hadn't been in the salon for two minutes before I was asked to leave.'

'If my staff thought you were possible opposition, then…'

'Now, that's the funny thing,' she said. She'd risen and moved over to one of the Christmas trees. The angel on top was askew and she started carefully to adjust it. Then she began to check the lights, twisting each bulb in turn, taking her attention from him. 'They didn't even ask why I was there,' she said over her shoulder. 'I could have been there to talk about my wedding. I could have been there to make enquiries about anything at all. But I was wearing jeans and a T-shirt, and carrying a small backpack Lorna had given me.' She gave a rueful smile. 'The backpack was pink. Anyway, they obviously sorted me as a type they didn't want. They asked me to leave, and suddenly there was a security guard propelling me onto the pavement.' She shrugged. 'Given my opinion of Carver Salons, I should have told you to take your very kind offer to buy this salon and stick it. But of course it's a very generous offer, and I need the money and the thought of me being in opposition to you is ridiculous.'

There was a moment's silence then. Guy thought about his Paris staff. They were the best. They ran weddings that were the talk of the world.

They'd kicked this woman out. She must have been humiliated.

Maybe he needed to be a bit more hands-on.

He didn't like to be hands-on.

He thought suddenly of the first wedding he'd planned. He'd been home from college, where he'd been studying law—a career his parents had thought eminently suitable but which bored him stupid. Christa—the girl he'd been dating since both their mothers had organised them to their first prom—had been managing his social life, and that had bored him, too. Then Christa's sister had announced her engagement to someone both families thought entirely unsuitable.

Louise had wept on Guy's shoulder. Without parental support, and with no money of her own, she'd been doomed to have a civil ceremony and go without the party she'd longed for.

Intrigued, Guy had set to work. He'd painted cardboard until his hands were sore, transforming a small local hall into a venue that looked like a SoHo streetscape. He'd organised the local hotdog vendor to set up in a corner. The pretzel seller had come as well—and why wouldn't he have? An inside venue in the middle of a hot August had been a welcome change. Guy had built and painted a bar, made of plywood, but it had looked fantastic. Guests had had to pay normal price for hot dogs and pretzels and beer, but the wealthy guests had been intrigued rather than offended. He'd persuaded buskers to come, including a rap dancer with a hat out for offerings. He'd been hands-on every step of the way, and he'd loved it.

The bride had been ecstatic. Christa and Guy's

mother had been less so. But when Guy had been approached the following week to do another wedding, and another, they'd been forced to stand by as Guy's career took off in another direction.

He remembered the family horror—his fledgling company had had to fly by the seat of its pants, and to risk money was unthinkable. Christa had been beside herself with rage. But he'd kept on. It had been fun, and he'd never known what fun was until he'd thrown aside the mantle of family responsibility.

When had he stopped having fun?

He could hardly remember. All he knew was that after Christa had been killed it had become his refuge—organising vast numbers of people in glittering social events that held no personal attachment at all.

His firm had grown, so he was now no longer hands-on. He employed hundreds—staff handpicked for their artistic and business acumen.

Would they have kicked this woman out on the street? He didn't know, and maybe he shouldn't care as long as they did their job well. But now he thought back to that first wedding, and remembered Louise's joy. He looked at Jenny, her face a trifle flushed and more than a trifle defiant, and he thought, Hell, she must have been demoralised.

What had she said?

A year ago I had a...well, I needed a holiday, and my parents-in-law sent me to Paris.

She'd had a what? A breakdown? What had happened to the husband?

'I'm sorry,' he said.

'It wasn't your fault.'

It was, though, he thought grimly. He took the credit for Carver weddings. He took responsibility for his staff.

'You don't really want to employ me,' she said. 'Do you?'

'I'd rather this place was kept open for business during transition. I had hoped to keep the acquisition quiet until I got my staff in place, but now it's got out… It's unfortunate, but nothing we can't handle. I want the place open for queries and future bookings. You need to be the front person. I'll give you a pricing structure so you can give brides an idea of what we offer. Run the weddings you have now under…' He hesitated, then said, without bothering to hide his disdain, 'Under Bridal Fluff. New bookings will be under Carver Salon.'

'New bookings will be expensive?'

'We're exclusive.'

'You don't need to tell me that.' She grimaced, and he was aware of a stab of…regret?

Once upon a time he'd tried to make his functions wonderful because they created joy. He hadn't heard of the concept of *exclusive*. He'd lived on a shoestring.

He'd learned the hard way that was nonsense. That last day with Christa… 'If you loved me you'd keep doing law. Your father's expecting you to take over the family firm. Your mother's scared you're gay. Guy, you play with paints. *Paints!* And me… How do you think I feel being engaged to a *wedding planner*?'

She'd said the words with such scorn. Then, two

hours later, she was dead. If she'd lived he was under no illusion that their relationship would have been over, but he knew that his life decision had killed her. And his father... His father had heard of Christa's death and it had been as if he'd said goodbye to the son he'd now never have. A wedding planner... Two days later he'd had a stroke, and he'd never recovered.

Guy hadn't gone back to law. He'd known he'd be good at this, but right there and then he'd vowed that he'd be a corporate success. Their deaths had been crazy and unnecessary. No one was going to throw *wedding planner* at him as a term of derision.

He worked hard. He kept to himself. He made money and he carefully didn't *know* people. His life decisions would never hurt anyone again.

He had become exclusive.

The telephone cut the stillness, and he welcomed it. He motioned Jenny to answer, then picked up a catalogue to flick through while she spoke.

Here were Bridal Fluff weddings over the past few years, catalogued down to the last ghastly feather.

He flicked through. And paused.

One bridal couple smiled out from the pages, dressed like a pair from the set of *Cabaret*. He looked more closely, taking in details of the setting.

The whole theme was *Cabaret*.

It was actually rather good. It'd be good even as a Carver Wedding.

He flicked through a bit more. Fluff, fluff... But every now and then something different.

There were just a few weddings in here that showed talent. He glanced up at Jenny, and she was smiling and making hand signals. A second phone lay on the reception desk. She was motioning to him to lift it.

He lifted it and listened.

'...be there for Christmas. About three hundred people. Barret's pulled strings and found someone who'll marry them, so you don't need to worry about the licence. All we need you to do is to turn a Christmas feast into a wedding feast. I'll outline details in my fax. The most important thing is that Anna needs a wedding gown, and she's caught up on location until she gets on the plane. But she trusts Carver implicitly. If he approves it, it'll be fine. There'll be six bridesmaids and six groomsmen. I'll fax through sizes. Anna's only stipulation is that she'd like a traditional wedding—the same as she saw at home when she was a little girl.' The woman hesitated. 'She said something about pink tulle.'

'Oh, we can do pink tulle,' Jenny told her, sounding chirpy and still smiling. 'Mr Carver's good at pink tulle.'

Guy stared at Jenny, astounded.

'You've been really lucky,' Jenny continued, ignoring Guy's astonishment. 'Mr Carver had stipulated there'd be no weddings from this salon until his people were in place. But as luck would have it Mr Carver himself arrived here this afternoon. I regret I personally won't be involved, but I know I'm leaving you in good hands. Sure, it's fine that you put out a press release. If you could fax us a copy it'll let us see exactly what tone we need to set. The figure per head is perfectly acceptable. Goodbye.'

And she replaced the receiver with a definite click.

Guy stared at her. Jenny stared straight back, still smiling. Her chin jutted out just a little, and she held his gaze and didn't break.

'What the hell have you done?' he demanded, and she smiled some more, a tight, strained smile that didn't reach her eyes.

'I just quit.'

'You quit?'

'The contract says my continued employment is optional. If I wish to leave at any time then I can. I know it was put there as a sop, so I'm letting you off the hook. I'm walking out now. Any remaining Bridal Fluff brides will be looked after by me from home. The salon's yours.'

'But you've just booked a wedding.'

'I have. It sounds just your style.'

'What wedding?'

'You were on the phone. Didn't you hear?'

'I heard nothing. Only Barret and Anna...' He paused as an appalling thought hit. 'Barret and Anna? You don't mean...'

'Barret and Anna,' she agreed, smiling benignly. 'Surely you of all people know Barret and Anna? Barret's just won...is it his second Oscar or his third? And Anna's on the front cover of this month's *Glamour*.'

'They're getting married?' he said stupidly, and she

nodded. She walked over to the desk and picked up her handbag. It was of ancient leather, he noticed, his mind settling on details as if they were important. It looked as if it was falling apart.

'On Christmas Day,' she said, following his gaze to her handbag, flushing, and putting it behind her. 'That gives you ten days to organise it. I'll send my father-in-law to clear the store of my gear. We'll have it out of here by tomorrow night, so you'll have a clear run. You'll need it,' she said thoughtfully. 'Three hundred people in ten days...'

'What the...?'

'It's a very good idea,' she said. 'You know Anna's a local girl? She's hardly been home for twenty years, and by local I mean Sydney, but she bought a property here two years back. She and Barret flew in here after *Amazon Trek* for a break, and the town went nuts. It seems they were planning a Christmas party, but suddenly they've decided it would be an excellent time to get married. Only nothing's organised. A blank canvas, Mr Carver, just how you like it. So now you have your very first Australian Carver Bride raring to go. Three hundred guests on Christmas Day.' She smiled some more. 'Ten days. You'll be very busy. But me... I have a little boy, who'll have Christmas with his mummy. Which is just as the world should be. Now me and my disreputable handbag will take ourselves out of your life. Good luck, Mr Carver. And goodbye.'

CHAPTER TWO

THIS was no drama. Guy watched her go with mixed feelings. There was a part of him that felt a strange lurch that she should walk away, and it had nothing to do with the bombshell she'd thrown at him. As usual, though, he attempted to shove personal thoughts aside and slip back into business mode.

It was difficult to shove the vision of Jenny away. The way she'd carried her handbag…

Barret and Anna. He had to think.

Barret Travers and Anna Price had a hugely powerful media presence. With Barret in a movie, an immediate box office hit was assured, and Anna's profile was almost the same. Their impending wedding would turn the eyes of the world right here.

To what? He couldn't put on a huge, media-circus-type wedding with this much notice. The booking was only five minutes old. He had to cancel, and fast.

That shouldn't be a problem. He'd phone Malcolm and get contact details straight away. But before he could lift his phone the fax machine on Jenny's desk hummed into life. Bemused, he watched the feed-out, recognising it for what it was. A press release.

'Barret and Anna to Wed!' the caption blared. 'Wedding to be in Sandpiper Bay, Australia. Guy Carver's first Australian wedding.'

They'd had it planned before they'd contacted Jenny, he thought. They'd had this press release ready to go.

Why? What could possibly add *more* media hype to this pair?

Carver's first Australian wedding. Guy thought about it, and his heart sank.

Anna had been pilloried in the press for her bad taste. Of course she'd want pink tulle, he thought. Pink tulle would be right in her league.

How to get pink tulle but still be thought cool by the cognoscenti?

Have a Carver wedding.

He had to cancel.

He stared down at the press release. Specifically at the tiny *cc*…

This was not a press release sent early just as confirmation to him. This was a press release which was simultaneously being read by every media outlet in the western world.

They'd been expecting his yes as perfunctory. Jenny had given them their yes, and they'd told the world.

If he pulled out now…

Carver Event Management pulling out would be news. People knew he was in Australia. Jenny had just confirmed it. So why couldn't he organise the wedding? No matter how carefully he explained it, Anna would take his refusal as a personal slight, and the world's press would agree.

Which meant problems for Anna.

The paparazzi spent their life reporting on Anna—and Barret. Barret was a loud-mouthed boor, but he was number one at the box office. In contrast, Anna was struggling a little. A few months ago she'd spent time in drug rehab. and the press had had a field-day. Her life seemed to be together now, but the media still wavered between idolatry and ridicule.

If they knew he'd knocked her back—*International Events Organiser Guy Carver Refuses Anna/Barret Wedding*—the world's press would say it served her right. They'd say she'd got what she deserved and the balance might well tip on the side of ridicule.

Which she didn't deserve.

Damn, he didn't get emotionally involved. He didn't.

He was. Right up to his neck.

He thumped the desk with his fist, and a fluffy stuffed dog, endowed for some reason with a disembodied head, started nodding in furious agreement. He stared down at the stupid creature and came close to throwing it through the pink-tinged windows.

Jenny was outside the window.

Over the road was the beach. A group of teenagers were clustered by the side of the road, leaning on their surfboards and chatting to Jenny. She was laughing at something one of them said.

She looked…free.

'Of course she looks free. You've just sacked her.'

Except he hadn't. She'd walked out on him. The thought was astonishing.

Focus on this wedding. How long did he have? Ten days?

The idea was ridiculous. He went through his top people in his head, trying to figure who could come.

No one could come. Everyone held parties at Christmas. And every event he had in his mental diary was major. There'd be repercussions if he pulled anyone out.

For a wedding like this, at this short notice, he needed local people. He needed…Jenny.

She was climbing into an ancient Ford, a wagon that looked more battered than the decrepit vehicles the surfers were using. While he watched, she backed out of the parking spot, then headed right. Her wagon passed the teenagers and did a backfire that made everyone jump.

'She'd be hopeless,' he told no one in particular, and no one in particular was interested.

'I can't ask her.'

No one was interested in that, either.

He stared at the fax again and swore. 'Do I care if the wonderful Anna's career goes down the toilet?'

He did, he thought. Damn, he did. Two months ago he'd catered for a sensational Hollywood ball. Anyone who was anyone had been present. He recalled a very drunken producer hitting on Anna. When she'd knocked him back he'd lifted her soda water, sniffed it, and thrown it away in disgust.

'Once a tart, always a tart, love,' he'd drawled at her. 'You're not such a good little actress that you can pretend to be something you're not for ever.'

Guy had intervened then, handing Anna another soda water, giving her a slight push away and deflecting the creep who'd insulted her by showing signs of investing in his latest project. But he'd seen Anna's white face, pretence stripped, and he'd also seen how she'd stared into the soda water, taken a deep breath, and then deliberately started to drink it. To change your life took guts—who should know that better than him?

If Anna wanted him to cater for her wedding then he would.

'Even if it does mean I have to go on bended knee to the Widow Westmere.'

Jenny pulled into the front yard of her parents-in-laws' farm, switched off the ignition, took a few deep breaths—how to explain all this to Lorna and Jack?—and a car pulled in behind her.

A Ferrari.

Ferrari engines were unmistakable. What are the chances of someone else with a Ferrari pulling into my yard? she thought, and decided she ought to head inside fast, close the door and not even look out to see whether Mr Guy Hotshot Carver was on her property.

'Mrs Westmere,' he called, and the moment was lost. She sighed, leant back on her battered wagon with careful insouciance—and folded her arms.

'What?'

'I'd like to talk to you about your contract.'

'It's clear,' she said, trying to be brusque. 'I have the right to work for you for a year, and I also have the right to walk away any time I like. Your business manager seemed to think I'd be jumping all over myself to stay, but the obligation is on your side; not mine.'

'I'd like you to stay.'

'Nah.' She should be chewing gum, she decided. She didn't have the insouciance quite right. 'You're pleased to be shot of me.' Then she broke a bit—she couldn't quite suppress the mischief. 'Or you were until I landed you with the wedding of the century. You're going to have to cancel on the biggest wedding we've seen in this place. What a shame.'

'I can't cancel.'

'Come on. You can afford to lose one wedding. All that hurts is your pride. And pride doesn't matter to you. Just look what you did to Kylie.'

'I—'

'Is that you, Jenny?' Jack's voice interrupted, and Jenny hauled herself away from the wagon and abandoned the insouciance.

'I need to go inside. You need to go…wherever rich entrepreneurs go when they're not messing with this town. See you later.'

'Do you have someone out there?' Jack called.

'Jenny, I need to talk to you.'

'Mrs Westmere,' she flashed. 'It's Mrs Westmere, unless I can call you Guy.'

'Of course you can call me Guy.'

'Bring your visitor in, Jenny.'

'Go away,' she said.

'I need you.'

'You don't need anyone. You come waltzing into town in your flash car...'

'It's borrowed from a friend.'

'You *borrowed* a Ferrari?' she demanded incredulously. 'Someone just tossed you the keys of a Ferrari and said, "Have it for a few days." Like he has one Ferrari for normal use and another to lend to friends.'

'His other car's an Aston Martin,' he said apologetically. 'And his wife drives a Jag.'

'I *so* much don't need this conversation.' She made to turn into the house, but he stepped forward and caught her shoulders. The action should have made her angry—and at one level it did—but then there was this other part of her...

He really was a ludicrously attractive male, she thought. She wasn't the least bit afraid of him. Well, why should she be when she had Lorna and Jack just through the screen door? But there was more than that. His grip felt somehow...okay.

It wasn't the least bit okay. This was those damned hormones working again, she thought. She'd been a widow for too long.

But she had protection—against hormones as well as against marauding males. She hadn't answered Jack, and Jack and Lorna had grown worried. Now the front screen slammed back and Jack was on the veranda. Jack was a wiry little man in his late seventies, tough as nails and belligerent to go with it. He was crippled with arthritis, but he didn't let that stop him.

'Who's this?' he growled, before Jenny could say a word. He stalked stiffly down the veranda, trying to disguise the limp from his gammy hip, trying to act as if he was going to lift over six feet of Guy Carver and hurl him off the property.

Guy dropped his hands from Jenny's shoulders. He didn't step away, though. He stood a foot away from her, his eyes filled with quizzical laughter.

'You have a security system?'

'I surely do,' she answered, taking a grip of her wandering hormones and turning to face her in-laws. 'Jack, Lorna—this is Guy Carver.'

Lorna was out on the veranda now. She'd pushed her wheelchair though the doorway, rolling to the edge of the ramp but no further. Lorna had once been a blousy, buxom blonde. Her hair was still determinedly blonde, and her eyes were still pretty and blue, but a stroke had withered one side of her body. One side of her face had very little movement and her speech was careful and stilted.

'Mr Carver,' she managed.

'He says we can call him Guy.'

'Why are you manhandling my daughter-in-law?' Jack barked, and the lurking laughter behind Guy's eyes was unmistakable.

'I was just turning her in the right direction. Towards you.'

'It's okay, Jack,' Jenny told him. 'Mr...Guy's just leaving.'

'Look at the car,' Lorna said, suddenly distracted. 'What is that?'

'A Ferrari,' Guy said, bemused, and at that the screen door swung open again.

'Don't come out, Henry,' Jenny said quickly, but it was too late. Henry was already on the veranda.

She winced. She badly didn't want Guy to see Henry. He'd already shown himself to be insensitive. How much damage could he do now?

For the crash that had killed his father had left Henry so badly burned that for a while they'd thought he might not live. The six-year-old was slowly recovering, but the scars on the right side of his face were only a tiny indication of the scars elsewhere. His chest and his right leg bore a mass of scarring, and he was facing skin graft after skin graft as he grew.

Henry should be a freckle-faced kid facing life with mischief and optimism. There were signs now that he could be again, but the scars ran deep. His thatch of deep brown curls stopped cruelly where the scarring began, just above his right ear. His brown eyes were alive and interested—thank God his sight had been untouched—but he'd lost so much weight he looked almost anorexic compared to most six-year-olds. His right leg was still not bearing weight, and he used crutches. His freckles stood out starkly on his too pale skin. Standing on the veranda in his over-big pyjamas— Lorna was sure he'd have a growth spurt any minute, and she sewed accordingly—he looked a real waif. The surgeons said that in time they'd have his face so normal that, as he matured, people would think of him as manly and rugged, but that time was a long way off from now.

'I want to see the car,' Henry said.

She held her breath, waiting for Guy to respond. If she had her druthers Jenny would keep her private life absolutely to herself. A private person at the best of times, these last two years had been hell. She'd been forced to depend on so many people. The locals had been wonderful, but now she was finally starting to regain some control of her shattered life, and the look of immediate sympathy flashing into Guy Carver's eyes made her want to hit him.

What's wrong with your little boy...?

How many times had that been flung at her since Henry had recovered enough to be outside the house? It was never the locals—they all knew, and had more sense than to ask about his progress in front of him. But the squillionaires who arrived for a week or two were appalling, and she wanted to be shot of the lot of them.

Maybe now she'd sold the business she could move, she thought. She could get a great place if she was prepared to go inland a little. But Jack and Lorna had lived here all their lives. She and Henry were all they had.

She couldn't leave.

So now she flinched, waiting for Guy to say something like they all did. *What's wrong?* or, *Gee, what happened to your kid? Why is he so scarred?* Or worse, *Oh, you poor little boy...*

But Guy said nothing. He had his face under control again, and the shock and sympathy were gone. Instead

he glanced at the Ferrari with affection. 'It's a 2002
Modena 360 F1,' he told Henry, man to man.

'It's ace,' Henry whispered, and something in Guy's
face moved. Something…changed.

'If it's okay with your mother, would you like a
ride?'

Henry's small body became perfectly still. Rigid. As
if steeling himself for a blow.

'I… Mum…?'

'You're kidding,' she said to Guy.

'I don't kid,' he said, and his voice had changed, too.
It had softened. 'I mean it. I'm assuming this is your son?'

'Yes, but…'

'I'm Guy,' he told Henry. 'And you are…?'

'Henry,' said Henry. 'Is this your car?'

'It's borrowed.'

'Do you have a car like this?'

'I have a Lamborghini back in New York.'

'Wow,' Henry breathed, and looked desperately at his
mother. 'Is it okay if I take a ride with him?'

'It's dinnertime.'

'Dinner can wait,' Jack growled. Jenny's father-in-
law was looking at the car with an awe that matched his
grandson's. 'If anyone offered me a ride in such a car
I'd wait for dinner 'til breakfast.'

'You're next in the queue,' Guy said, and grinned.
'I'd take you all at once,' he added apologetically, 'but
it's hard to squeeze three people in these babies. Jenny,
you can go third.'

'I don't want to go.'

'Is it okay if I take Henry?'

'Of course it's okay,' Jack snapped, as if astounded that anyone could ask that question. 'Isn't it, girl?'

'Fine,' she said, defeated, and Henry let out a war-whoop that could be heard back in Main Street. Then he paused.

'You don't mean just sit in it?'

'Of course not.'

'Can we go out on the coast road?' Henry asked, eyeing his mother as if she'd grown two heads. *Never go with strangers...* Her consent meant she knew this guy and trusted him. His mother had a friend with a Ferrari. She could see she'd just raised herself in his estimation by about a mile. 'The coast road winds round cliffs. With this car...it'll go like it's on rails.'

'You won't go fast?' She knew her voice was suddenly tight, but she couldn't help it.

'We won't go fast,' Guy told her, and there was that tone in his voice that said he understood.

How could he understand?

The remembrance of his hands on her shoulders slipped back into her mind. Which was dumb.

'Henry's in his pyjamas,' she said, too quickly, but suddenly that was how she felt. As if everything was too quick. 'Does he need to change?'

'No one notices who's in a Ferrari,' Guy told her. 'They only notice the Ferrari. If you're in a Ferrari you can wear what you d— whatever you like. You're cool by association. Are you ready, Henry?'

'Yeah,' Henry breathed, and tossed aside his crutches

and looked to his mother for help to go down the ramp. 'Yeah, I am.'

'He seems lovely.'

'He's not.' Back inside, Jenny was trying to explain the extraordinary turn of events to her in-laws. 'He won't do Kylie's wedding. She's not good enough to be a Carver Bride.'

'Kylie is a bit...' Lorna said, and Jenny glowered and tossed tea into the pot with unnecessary force.

'Don't you come down on his side. Kylie and Shirley were great to us.'

They had been. All of those dreary months when Jenny had needed to be in the hospital—for three awful weeks Henry had not been expected to live—Kylie and Shirley and a host of other locals had run this little farm, had ferried Lorna and Jack wherever they'd wanted to go, had filled the freezer with enough casseroles to feed an army for years, had even taken over the organisation of local weddings. The town had been wonderful, and Jenny wasn't about to turn her back on them now.

'I know they're fabulous,' Lorna told her. 'And of course I promised we'd do Kylie's wedding. But they won't hold us to more than that. I was just so upset. With Ben dead, and we thought we'd lose Henry...'

'You would have promised the world,' Jenny said. 'Shirley knows that. She tried it on with Guy this afternoon—and why wouldn't you? But I will do Kylie's wedding for cost, and Guy can't stop me. I'll just organise it from here.'

'And the rest?'

'He can have the society weddings. I don't want them.'

'They're the only ones that make us money.'

'We'll survive. He paid heaps for the business—more than its worth. But I don't want Guy Carver as my boss.'

'There'd be worse bosses,' Jack said, and Jenny sighed.

'Just because the man has a Ferrari…'

'What's he driving Henry for?'

'To wheedle his way into getting me to work for him,' she snapped. 'The man's a born wheedler. I can see it.'

'He doesn't look like a wheedler to me,' Lorna said. She'd been laying plates on the table, but now she stilled her wheelchair and turned to face her daughter-in-law. 'Jenny, it's been two years. We know you loved Ben, but maybe it's time you moved on?'

'What are you talking about?'

'He looks quite a catch,' Jack said, crossing to the door to look—hopefully—out. With a bit of luck there'd be time for a ride for him before dinner was on the table. 'A Lamborghini at home, eh?'

'You think I should jump him because he owns a Lamborghini?' Jenny asked incredulously, and Jack had the grace to look a bit shamefaced.

'I just meant…'

'He just meant don't look a gift horse in the mouth,' Lorna said decisively. 'I'm asking the man to tea.'

'You can't.'

'Watch me,' Lorna said, plonking a fifth plate on the table. 'I just know the nice man will stay.'

* * *

The night was interminable. Jenny couldn't believe he'd accepted Lorna's invitation. She couldn't believe he was sitting at her dining table with every appearance of complacency.

This was a man international jet-setters regarded as ultra-cool—the epitome of good taste. If they saw him now...

For a start he'd walked in the front door without even appearing to notice Lorna and Jack's decorations. The Christmas after Ben had been killed, when Henry's life had hung by a precarious thread, Lorna had decreed Christmas was off. 'It doesn't mean anything,' she'd declared. 'I'm tossing all my decorations.'

Twelve months later she'd rather shamefacedly hauled out her non-tossed decorations. Jack and Jenny had been desultorily watching television, with Henry on the sofa nearby. They'd been miserable, but they'd fallen on the decorations like long-lost friends. That night had been the first night when ghosts and fear and sadness hadn't hung over the house, and this year Henry had demanded his grand-parents start sorting the decorations on the first day of November.

So there was a reason why the decorations were just ever so slightly over the top, Jenny conceded. She'd hauled Henry's chair close beside her. He was leaning on her, still lit up after his ride in Guy's wonderful car. He was tired now, but Jenny thought there'd be trouble if she tried to send him to bed. Lorna and Jack were chatting to Guy as if they were entertaining an old friend, and Henry was soaking in every word.

He had a new superhero.

As for Jenny...Jenny was trying to block out the flashing lights from the real-sized sled in the front yard. The house and the yard were chock-full of Christmas kitsch. She loved every last fluffy pink angel, she decided defensively, trying not to wonder what he was thinking of her. If Guy didn't like them, then he could leave.

Guy Carver would be a minimalist, Jenny thought, watching Lorna ladle gravy over his roast beef and Jack handing him the vast casserole of cauliflower cheese. He'd like one svelte silhouette of a nativity scene in a cool grey window.

Jenny could count five nativity scenes from where she was sitting.

'The decorations are wonderful, Mrs Westmere,' Guy told Lorna, and Jenny cast him a look of deep suspicion as Lorna practically purred.

'Jenny thinks maybe the front yard is a bit over the top.'

'How could you, Jenny?' Guy said, and cast reproachful eyes at her.

She choked.

'Are you staying until Christmas?' Jack asked, and Guy said he wasn't sure.

'Why I'm asking,' said Jack, obviously searching for courage, 'is that every year Santa comes to Sandpiper Bay.'

'If you're asking me to wear a Santa suit...' Guy

said, suddenly sounding fearful, and Jenny looked at Guy's Mediterranean good looks and thought, *Yeah, right. Santa—I don't think so.* 'Then, no.'

'No, no,' Jack assured him. 'We have a very fine Santa. Bill went to a training course in Sydney and everything. But the thing is that every Christmas morning Santa drives through the town tossing lollies—'

'From the fire truck,' Henry interrupted, which just about astounded Jenny all by itself. Normally when visitors came Henry was seen but not heard. Henry had been a happy, cheerful four-year-old when his father's car had collided head-on with a kid spaced out of his brain on cocaine. Now Henry's world was limited to hospital visits, physiotherapy clinics and his grandparents' farm. For Henry to go with Guy tonight had been astonishing, and the fact that he was chirping away like a butcher's magpie now was even more so.

'See, there's the problem,' Jack explained, growing earnest. 'The problem with Christmas in Australia is that it's at the height of summer. In summer there's fires. Last year the fire truck got called away. One minute Santa was up top, handing out lollies, the next he was standing in the middle of Main Street with a half-empty Santa sack while the fire truck screamed off into the distance to someone's burning haystack.'

'Goodness,' Guy said faintly; *Goodness*, Jenny thought, suddenly realising where this was going.

'Now, if you were here, young man, in your Ferrari...'

'Santa could use your Ferrari,' Henry said, suddenly wide-eyed. 'Cool. Course it's not the *real* Santa,' he explained, while Guy looked as if he was trying to figure how he could escape. 'He's a Santa's helper. Mum told me that last year. I sat in the back of our car and the fire engine came right up and Santa gave me three lollies.'

'That was before it was called away,' Jenny said, trying not to get teary. Too late—she was teary. Dratted tears. She blinked them away, but not before Guy had seen. She knew he'd seen. He had hawk-like eyes that could see everything.

'Mr Carver's going home before Christmas,' she told Henry, feeling desperate. 'Aren't you, Mr Carver?'

'I'm not sure,' Guy told her. 'And the name is Guy.'

'You're not seriously thinking of doing the Anna/Barret party?'

'I'd need help.'

'A party?' Lorna intercepted, bright-eyed. 'What sort of party?'

'Anna and Barret's wedding.'

'Anna and Barret...' Lorna paused, confused, and then confusion gave way to awe. 'You don't mean *Anna and Barret*?'

'I mean Anna and Barret.'

'They're getting married? Here?'

'If we can cater. If your daughter-in-law will come back as a member of my staff.'

'Jenny,' Lorna said, eyes shining. 'How wonderful.'

'It's not,' Jenny said. 'He won't do Kylie's wedding.'

'We can do Kylie's wedding,' Guy said.

She eyed him with disbelief. 'As a Carver Wedding?'

'I don't think—'

'Ha!'

'She wouldn't like my style of wedding.'

'Anna wants pink tulle. Surely you give the clients what they want?'

'If it fits into my—'

'That is such an arrogant—'

'Will you two stop it?' Lorna said, stuttering in an attempt to get this sorted. 'Jenny, you need to help him.'

'I don't.'

'As a matter of interest,' Guy said calmly, '*could* you help me if you wanted to?'

'Do what?' she said, trying to disguise a child-like glower. But he saw it and his lips twitched. No wonder the glossies described him in glowing terms, Jenny thought. Until now she'd wondered how the head of what was essentially a catering company had become someone that the gossip columnists described as hot property. Now she knew. Guy would just have to look at you with those eyes, that held laughter...

The man was seriously sexy.

'Do you have the resources to run a wedding for three hundred on Christmas Day?' he asked, and she had to make a sharp attempt to haul her hormones into line. 'Are we arguing about something that's an impossibility?'

'It's not impossible,' she said, and then thought maybe she shouldn't have admitted it.

'Why is it not impossible?'

'Anna says she wants pink tulle?'

'So?' The laughter was gone now, and she could see why he was also described as one of the world's best businessmen. She could see the intelligence…the focus.

'So we could give her a country wedding. Kylie-style. It would be so unexpected that she'd love it.'

'We could put on a country dance,' Jack contributed. 'It's great weather this time of year. Haul some hay bales out into the paddock for seats, some more for a bar, and shove a keg on the back of the truck.'

'Keg?' Guy asked faintly.

'Fosters,' Jack told him. 'Gotta be Fosters.'

'He means beer,' Jenny told him, putting him out of his misery. 'I don't think this crowd would be happy with only beer.'

'Drink's the least of my problems.'

'So what's your problem?'

'Finding clothes for the wedding party in ten days. Sourcing food. Finding staff to wait on tables and clear up afterwards.'

'Piece of cake,' Jenny said, and then thought that was stupid. What was she letting herself in for?

'How is it a piece of cake?'

'Make Kylie's wedding the first Australian Carver Wedding and I'll tell you.'

'Kylie doesn't want a Carver Wedding.'

'You're making huge assumptions here,' she flashed, and Henry stirred and looked up at his mother in surprise. Lorna shifted her wheelchair sideways so she could take his weight, and he moved his allegiance to his grandmother. As if he wasn't quite sure who his mother was any more. 'What's the difference between Anna and Kylie?' she demanded. 'Career choice and money. Nothing more. Kylie's got herself pregnant, but Anna ended up in drug rehab. Two kids getting married. Kylie does want a Carver Wedding, and she asked first.'

'You'd seriously make me—'

'No one's making you do anything,' she told him. 'Including staying at our dinner table.'

'You're telling me to leave?'

'I don't like what money does to people.'

'The man hasn't finished his dinner yet,' Jack protested. 'Have a heart.'

'It's a bit rude to invite him to eat and put him out,' Lorna added, looking curiously at Jenny.

'Jenny's just itching for a fight,' Jack told Lorna, speaking across the table as if no one else was there. 'Dunno what's got into her, really.'

'It's hormones,' Lorna decided. 'You have a nice cup of tea, Jen.'

'Lorna…'

'She could do the wedding if she wanted to,' Lorna said, turning to Guy. 'She's the cleverest lass. I used to run the salon, making dresses for locals and organising caterers for out-of-towners. Only then the out-of-towners grew to so many that I had to employ Jenny. It was the best thing I ever did. Her mum didn't have any money, and her dad lit out early, so there wasn't enough to send Jenny to anywhere like university. She took on an apprenticeship with me. She's transformed the business. She's just…'

'Lorna!' Jenny said, almost yelling. 'Will you cut it out? Mr Carver doesn't want to know about me.'

'Yes, I do,' he said mildly. 'I need to persuade you to use some of your skills on my behalf. Where could you get caterers on Christmas Day?'

'I don't—'

'You tell him, lass,' Jack said. 'Don't hide your light under a bushel.'

She stared wildly round, but they were all watching her expectantly. Even Henry.

'This town is full of retirees,' she said at last, trying desperately to get her voice under control. 'Most of them have a very quiet Christmas. If we had all the food planned the day before—if we settled on country fare that all the women round here can cook—if Anna settled for a late wedding and if we told the locals that they could come to the dance afterwards—there'd be queues to work for us.'

'Locals come to the *ceremony*?' he said, incredulous.

'Not the ceremony. The idea would be that there'd be a huge party afterwards, with workers welcome. Think of the publicity for Anna and Barret. If you got onto that nice PR person I talked to this afternoon…'

Guy stared at her, poleaxed. 'It might…'

'It might well work,' she said. 'She's not squeaky clean, our Anna, and this would be great publicity.'

'You know about Anna's past?'

'The world knows about Anna's past. This wedding will be great for her.'

'It would,' he agreed, and suddenly Jenny's eyes narrowed.

'That's why you're thinking of doing it,' she said softly, on a note of discovery, thinking it through as she spoke. 'I couldn't understand…' But suddenly she did, seeing clearly where her impetuous nature had landed Guy. 'The Carver empire doesn't need this wedding, but Anna needs the Carver emporium.' She bit her lip. 'I should have thought about that when I was contacted. Oh, heck. I was angry with you, and I didn't think.'

To say Guy was bewildered was an understatement. That Jenny was sensitive enough to see connotations that he'd only figured because he moved in those circles….

His estimation of the woman in front of him was changing by the minute. Gorgeous, smart, funny…

He didn't do gorgeous, smart and funny. He didn't do complications.

He rose, so sharply that he had to make a grab to catch his chair before it toppled. 'I need to go.'

'You haven't had coffee,' Lorna said mildly, but he didn't hear. He was watching Jenny.

'You agree to staying on my payroll until Christmas?'

'Can Kylie have a Carver Wedding?'

'Yes,' he said, against the ropes and knowing it.

She hesitated, but then gave a rueful smile. 'Okay, then. I've never worked for a boss before.'

'What about me?' Lorna said, indignant, and Jenny grinned.

'That's different. I walked into your shop for the

interview and Ben was there. I was family from that minute on.'

'You were, too,' Lorna said, and reached over and squeezed her hand.

Family.

Something knotted in Guy's gut that he didn't want to know about. He backed to the door.

'Where are you staying, young man?' Jack asked.

'My secretary booked a place for me. Braeside?'

'You been there yet?'

'No. I—'

'You'll never find it,' Jack said with grim satisfaction. 'It's up back of town, by the river. Tourists get lost there all the time.' It seemed a source of satisfaction. Jack was looking at him with what seemed to be enjoyment.

'I have directions.'

'I've seen the directions they use. You'll be driving through the mountains 'til dawn. Jenny'll have to take you.'

Jenny stilled. Then she nodded, as if she agreed. 'You will get lost. I'll drive there, and you can follow me.'

'What fun is that?' Jack demanded. 'You haven't had a drive in his Ferrari. I've got a better idea. You drive him home in his Ferrari and then bring it back here. Then pick him up on the way to work tomorrow morning.'

'I can't drive a Ferrari,' Jenny said, astonished.

'Course you can,' Jack said roundly. 'If you can make your ancient bucket of bolts work, you can make anything work. Her wagon's held together with string,' he told Guy. 'She ought to buy another, but she's putting every cent she owns into a fund for Henry's schooling.' His face clouded a little. 'There's been a few costs over the last couple of years we hadn't counted on.'

Of course, Guy thought, his eyes moving to Henry's face. The little boy's face was perfect on one side, but on the other were scars—lots of scars.

'I can't drive a Ferrari,' Jenny said again, and he forced himself to think logically. Which was hard when his emotions were stirring in all sorts of directions.

'Yes, you can,' he said, and managed a smile that he hoped was casual.

'There you go, then,' Lorna said, triumphant. 'Jack and me will put Henry to bed. Henry, your mother is going to have a drive in the lovely car. Isn't that great?'

'Ace,' said Henry.

CHAPTER THREE

IT FELT weird, Jenny thought as they walked across the yard towards his car. It was almost dark. She should be reading her son his bedtime story.

She shouldn't be climbing into a Ferrari.

'You drive,' Guy said, and tossed her the keys.

'This is a bad idea,' she muttered. 'This is a borrowed car. Surely your friend wouldn't agree to me using it?'

'If you crash it I'll buy him another.'

The idea made her stop in her tracks. 'You're kidding.'

'Why would I kid?'

'I don't want to go with you,' she said, and it was his turn to pause and stare.

'You have ethical objections to money?'

'No, I...'

'You should be charging Kylie. There's no need for you to be broke.'

'Isn't there?' she snapped, and glared.

'Giving your services for free is noble, but...'

'You have no idea, do you? This community...we're

here for each other. We do what has to be done, and asking for payment—'

'Your career is a bridal planner. Selling yourself short is stupid.'

'When Ben was killed, Henry was injured, and he had to spend months in a burns unit in the city,' she snapped. 'Jack has macular degeneration—his eyesight's not what it should be—and Lorna hasn't driven since her stroke. Shirley Grubb was one of a team who took it in turns to drive Jack and Lorna down to see us. Twice a week for nearly six months. Every other day they drove Lorna into the bridal salon and someone stayed with her all the time. The business stayed open. There were casseroles—you can't believe how many casseroles. And you know what? Not a single person charged us. Did they sell themselves short, Mr Carver?'

'Guy,' he said automatically, and opened the driver's door of the Ferrari. 'Get in.'

'I'm not driving.'

'You are driving. You need to bring it home yourself, so you can try it out now.'

'We can take my wagon.'

'Your wagon backfires. Backfiring offends me. And I have no intention of being lost in these mountains for want of a little resolution on your part. Get in and drive.'

It was such a different driving experience that she felt... unreal.

The road up to Braeside was lovely. It followed the

cliffs for a mile out of town, and the big car swept around the curves with a whine of delight. By the time the road veered inland, following the river, she had its measure, and was glorying in being in control of the most magnificent piece of machinery she'd ever seen.

'Nice, huh?' Guy said, five minutes into the drive, and she flashed him a guilty look. She'd been so absorbed in her driving that she'd almost forgotten he was there. Almost.

'It's fantastic.'

'You get this wedding working for me and you can keep it.'

She almost crashed. She took a deep breath, straightened the wheel, and tried to remember where she was.

'Don't be ridiculous.'

'I'm not being ridiculous. I'll merely pay my friend out. It's not like it's a new car.'

'*It's not like it's a new car,*' she said, mocking. 'No, thank you, Mr Carver. My salary is stipulated in the contract. I'll take that, but that's all. I'd be obliged to you for ever, and I've had obligations up to my neck. So leave it.'

He left it. There were another few moments of silence while Jenny negotiated a few more curves. It was so wonderful that she could almost block Guy out—and his preposterous offer.

'Feels great, doesn't it?' he said, and she was forced to smile.

'It's magic.'

'Yet you don't want it?'

'I couldn't afford the trip to Sydney to get this serviced,' she told him. 'Much less the service itself. Leave it alone.'

'I'm not used to having my gifts knocked back.'

'Get used to it.'

'Jenny…'

'I'm not for sale, Guy,' she said roughly. 'And don't interfere with my life. I intend to do these two weddings and then get out of your business for ever. You'll go back to Manhattan and live your glamorous life, a thousand miles from mine—'

'What do you know about my life?' he said, startled, and she screwed up her nose in rueful mockery.

'I've spent the last two years in doctors' waiting rooms.'

'So?'

'So I reckon I've read every issue of *Celebrity* magazine that's ever been printed. With you being rich and influential, and associated with every celebrity bash worthy of the name, your life is fair game. I know how rich you are. I know you don't like oysters and you never wear navy suits. I also know you were in a car crash with your childhood sweetheart about fifteen years ago. Her father and your father were partners. She'd been at your parents' company Christmas dinner alone, and then she'd collected you from some celebrity bash you'd been organising. She was killed outright. Your parents disowned you then. They said she'd been drinking because she was angry. They said if you'd stayed in the family law firm like you were supposed to it would never have happened. And you…

The glossies say you're still grieving for your lost love. Are you?'

'No,' he said, stunned.

'I hope you're not.' She took a deep breath, deciding whether to be personal or not. What the heck? 'It's hard,' she confided. 'Ben's only been dead for two years, but you know, my photographs of Ben are starting to be clearer than the image I hold in my head. I hate that. Are you better at it than me? Can you remember…what was her name? Or do you only remember photographs?'

'It was Christa,' he said, in a goaded voice. 'I can't imagine why you'd be interested enough to read about us.'

'I wasn't very,' she admitted. 'It was just something to read in the waiting room—something to take my mind off what was happening to Henry. But I remember thinking it was crazy, wearing the willow for someone for fifteen years.'

'So how long do *you* intend to wear the willow for Ben?'

'I'm not.'

'You're living with his parents.'

'That's because they've become my parents,' she said. 'Sometimes I wonder whether I fell in love with Ben himself or if I fell in love with the whole concept of family. Like you tonight, looking round the dining table and looking…hungry.'

'I didn't,' he said, revolted. 'Can we leave it with the inquisition?'

'Sure,' she said, and she thought maybe she had pushed it too far. This man was supposed to be her boss. She should be being a bit deferential. Subservient.

He didn't make her feel subservient. He made her feel…

She didn't understand how he made her feel. She tried to conjure Ben up in her mind. Kind, gentle Ben, who'd loved her so well.

'It's tough,' he said into the stillness, and she wondered what he was talking about. 'The first Christmas was the worst, but it's still bad,' he added, and she knew he knew.

'It's okay.'

'But it's tough.'

'I've got thirteen years before I catch up to you in the mourning stakes,' she snapped, and turned the car into the front yard of Braeside. 'Here's your guesthouse.'

It was a fabulous spot, Guy thought, staring around with appreciation. The moon was glinting through bushland to the river beyond, hanging low in the eastern sky over the distant sea. The guesthouse was a sprawling weatherboard home, with vast verandas all around.

'I've heard it's sumptuous,' Jenny said, climbing out of the car to stretch her legs.

'You've never been inside?'

'The likes of me? I'd be shown out by security guards.'

'I'm sorry about Paris.'

'I shouldn't have told you about Paris.' She hesitated

A BRIDE FOR CHRISTMAS

while he hauled his gear from the trunk. 'Are you serious about me driving this thing home? You realise it'll be parked near chooks.'

'Chooks?'

'Feathery things that lay eggs.'

'Park it as far away as possible,' Guy said, sounding nervous.

'Okay. I was just teasing. I might even find a tarpaulin. I'll collect you tomorrow at nine, then. With or without chook poo.'

'Fine,' he said. He turned away. But then he hesitated.

'Thank you for tonight,' he said. 'And we really will give Kylie a great wedding.'

'I know we will.' She trusted him, she thought. She wasn't sure why, but she did.

But suddenly she didn't trust herself.

She should get into the driver's seat, she told herself. Guy needed to walk away.

But then…and why, she didn't know…it was as if things changed. The night changed.

'Jenny?' he said uncertainly.

'I know,' she said, but she didn't know anything. Except that he was going to kiss her and she was going to let him.

She could have pulled back. He was just as uncertain as she was—or maybe he was just as certain.

He dropped his holdall. Moving very slowly, he reached out and caught her hands, tugging her towards him. She allowed herself to be tugged. Maybe she didn't need his propulsion.

'Thank you for dinner,' he said, and she thought, *He's making this seem like a fleeting kiss of courtesy.* Though both of them knew it was no such thing.

'You're welcome,' she whispered.

His lips brushed hers, a feather touch—a question and not an answer.

'You're very welcome,' she said again as he drew back—and suddenly she was being kissed properly, thoroughly, wonderfully.

She'd forgotten...or maybe she'd never known this heat. This feeling of melting into a man and losing control, just like that. There was warmth spreading throughout her limbs. A lovely, languorous warmth that had her feeling that her world was changing, right there and then, and it could never be the same again.

She kissed him back, demanding as much as he was demanding of her. Tasting him. Savouring the feel of his wonderful male body under her hands. Guy Carver...

Guy Carver.

This was crazy.

She, Jenny Westmere, mother of Henry, wife of Ben... To kiss this man...

She was out of her mind. Panicked, she shoved her hands between her breast and his chest, pushing him away.

He released her at once. He tried to take her hands but she'd have none of it. She was three feet away from him now. Four.

'No.'

'No?' His eyes were gently questioning. Not laughing.

She couldn't have borne it if he was laughing. 'No, Jenny?'

'I only kiss my husband,' she said, and the words made perfect sense to her, even if they didn't to him.

But it appeared he understood. 'You're not being unfaithful, Jenny. It was only a kiss.'

Only a kiss? Then why was her world spinning?

'I'm not some easy country hick…'

'I never thought you were.'

'You're here until Christmas. Will we see you again after that?'

'Probably not.'

'We're ships passing in the night.' She took a deep breath and steadied. 'So maybe we'd better do just that—pass.'

'I'm not into relationships,' he said, not even smiling. 'I'm not about to mess with your tidy life.'

'My life's not very tidy,' she confessed. 'But thank you. Now…I think I'd better go home.'

'You're brave enough to drive the Ferrari by yourself?'

'Something tells me it'd be far more dangerous to stay here with you,' she muttered. 'But I'll pick you up in the morning. As long as you promise not to kiss me again.'

'You want me to promise?'

'Yes, I do,' she said, and if her voice sounded desperate she couldn't help it.

'I won't kiss you again. I know a mistake when I see one.'

'I'm a mistake?'

'Absolutely,' he told her. 'This whole place is a mistake. I should leave now.'

Only of course he didn't. He couldn't. He booked into the fantastic guesthouse he'd been delivered to. He rang Malcolm in New York and confirmed that there was no one who could get here on short notice to take over organisation.

'Scooping the Barret and Anna wedding is fabulous, though.' Malcolm was chortling. 'Every bride in Australia will want you after this. It's just as well you're there to do it hands-on. You'll use the local staff? Great. Make sure you don't mess up.'

The local staff? Guy thought of what he had to build on—Jenny and, by the sound of it, a crew of geriatrics—and he almost groaned.

'It's the best publicity we could think of,' Malcolm said jovially. 'I'll manage the Film Conglomerate do. We're fine.'

Only they weren't. Or he wasn't. Guy lay in the sumptuous four-poster bed that night, listening to owls in the bushland outside, and wondered what he was getting into.

He didn't know, and he didn't want to find out.

And five miles away Jenny was feeling exactly the same.

When she got back to the farmhouse Henry was asleep and Lorna and Jack were filling hot water bottles from the kitchen kettle.

'Did you have a nice ride, dear?' Lorna asked, and for the life of her Jenny couldn't keep her face under control. Lorna watched her daughter-in-law, her eyes twinkling.

'He seems very… personable,' she said, speaking to no one in particular, and Jenny knew her mother-in-law was getting ideas which were ridiculous.

They *were* ridiculous.

She scowled at her in-laws and went to bed. But not to sleep. She stared at the ceiling for hours, and then flicked on the lamp and stared at the picture on her bedside table. Her lovely Ben, who'd brought her into this wonderful family, who'd given her Henry.

'I love you, Ben,' she whispered, but he didn't answer. If he was here he'd just smile and then hug her.

She ached to be hugged.

By Ben?

'Yes, by Ben,' she told the night. 'Guy Carver has been here for less than twenty-four hours. He's an international jet-setter with megabucks. He kissed me tonight because I'll bet that's what international jet-setters do. He's your boss, Jennifer Westmere. You need to maintain a dignified employer-employee relationship. Don't stuff it up. And don't let him kiss you again.

'He won't want to.

'He might.'

She wasn't sure who she was arguing with. If anyone could hear they'd think she was crazy.

'Ben,' she whispered, and lifted the frame from the bedside table and kissed it.

She turned off the lamp and remembered the kiss.

Not Ben's kiss.

The kiss of Guy Carver.

CHAPTER FOUR

JENNY arrived at Guy's guesthouse the next morning wearing clothing that said very clearly she was there to work. Plain white shirt, knee-length skirt, plain sandals. Guy emerged dressed in fawn chinos, a lovely soft green polo shirt with a tiny white yacht embroidered on the chest—Jenny bet it had to be the logo of the world's most exclusive yacht club—and faded loafers. He looked at what Jenny was wearing and stopped dead.

'The Carver corporation has a dress code,' he said.

'What's wrong with this?'

'It's frumpy.' It was, too. In fact, Jenny had worked quite hard to find it. There'd been an international lawn-bowls meet in Sandpiper Bay two years ago, and she'd helped organise the catering. The dress code for that had meant she'd had to go out and buy this sophisticated little outfit, and she hadn't worn it since.

'It's my usual work wear,' she lied. 'Yesterday I was too casual.'

'We were both too casual,' he agreed, and she blushed.

Right. Get on with it.

'So where do you want to start?'

'I've come here to plan the refurbishment of the salon.'

'That's important. But there's the little manner of two weddings…'

'Leave the planning to me,' he said, and she subsided into what she hoped was dignified silence. She was this man's employee.

He'd kissed her. She should forget all about that kiss. She should…

Let's not aim at the stars here, she told herself. Let's just be a good little employee and put the memory of that kiss on the backburner.

But not very far back.

He was out of his depth.

They'd purchased three salons so far in this round of expansion. In each of those, Guy had visited early, taken note of the features of the building as they were, then brought his notes back to his cool grey office in Manhattan and drawn them up as he'd like them to be. With plans prepared, he'd sent a team of professionals to do his bidding, and six months later they'd opened as a Carver Salon.

Now, thanks to Lorna's indiscretion, the Carver name would be used before he could leave his imprint.

He had to get rid of the fluff, and fast. Instead of sitting down, calmly planning for the future, he was trying to figure how he could get this place clear so if the media arrived to see the latest Carver Salon they'd see something worthy of the name. How to transform fluff to elegance in a week?

And how to ignore Jenny, sitting silently at her desk? She sat with her hands folded in front of her, a good little employee, waiting for instructions.

What was it about this woman that unnerved him?

Why was she so different?

He didn't do relationships. He didn't…

'Phone Kylie,' he said at last, goaded. 'Tell her she's having a Carver Wedding.'

'I already have,' she said meekly.

He was out of his depth. He needed help here.

'I need your assistance,' he snapped, and she nodded, ready to be helpful.

'Yes, sir.'

'Jenny…'

'Sir?'

'Will you cut it out?'

'Cut what out?'

'I don't know where the hell to start,' he confessed, and watched as she struggled to keep the expression on her face subservient.

'You're asking for my input?'

'I want some solid help here,' he told her. 'I assume you're not just the girl who mans the desk? You've been running this place on your own since Lorna's stroke.'

'But you're in charge. I'm waiting for orders.'

'We need to get a dumpster,' he said in exasperation. 'Something to get rid of this lot.'

'You have two weddings to organise before

Christmas and you're planning to redecorate the salon?' she said cautiously. 'Right.' She lifted the phone. 'I'll order a dumpster.'

'Dresses,' he said, in increasing frustration. 'We need to organise a wedding dress and attendants' outfits.'

'They might take some time,' Jenny said, and started dialling.

He lifted the phone from her hand and crashed it down onto the cradle.

'If I don't get some solid help here I'll—'

'Sack me?' she said, and smiled.

Damn the woman. He knew she was competent. He wanted to take her shoulders and shake her.

He wanted to kiss her.

That thought wasn't helping things at all. His normally cool, calculating mind was clouded, and it was clouded because this woman was looking up at him with a strange, enigmatic smile.

This woman who was as far from his life as any woman he'd ever met. This woman who was up to her neck in emotional entanglements.

His employee.

He took a deep breath, turned, and paced the salon a couple of times, trying to clear his head. He knocked one of the bridal mannequins and spent a couple of minutes righting it.

He turned to Jenny and she was watching him, her eyes interested, her head to one side like an inquisitive sparrow.

Forget she's a woman, he told himself. And forget she's an employee. Let's get this onto some sort of even keel.

'Jenny, I'm out of my depth here,' he told her. 'I don't know where to start.'

She stilled. The faint smile on her face faded. He'd shocked her, he thought. Whatever she'd been expecting it hadn't been that.

There was a long silence.

She could keep up the play-acting, he thought. And she was definitely considering it. The role of subservient employee was a defence. He watched as indecision played on her face. Finally she broke. Her face was incredibly expressive, he thought. He saw the exact moment she put away the play-acting and decided to be up-front.

'Two weddings,' she said. 'The biggest problem is the dresses. We need to get things moving. There are three local women with the capacity to sew fast and well.'

'Contact them.'

'No.' She shook her head. 'They're all up to their ears in Christmas preparations.'

'Then what—?'

'There are a couple of oldies I know who love baby-sitting,' she said. 'They have very quiet Christmases, so they may be prepared to help. Jonas Bucket had an accident at work some years ago and is confined to a wheelchair. He loves Christmas cooking. So if I...'

'What are you talking about?' He was lost.

'Mary, Sarah and Leanne are my seamstresses,' she said patiently. 'Mary and Sarah have small kids, and Leanne's having eighteen people for Christmas dinner. If I ask them to sew for me they'll say no. But if I say I've already organised childminding and cooking and house-cleaning—and someone to set Leanne's table—then they'll jump at the chance to escape by sewing. Now...'

'Now what?' he said, stunned.

'You're the boss,' she said, 'but if I were you I'd sit down and write the menu for the Barret and Anna wedding. We need to get the food ordered right away. They've elected to do a Christmas theme, so we'll keep it like that. Roast turkey and all the trimmings.'

'For a sophisticated—?'

'She *did* say pink tulle,' Jenny said, though she sounded a bit less certain of her ground.

'So she did,' Guy said, thinking fast, and then looked up as the doorbell tinkled.

It was Kylie. She was dressed in pregnancy overalls with a white T-shirt underneath. With her face flushed with either nerves or excitement, and her blonde curls tied up in two pigtails, Guy decided she looked like one of those Russian Mazurka dolls. If you pushed her she'd topple over and then spring right up.

'Hi, Kylie,' Jenny said, and Guy winced. This woman was a client. His first Australian Carver Wedding...

'Mum just rang me,' Kylie said, with a nervous look aside at Guy. 'She says Mr Carver's agreed to do my wedding.'

'He has,' Jenny said. 'But there's no need to change your plans. We'll do your wedding exactly as we've planned it.'

'No,' said Kylie.

There was a moment's silence. 'No?' Jenny said at

last, cautiously, and received a furious shake of her head in reply. 'You don't want a wedding?'

'Of course I want a wedding,' Kylie said. 'Me and Daryl are really excited. But...'

'But what?' Jenny asked.

'It's *Mum's* wedding,' she burst out. 'And Daryl's mum's. They've been at us for ever to get married, and of course we want to, but we didn't want this. We thought maybe we'd just have the baby and then go somewhere afterwards and get married quietly. But from the minute we told them we were expecting they've been at us and at us, until finally we cracked. And that dress... Mum had you make it for me when I was sixteen. She chose it. Not me. Every week since then Mum gets it out and pats it. Do you know how much I hate it?'

'No,' Jenny said, stunned.

'I can't tell you,' Kylie declared. 'But I loathe it. I would have gone along with it. Fine, I said to Daryl, whatever makes them happy. But when Mum rang and said I could have a Carver Wedding I thought suddenly, *A Carver Wedding!* I could maybe have it like I want. Elegant. Sleek. Sophisticated. Something so when our kids grow up they'll look at our wedding photos and think, Wow, just for a bit our parents weren't assistants in a butcher's shop. If you knew how much I hate pink tulle...'

'Your six bridesmaids are in pink tulle,' Jenny murmured.

'Exactly.' Kylie's colour was almost beetroot as she desperately tried to explain herself. 'It was bad enough when I was skinny, but now I'll look like a wall of cupids coming down the aisle, with a sea of pink tulle coming after.' She turned to Guy. 'They say in the fashion magazines that you can perform miracles. Get me out of cupids and pink tulle. Please.'

There was a deathly hush.

'We can't,' Jenny said at last. 'Kylie, the dresses are finished. There's less than a week to your wedding, and we have another enormous wedding to cater for on Christmas Day.'

The passion went out of Kylie like air out of a pricked balloon, and defeat took its place in an instant. She'd expected this, Guy thought. Her request had been one last stand, but defeat had been expected.

'That'll be for someone rich, I'll bet,' Kylie said, but it wasn't said in anger. It was said as a fact, and there was a wealth of resignation in her voice. 'Someone who can afford any wedding she wants and who has enough guts to stand up for it.'

Guy looked suddenly at the girl's hands. They were scrubbed almost raw. There were jagged scars on two fingers.

'You work in a butcher's shop, Kylie?' he asked her, and Kylie bit her lip.

'Yeah. Morris's butchers next door. That's why I could come so quickly. But I should be back there now.'

'You'll work there after you're married?'

'Course I will,' she said. 'It's Daryl's dad's shop, and there's no way we can afford for me to stay home. We're having a week's honeymoon staying at Daryl's auntie's place. I'll have another week off when the baby's born.

Then we'll set up a cot in the back.' She shook her head. 'Sorry. It was dumb to ask. I gotta get back.'

She sounded totally resigned, Guy thought. Accepting.

Jenny was watching him.

What had Kylie said when she first arrived? *They say in the fashion magazines that you can perform miracles.*

He couldn't perform miracles. Of course he couldn't. But…

'Anna wants pink tulle,' he said slowly, and Jenny nodded. She seemed…cautious.

'That's no problem. We can order more.'

'But Anna will be more than happy with a kitsch wedding,' he continued, thinking it through as he spoke. 'From the sound of the fax they sent me, kitsch is exactly what she wants. And Anna has six bridesmaids.'

'So?'

'So we swap,' he said, and his organisational mode slipped back into place, just like that.

Jenny's presence—Jenny herself—had somehow thrown him off course. He'd been feeling out of control since yesterday, but suddenly now he'd slipped back behind the wheel, knowing exactly where he was going.

'We'll take Kylie's wedding dress and bridesmaids' dresses and we'll alter them to fit Anna and her followers,' he said. 'Jenny, you said you have three dressmakers ready to go? Let's get the measurements and get them started. Kylie, your bridesmaids…'

'Mmm?' She was staring, open-mouthed. 'What's kitsch?' she said.

'What your wedding was, and what it won't be any

more,' he said. 'My alternative bride and her friends will think it's fun. It's fun when you're not forced into it. Do your bridesmaids all have little black dresses? The sort of thing you wear when you want to be elegant?'

'Course,' Kylie whispered, not seeing where he was going. 'I mean, everyone has to have a black dress. For when you dunno what else to wear.'

'Would they be upset to lose the pink tulle?'

'You have to be kidding. They hate pink tulle as much as I do. Two of them are my sisters, and three of them are Daryl's sisters, so they have to do what our mums say. The other one's my best friend, and Doreen says the pink tulle makes her look like a Kewpie doll.'

'Right,' Guy said. 'Let's go for an elegant Christmas theme. Deep crimson and a rich, dark green.'

'Seven dresses?' Jenny said faintly.

'Six bridesmaids in their lovely black dresses. It means they won't have to spend a cent, and they'll have already chosen something that looks great on them. There'll be no one-style-suits-all disasters. They'll wear their hair sleek and elegant—up if it's long, in sophisticated chignons, or if it's short I'll arrange really good cuts. I'll do it myself if need be. Black strappy shoes. The only colour about them will be a beautiful crimson and green corsage. That'll bring in a tiny Christmas theme, which seems appropriate at this time of the year. I'll get onto a Sydney florist this afternoon and organise the best.'

'What about me?' Kylie whispered. 'And the men?'

'Gangster-style suits and hats,' Guy decreed. 'We'll

hire them from Sydney or fly them from New York. What do you think?'

'Gangsters?' Kylie said, the beginnings of anticipation curving the sides of her mouth into a smile. 'Hats and braces and white shoes?'

'You've got it.'

'Daryl will love it.'

Guy smiled. 'Great. And you…' He looked at Kylie for a long minute while Jenny watched in dumbfounded silence. 'Kylie, let's not try to disguise your pregnancy. Let's be proud of it. I'm thinking pure white shot silk— Jenny, can we get shot silk?'

'Sure,' Jenny said, dazed.

'A really simple dress,' Guy said. 'Shoestring straps and a low sweetheart neckline that accentuates those gorgeous breasts.' Kylie started to blush, but he wasn't distracted. He'd grabbed the pad beside the phone and was sketching. 'Like this. Practically bare to the breasts. Softly curving into your waist, accentuating the swell of pregnancy, curving in again, and then falling with a side slit from your thigh to your ankles. I bet you have great legs.'

Kylie was staring at the sketch, entranced. 'Daryl says…' She subsided. 'Yeah,' she whispered. 'My legs are…okay.' The sketch was growing under Guy's hands and she couldn't stop watching. 'Wow. That even looks like me. What are you doing to my hair?'

'Piling it up in a thousand tiny curls on top of your head,' he said. 'The simplicity of your bridesmaids' hair will accentuate yours. We'll thread the same crimson and green though your hair—just a little. You'll carry a tiny bouquet of fern and crimson rosebuds. And if you want…'

'Wh-What?' she stammered.

'We'll thread tiny silver imitation pistols through the ribbon of your bouquet. You're a gangster's moll. This is a shotgun wedding and you've got your man.'

Kylie stared. Jenny stared. Then, as one, they burst out laughing.

'My mum will hate it,' Kylie said when she finally recovered.

'It's a Carver Wedding. Take it or leave it.'

'Oh, I'll take it,' Kylie whispered, smiling now through the beginning of unshed tears. 'Yes, please.'

'You're a magician.' Kylie had left them to spread her news. Guy was left with Jenny, who was staring at him as if he'd grown two heads.

'I'm no magician,' he said, but he was aware of a tinge of pleasure. It was a pleasure he hadn't felt for a long time. And…was there also a tinge of excitement? He wanted to do this well, he thought, and when he tried to figure out why he knew that it had little to do with the reputation of the Carver empire. It was all to do with making Jenny smile.

And he had made her smile. She was definitely smiling.

'I need to organise cars,' he said, trying to move on.

'There are limousines booked.'

'Limousines won't do. Transfer that booking to Anna's, if you can. For Kylie we need to get Buicks, or something similar. We'll take the theme right through.'

'We'll never get them locally.'

'I'll try Sydney.'

'Kylie can't afford—'

'We'll cover the cost ourselves,' he said. 'As the first Australian Carver Wedding, it'll more than pay for itself in publicity. As for dress, we've done gangster-type weddings in my other salons, so gear shouldn't be a problem. I'll fly in costumes for the waiting staff.' He paused. 'I assume you have staff booked?'

'Of course I have staff booked,' she said, incensed. 'This wedding is planned down to the last pew ribbon.'

'We'll use some of those resources for the Anna and Barret wedding. We'll design the wedding for Kylie from scratch, and use the basis of Kylie's for Anna's. It'll work. I'll need to paint sets for the gangster setting. I'll see if we can get a smoke machine from Sydney.'

'A smoke machine…'

'It creates the haze without the health risk. I should have everyone smoking either cigars or Gauloise, but I'll bet you have laws preventing it.'

'We do.'

'There you go, then. A smoke machine it is. Now, let's look at these dresses and see if any of them might fit without alterations.'

'You're good,' she said, on a note of discovery, and Guy stopped making lists and glanced up at her.

'You're surprised?'

'You said you could even cut hair?'

'There's nothing I haven't been landed with in the years I've been building this business. I know my stuff,

Jenny. I wouldn't be here if I didn't.' He smiled at her look of scepticism. 'You don't need to worry,' he said softly. 'We'll look after Kylie. The first Australian Carver Wedding will go off with a bang.'

'It surely will,' she said, awed, and then suddenly, as if she couldn't help herself, she slipped out from behind the counter, took two steps forward and kissed him.

It was nothing like the kiss they'd shared last night. It was a kiss of gratitude, nothing more, and why it had the capacity to make him feel as if his feet weren't quite on the ground he couldn't say.

'You're making Kylie happy,' she said softly. 'Thank you.'

'Think nothing of it,' he said, or he tried to say it, but the words weren't quite there. He was staring at Jenny as if…

He didn't know what.

This wasn't the type of woman that attracted him.

He hadn't exactly been celibate since Christa had died. What had Jenny said? *It was crazy, wearing the willow for someone for fifteen years.* He hadn't. Or maybe he had, but only in the sense that he never got emotionally involved. Where relationships went he used his head and not his heart. It did his firm's reputation good if he was seen with A-listers on his arm. He chose glamorous women who could make him laugh, but who knew commitment was neither wanted nor expected.

But Jenny…

She was dressed like a prim secretary. Like a repressed old maid. Like something she wasn't. He knew she wasn't.

Because otherwise why would his body be screaming that it wanted this woman—*he* wanted this woman?

She was a complication, he told himself desperately, and he'd spent his entire adult life making sure that he had as few complications in his life as possible.

'I need to go check the facilities at Anna's property,' he said, and if he sounded brusque he couldn't help it.

She grabbed her bag. 'It's in the hills, north of town.'

'I'll find it,' he said, and she hesitated and then put her bag down again.

'You want me to stay here?'

'Yes.'

'Fine.' Back to being subservient. 'I'll make lists of what's needed.' She hesitated. 'That is, if you want me to?'

'I want you to.'

'Fine.'

What was it between them? What was this…thing? It felt like some sort of magnetic charge, with both of them hauling away from it.

'Fine,' he repeated, and he left—but some important part of him stayed behind. And he couldn't for the life of him think what it was.

CHAPTER FIVE

THEY worked brilliantly as a team—apart.

For the next few days plans for the two weddings proceeded as swiftly as for any function Guy had organised in Manhattan. Most of it was down to Jenny. Guy just had to hint at a suggestion and she had it organised. She seemed to know every last person in a twenty-mile radius of Sandpiper Bay. He needed oysters? She knew the couple who leased the best oyster beds. He wanted lobsters? She knew the fisherman. Fantastic greens? Her husband's best friend had a hydroponic set-up where they could get wonderful produce straight from the grower.

Jenny wrote out a menu for Anna's wedding, and when Guy read it he grinned. It was inspired. Yabbies, prawns, oysters, lobsters, scallops—seafood to die for, and all in enough quantities to make their overseas guests drool. After the main courses the menu became even more Australian—pavlovas with strawberries and cream, lamingtons, ginger fluff sponges, chocolate éclairs, vanilla slices, lashings of home-made berry ice-cream, bowls and bowls of fresh berries…

Guy thought of how much this would cost in New York, and then he looked at the figures Jenny had prepared and blinked—and then he thought he'd charge New York prices anyway. It would mean he could put more into Kylie's wedding. He could employ a really excellent band…

But this was all discussed by phone. Guy had left Sandpiper Bay to make a sweep of Sydney suppliers. The time away let him clear his head. In truth, the day he'd tried to find Anna's property he'd become thoroughly lost. He'd got back to the salon flustered and late, and Jenny had merely raised her brows in gentle mockery and not said a word. She'd known very well what had happened, he thought, and he didn't like it. He didn't like it that she could read him.

So he'd gone to Sydney. He wasn't escaping, he thought. It was merely that things needed to be organised in Sydney.

On Monday, three days before Kylie's wedding, five days before Christmas, he returned.

The beach was crowded—summer was at its peak and there were surfing-types everywhere.

Bridal Fluff was closed.

What had he expected? he asked himself. Jenny had told him things were going well. And besides, he didn't want to see her.

Did he?

He let himself into Bridal Fluff. There was a typed

list on the desk, of everything that had to be done for the two weddings, with a neat tick beside everything that had been done.

She was good.

He didn't want to think about how good she was.

He drove back to his guesthouse, dumped his gear and made his way disconsolately down to the lobby. He needed something to do. Anything. Even if it was just to stop him thinking about Jenny.

Especially if it was to make him stop thinking about Jenny.

'You should go to the beach,' the guesthouse proprietor told him. 'It's a wonderful day for a swim.'

'I need to—' he started, and then thought, No, he didn't need to do anything. 'The beach looks crowded.'

'That's just the front beach,' his host told him. 'There's no need to be crowded at Sandpiper Bay. All the kids go to the front beach. They say the surfing's better there, but in truth it's just become the place to be seen. And being so near Christmas there'll be lots of out-of-towners coming for picnics. Family parties and such. If you want a quiet beach, I can draw you a map showing you Nautilus Cove, which has to be one of the most perfect swimming places in Australia.'

So ten minutes later he was in the car, heading south for a swim.

There were two cars at the side of the road when he pulled up—expensive off-roaders—and he was paranoid enough to be thankful they weren't Jenny's.

'There might be a couple of locals there,' he'd been told. 'But they won't mind sharing.'

Actually, *he* did mind sharing, but it was a bit much to expect to have the beach to himself. And two cars hardly made a crowd.

There were a few empty beer cans by the side of the road. That gave him pause for a moment. In this environmentally friendly shire, roadside litter was cleared almost as soon as it happened. Were the owners of the off-roaders drinking?

No matter. He could handle himself. He just wanted a quick swim. He tossed his towel over his shoulders and strode beachwards. As he topped the sand hill, the cove stretched out before him, breathtakingly beautiful. Golden sand, gentle surf, sapphire sea. There was a group of youths at the far end of the beach—the off-roaders' occupants? Surely not, he thought, frowning. They looked too young to be driving such expensive cars. Someone was yelling. It looked a small but intimidating group of youths. Drunken teenagers showing off to each other?

He didn't want trouble, and they looked like trouble. He'd find another beach.

But then he hesitated. A figure broke from the group. Someone shoved and the figure stumbled. There was raucous laughter, cruel and jeering.

Someone was in trouble. They were a few hundred yards from him, and it was hard to see. But then... He focussed. It was a woman, he thought, and the woman seemed to be carrying a child. She took a few more steps towards him.

Jenny.

She was trudging through the soft sand, carrying Henry. Henry was clinging to her, his face buried in her shoulder, as the taunts followed them.

'Get the hell off our beach!' they yelled. 'Take your deformed kid with you.' A beer can hurtled through the air. It didn't hit Jenny, but it hadn't landed before Guy was hurtling down the slope as if the hounds of hell were after him.

Jenny.

She was carrying a bag which looked a load in itself. She was concentrating on putting one foot in front of another, making sure she kept her balance in the soft sand. She didn't see him approach, every fibre of her being concentrating on getting off the beach—fast.

He reached her and put out his hands and stopped her. She flinched backwards.

'Jenny.'

She looked up at him, her face pale and gaunt, but as she saw who it was relief washed over her. She almost sagged. 'G…Guy. Get us out of here,' she stammered.

Another beer can headed in their direction. 'You're not moving fast enough,' someone yelled from the group. 'Hey, mister, keep away from them. The kid's a mutant.'

'Go,' Guy said urgently, and put his body between her and the barrage of cans and foul language. If he could have picked her up and carried her he would have, but picking up Jenny and Henry *and* their gear was a bit much even for someone with superhero aspirations. 'Go on up to the road,' he told her. 'Get to my car and wait for me.'

'But—'

'Go.' He tugged his cellphone from his belt. 'It's 000 for emergency here, isn't it?'

'Yes, but—'

'Go.'

She went. She didn't have a choice.

He stood his ground and dialled, and two seconds later he had a response. He stood facing the teenagers and spoke into the phone, loudly and firmly. Loud enough for them to hear.

'There's a group of what looks like under-aged drinkers on Nautilus Cove,' he told the officer who'd answered his call. 'I'm guessing they've been driving drunk, and none of them look old enough to hold a driving licence. Their cars look expensive. The kids' average age is about sixteen, so I'm guessing the cars are stolen. They're throwing beer cans at a woman and child on the beach. It's ugly.'

'We'll have someone there in minutes, sir,' the operator said. 'Can you stay on the line?'

'Sure. You'll hear everything that goes on.' Ten or eleven youths were staring at him now, with the uncertainty that stemmed from being drunk and out of control and seeing someone acting *in* control. They could turn on him, he thought, but he had a window of opportunity to stop that happening. They didn't know who he was, he sounded authoritative, and they were too drunk to act fast.

'If those cars are stolen,' he said, loudly but calmly, 'then you all have a major problem. The police are on their way. You can stay and get arrested, or you can go now.'

They stared at him in silence, drunk and still aggressive, but obviously trying to think. One took a menacing step forward.

Guy didn't budge. His face stayed impassive. 'The road into this beach is a one-lane track,' he said, conversationally, as though informing them of something important they should have remembered. 'If you try and drive out, you'll meet the police coming in. They'll block your way.'

There was a further uneasy silence. Then, 'Hey, Jake, I'm off.' One of the kids at the back of the group sounded suddenly scared. 'It's my old man's car. If I'm found in it I'll be grounded for years. As far as I'm concerned *you* pinched it. Not me.' He turned and stumbled away, half-running, half-walking, heading northwards along the beach. Around the headland were more beaches and bushland, where maybe he could hide himself and then head home to be innocent when his father found the car missing.

'Geez, Jake, my old man'll do the same,' another said, already backing and starting to run. 'Mac—wait up.'

'But you guys've got the keys,' Jake yelled, and hurled another can after his retreating mates.

Some of the other kids were backing away now. Half seemed inclined to stay with Jake. The others seemed inclined to run.

'We're on our way,' the policeman said on the other end of the phone line, and Guy nodded and held the phone helpfully out towards the kids.

'The police are on their way. This officer says so. He'd like to talk to you. Jake?'

'Go to hell,' Jake yelled.

'Is that Jake Marny?' the officer asked.

'I'll ask him,' Guy said, and held out the phone again. 'He says are you Jake Marny?'

'Geez—he knows us. The cops know us,' one of the kids yelled, panic supplanting aggression in an instant. And that was enough for them all. They were stumbling away, heading after the first two boys. For a long moment Jake stared at Guy, murder in his eyes, but it was the drink, Guy thought. Underneath, Jake was nothing but a belligerent kid—and a kid alone now, as his friends deserted him. He picked up another can and hurled it, but he didn't have his heart in it.

'What will you do, Jake?' Guy said, and Jake turned and found all his mates had gone without him.

He turned and ran.

The police arrived before Guy had made it up to where he'd parked his car. He told them what had happened, briefly and succinctly, and left them to it. They'd radioed in the registrations of the cars as soon as they saw them. They knew the kids.

'You'll take care of Mrs Westmere and Henry?' they asked.

'Sure,' he told them, and headed up the track to find them.

They'd reached his car. Jenny was leaning back on

the bonnet, still hugging Henry, her face buried in his hair

'Jenny?'

She looked up, and he saw that her face was rigid with tension and with anger. She was fighting back tears.

The little boy was huddled against her, and clinging. His body language was despairing.

Guy had never had anything much to do with children. He'd met Malcolm's kids, beautifully dressed and with precocious social manners. He was godparent to their youngest, and sometimes he even took them gifts.

'Thank Mr Carver,' their father would say, and the appropriate child would smile.

'Thank you, Mr Carver. This is a cool present.'

They were well-trained, well-adjusted kids, with two solid parents and all the advantages in the world.

But this mite… He was too thin. He was wearing some sort of elastic wrap on one of his legs and around his chest. His face was scarred and it was creased with crying. But now he faced Guy with the same sort of determination Guy saw in his mother. He wouldn't show the world he was upset. He blinked back tears and gulped.

Guy's heart twisted. This had nothing to do with how he felt about Jenny. Here was a whole host of other emotions.

He didn't get involved.

Too late. He looked from Jenny's face to Henry's and back again, and he was so involved he knew that from this minute on nothing would be the same again.

324   A BRIDE FOR CHRISTMAS

'Tell me what happened,' he said, and something about his voice made Jenny's face change. Her defences slipped a little.

'We were going to have a picnic,' she whispered, and he reached forward and took the basket from her grasp. It suddenly seemed to be unbearably heavy. He would have liked to take Henry, too, but Henry was clinging to his mother as if he'd never let go. 'Jack's been delivering Christmas presents. He dropped us off at one, and was going to pick us up at three. But…'

'But?'

'But I reckoned without Henry's scarring,' she whispered. 'Those kids… They arrived about fifteen minutes after we did. They were dreadful—weren't they, Henry?'

'What happened?'

Jenny shook her head, but Henry, surprisingly, took over. 'We had a ball,' he said. 'Mummy threw it to me and I missed it, and it rolled along the beach and ended up near one of the men's beer cans. When I went to get it he said I was deformed. He said, "Get lost, you ugly, deformed little s…"'

Henry's words were spoken almost exactly as he'd heard them. Guy heard the vindictiveness in the child's bleak recital, and he flinched. He tried to find his voice but it wasn't there. There weren't words.

He wanted to—

'Don't,' Jenny whispered, and he knew she was reading the primitive desire that was starting to build— to launch himself back down the beach and punch Jake and his mates until they bled.

It would achieve...nothing. And the police were there. They'd be taken care of.

'Why do you think they said that?' he said at last. He didn't recognise his voice. He didn't recognise his feelings. Dumb fury and more...

'I don't know,' Henry whispered.

'I don't know, either.' He was fighting desperately for the right words here. For any words at all. 'It surely isn't because you're deformed, Henry. You're wearing an elastic bandage and you have a couple of manly scars. That doesn't make you deformed.'

'The boy kicked me.'

'He was probably jealous,' Guy said, swallowing his anger with a huge effort.

He set Jenny's picnic basket on the ground and hauled it open, inspecting its contents with a critical eye. It gave him something to do. Independent or not, afraid of relationships or not, he wanted to hug them and hold them close, but he knew they'd accept no such gesture. And such a gesture wouldn't help. Nor would violence. He had to come up with something better.

'I thought so,' he said, feeling his way. 'There's pink lemonade in here. And *great* food. They only had beer. Jealousy makes people say funny things. Do you think that's it?'

'I don't know,' Henry said, staring down at the pink lemonade. 'That's silly.'

'Not as silly as calling you names.' Guy took a deep breath and turned his back to them both. 'When people have been angry about things they've called *me* names, too. A lady burst into tears at a swimming pool once. She called me a poor thing. She was stupid. I'm not a poor thing at all. Take a look at this.'

He tugged his shirt over his head, baring his back. They'd be seeing the myriad of scars running down the left side of his body. He heard Jenny's intake of breath and he winced. The last thing he wanted was sympathy, but this was the only thing he could think of to do.

His scars were a bleak reminder of the night Christa had been killed. She'd been speeding in her father's Maserati and she had been furious. 'Why can't you be a lawyer?' she'd screamed. 'I refuse to be married to some dope who organises tinpot weddings and doesn't have any money to even pay for a decent car. You drive a van with a wedding logo on it. I'll be damned if I'm ever seen in it.'

She'd slammed her foot on the accelerator, making the point that the van he drove could never be as fast as this. Guy could still see the truck in front of them, the driver's face frozen in horror as their car slid on black ice, over to the wrong side of the road, straight into him. They'd hit almost broadside, killing Christa instantly and throwing shards of splintering metal into his side.

He'd learned not to hate his scars, but until now he'd never been grateful.

'Would you call *me* deformed?' he asked Henry, his tone carefully neutral.

'You've been cut,' Henry whispered.

'And you've been burned. Most people start out as babies with no marks on them, but as interesting things happen they get marked. We all get marked from life. Somewhere I read that the native people in Australia deliberately make scars on their chests to show they're grown up. I think the more marks you have on you, the more interesting you become.' He smiled at the little boy, searching for a response. 'So you and me, Henry…we're really interesting. And drunk people, stupid people, get jealous. Or sad that they're not mature. Those guys on the beach were stupid kids who'd drunk too much. They'll be sick soon, and they'll go to sleep and wake up with a headache, and then they'll know they've been dumb and they've been wrong. But meanwhile we should enjoy our day.'

Enough. He'd made his point. Now he needed to lighten up. 'Hey, there's more here than pink lemonade,' he said, turning back to the basket. 'Do you have enough picnic for me, too?'

'Yes,' said Henry.

Jenny was doing a lot of silent blinking.

He glanced back to the beach, where a couple of the youths had been caught before they'd disappeared round the headland. He could see glimpses of them though the trees—police and kids. The kids were gesticulating wildly after their mates.

They needed to leave here, he thought. He didn't want any more invective as the police brought the kids up to the cars. 'Are there any more beaches around here, Jenny?' he asked.

'There's another cove about a mile south,' she managed, in a voice that was none too steady. 'But...we haven't got a car.'

'So it's the Ferrari,' Guy said, and grinned. 'Three people and a picnic basket in a Ferrari? We need to squash. And we need to leave now, before we have police watching. I think what I intend to do might be just a little illegal. But desperate times call for desperate measures.'

'Everyone in your car?' Henry said, brightening immediately. 'Now?'

'Absolutely now,' Guy said, with a lot more certainty than he was feeling. 'Let's go.'

So independent, aloof Guy Carver had a family picnic. Jenny couldn't believe it. She'd seen this man in celebrity magazines. She'd never dreamed he could be...human.

But human he was. From squashing them all into his Ferrari, from helping her to put on suncream, from making sand bombs...

He was more than human. She thought of the gift he'd given Henry by showing him his scarred back and the tears kept welling. Such a gift was beyond value. Henry had been given back his pride.

But she couldn't say anything. Guy was acting as if the whole ugly incident hadn't happened, and so must she.

They ate lunch, and Henry chattered about anything and everything, a contented six-year-old having a blissful day out with a man who drove a Ferrari and had life scars. What a hero. She watched as Guy spoke to him man to man, and her son's dreadful day disappeared to nothing and hero-worship took its place.

She didn't blame Henry. She was getting pretty close to hero-worship herself.

Guy lent her his cellphone. She contacted Jack to tell him Guy would be bringing them home, so not to worry about collecting them. Then they spent a couple of hours in the shallows, teaching Henry to float. The little boy hadn't spent much time in the water since his accident and he was nervous. Up until now Jenny hadn't persuaded him to put his face under water, but he'd do anything Guy asked. By mid-afternoon he was floating, kicking his scarred little legs, taking a brief gasp of air and floating again.

'I'm swimming,' he gasped, exultant, lit with happiness, and Jenny had to do a whole heap of blinking all over again.

Finally he was exhausted. Guy carried him up the beach and towelled him dry while Jenny packed the picnic gear. They loaded everything once more into the Ferrari, and Guy drove home with Henry's legs on his knee, picnic gear covering Jenny and a liberal supply of sand coating everything.

'Every Ferrari should look like this,' Jenny said, squashed and happy. 'It's perfect.'

'It is,' Guy said, and smiled at her, and Jenny felt her heart flip and flip again.

She was so close…

Don't, she told herself fiercely. This man is not of

your world. He is nothing to do with you. He just happens to be wonderful right now.

But not tomorrow?

Then they were pulling into the farm and Jack was limping down the steps to greet them, looking worried.

'There's been news about trouble with some kids on the beach,' Jack growled. 'Jenny, the police rang and say they want a statement from you. What happened? What's wrong?'

'Nothing's wrong,' Jenny said quickly. 'Something's right. Mr Carver taught Henry to swim.'

'I can swim, Grandpa,' Henry said sleepily. 'I can really, really swim, and Mr Carver says one day I'll be a champion.'

'You're a champion already,' Jack said gruffly, and lifted his grandson out of the car. He looked from Jenny to Guy, and then looked at his little grandson. His mouth twisted. Maybe the police had told him what had happened, Jenny thought, but he had the sense to let it go.

'Mother, Mr Carver's taught our Henry to swim,' Jack boomed, and Lorna waved her delight from the veranda.

'How wonderful. Mr Carver, what are you doing for Christmas?'

'It's Guy,' Guy said. 'And we're putting on a wedding on Christmas Day.'

'But not until late,' Lorna called. 'Christmas dinner's always at midday. You're to come to us. Now, no argument. A place will be laid.'

'You're coming for Christmas?' Henry said sleepily, and Jenny watched Guy's face as he stared at Henry.

He was fighting something, Jenny thought. And he was... losing?

'I'll come,' he said. 'If I can get all the arrangements in place...I'll be here.'

'He's lovely.' Late that night Jenny was sitting on the veranda with her mother-in-law, watching the stars over the distant ocean and listening to the soft clicking of Lorna's knitting needles.

'Guy?'

'Of course Guy,' Lorna said, and smiled. 'Jenny, he's just what you need.'

'I don't need anyone.'

'Of course you do,' Lorna said equitably. 'You're a lovely, healthy young woman. You've lost Ben, and that's dreadful, but Ben would be the first one to say you shouldn't spend the rest of your life grieving.'

'I could never leave you,' Jenny said, and Lorna looked at her face and saw the emotions working there.

'So you *are* feeling...?'

'Of course I'm feeling,' Jenny burst out. 'He's gorgeous, and I'd have to be non-human not to feel that. But he can have any woman he wants. He's a squillionaire. As soon as this wedding's over he'll go back to his life in New York.'

'And if he asked you to go with him?'

'He won't.'

'Jenny...'

'He won't,' she said definitely. 'And even if the impossible happened and he did, do you think I could take Henry away from all this? There's no way, and you know it.' She gave herself a mental shake and managed a grin. 'Okay, he's gorgeous, and if he happened to kiss me again…'

'He *kissed* you?' Lorna squeaked, and Jenny's grin firmed.

'There's things that even you don't know, Lorna Westmere. It's true I find him enormously attractive, and the memory of Ben won't hold me back. But it's only for a few days and then it'll be over.'

Guy spent much of that night awake. Thinking of Christa.

Thinking of Jenny.

He'd loved Christa, he thought. He remembered the bleakness, the guilt, the horror of those weeks after she'd been killed, but in contrast… He remembered the joy of Christa's life, how she'd made him laugh, how when she'd agreed to marry him he'd felt like the luckiest man in the world.

But then things had changed. She'd hated his new career. There'd been fight after fight. The relationship had soured to the point where if she hadn't been killed it would have been over.

He'd thought he'd been in love and he'd been wrong, and such a fundamental mistake had stayed with him ever since. Hell, if he could be so wrong about someone he'd believed he loved so much, how could he ever commit again?

He couldn't.

'So what the hell are you thinking of now?' he

demanded of himself aloud, and there was only one answer.

'You're thinking she's gorgeous. You're thinking that she's been through hell and her little boy needs someone and...

'You're thinking of *marrying*?' It was an incredulous demand into the darkness. 'You're thinking of taking them *home*?'

Why not?

The idea was so far out of left field that he almost laughed.

But...

But.

It wouldn't mess with my life, he told himself. She'd come back to New York. We'd get the best medical attention for those scars. Henry could go to school. Jenny could work in the company.

And live with you?

Of course live with me, he told his alter ego, letting the picture of domestic bliss build. I have a huge apartment. There's room to spare. Henry could have his own wing, and Jenny and I...

There was the nub of the matter. Jenny and I.

Jenny. Jenny as she'd been today, dressed only in a bikini, all womanly curves, defending her son, defiant, taking on all comers. Jenny squashed into his Ferrari, giggling with her son, meeting his eyes over Henry's head and sharing his laughter.

Jenny.

You haven't even slept with the woman, he told

himself, and he sounded desperate, even to himself. How do you know you want her every night for the rest of your life?

Because I do, he thought, suddenly sure.

It was crazy. It was way too fast. But the thought of Jenny in his bed was suddenly immeasurably enticing.

It's too soon, he told himself, his heart for once agreeing with his head. The way you're feeling… It might just be sympathy.

It's not sympathy and you know it.

It might be. You thought you loved Christa.

You wouldn't be committing in the same way, he told himself. You can stay independent. What's the harm? If it doesn't work, what do you have to lose?

Nothing if you stay independent.

Can you stay independent?

Maybe. I can try.

CHAPTER SIX

KYLIE'S wedding took place two days before Christmas, and it was more than Kylie and Daryl had ever dreamed of.

Kylie moved though her wedding day in a blissful whirl. She looked totally in love with her wedding—and totally in love with her man. Daryl, too, looked as if all his dreams had come true. He had the woman he loved, and he had a wedding ceremony that would be the talk of the district for years.

For it was a true Carver Wedding.

The man had brilliance, Jenny thought, gazing round the transformed hall where the reception was being held. It was no longer a hall. Instead it was a smoky gambling den, straight out of the nineteen-twenties. Guy had spent the last few days painting sets, organising props, training a couple of acting students he'd flown in from Sydney, throwing himself into this wedding as if it was a vastly publicised celebrity wedding instead of the wedding of two butcher's assistants with no profit to be made at all.

His work was worth it for the sheer pleasure it gave, Jenny decided. It was fantastic. As every guest arrived they gasped in wonder, joining instantly into the pleasure of make-believe mingled with a true-love wedding. The press, arriving to see the first Carver Wedding in Australia, were hauled right into the theme, being directed to point their cameras at the groom's right side and make him look good or they'd be wearing concrete shoes before they knew what had hit them.

The photographers didn't know where to point their cameras next. Even Shirley Grubb abandoned her need for pink tulle and embraced the theme with enthusiasm.

'Oh, Jenny… I've been dreaming of this wedding since Kylie was born, and I so wanted everything to be right,' she confided towards the end of the evening. 'I was so upset when Kylie told me she wasn't doing it my way. But now… My two sisters are here. Their daughters had flash weddings in Sydney—no money spared—and you know what? They're *jealous*. They're jealous of their little sister who married Fred Grubb and never has any money to her name.' She hugged Jenny, and there were tears slipping down her face. 'He's fabulous,' she whispered. 'You're so lucky.'

Guy was fabulous? Jenny was lucky? Jenny examined the comment from all sides, then decided to ignore it and hand out a few more drinks.

She couldn't quite ignore it.

Guy was everywhere, working hands-on, making sure the event went without a hitch. He was dressed as a body-guard, armed and dangerous, his slicked-down hair making his face look somehow menacing, his mock pistols too obvious, moving among the crowd, making amiable if-you-don't-have-a-good-time-I'll-punch-your-lights-out comments—sure his wedding couple were safe.

I'd think *I* was safe if I had him for a bodyguard, too, Jenny thought while she dispensed drinks. But she shoved the notion aside and went to make sure the cake, an overblown affair, adorned with a miniature gangster and his bride driving away in their fancy car—*where had Guy found these props?*—was ready for cutting.

She put the thought of Guy to one side.

But she stayed achingly aware of him.

And Guy…?

He moved through the wedding with his customary efficiency, ensuring each and every guest took home memories to cherish. Whether it was adroit flirting with the bridesmaids, bullying Uncle Ern to take Cousin Cecilia onto the dance floor, or removing the third glass of champagne from fifteen-year-old Bert's grasp and re-placing it with cola. 'That stuff is a lady's drink—I never touch it,' he told the kid, who gazed at Guy in sus-picion and then decided that maybe cola really was okay. Wherever there was a need, there he was.

But at any given moment Guy knew Jenny's where-abouts. She was dressed in a pert maid's uniform, doing the same as him, working the crowd. He watched her laughter and her affection for these people. He watched as people responded to her with affection, and the more he saw of her the more his mind had to dwell on.

Jenny.

The night wore on. The crowd started to thin.

His awareness of Jenny built.

And the crazy idea from the night after the beach incident became louder and louder in his head. *You're thinking of marrying?*

Yes. Yes, he was.

He couldn't stay independent without her, he thought. It was a dumb notion, but maybe if he married her and kept her safe he could get her out of his system?

Or not. Whatever.

You're thinking of marrying.

Jenny had no time to talk to Guy until Daryl and Kylie had driven away, their found-for-the-occasion Buick trailing a suitable clattering of ancient shoes and tin cans. The guests dispersed with reluctance, the crew cleared the mess, and Jenny was left with Guy.

'That was fantastic,' she told him as they emerged into the warm night air, glad to be free of the fog inside. 'It was the *best* wedding.'

'It was, wasn't it?' Guy said. He flicked a switch and the lights of the hall disappeared. They were left in darkness, their two cars standing in solitary state in the abandoned car park. 'I'd forgotten how much fun it was to be hands-on.'

'I loved it.' She sighed in exhausted pleasure. 'There's no nicer thing than a truly happy wedding.'

'No,' he said, and paused.

It was one a.m. It was time she was home, Jenny thought ruefully. Henry would be awake at six, and the next day was huge. There was still planning to do for Anna and Barret's wedding, and Christmas was in two days' time.

Christmas…

Christmas without Ben was awful. She'd hated the last two Christmases. But now…things had changed, she thought, and she wasn't sure how. All she knew was that in the last few days she'd changed. She was no longer dreading Christmas.

Because of this man?

Maybe, but he didn't have to know it, she thought. He'd set something free in her that she hadn't known was imprisoned. She felt light and happy and young.

Whoa. This man was dangerous, she decided. Happy and young or not, she was Henry's mother, and she needed to go home to bed.

'Goodnight, Guy,' she said, and turned away, but his hands came out and caught her shoulders, turning her back to face him.

'Jenny…'

'Mmm?' She had to stay cool, she told herself. She mustn't let him see that just by touching him he could…he could…

He kissed her.

She let him kiss her. How could she not? It was a lovely, languorous kiss, a kiss to melt into, a kiss to lose yourself in. He was so big and dangerous and warm and safe and wonderful…

These were crazy thoughts. *She* was crazy, she decided, as the kiss went on and her entire being was consumed with the feel of him, the thought of him. Guy...

It was a magic end to a magic evening —to be kissed by Guy. Her life had been barren for too long. To have this man's hands hold her, to have this magic sensation drifting through her... It was wondrous.

The kiss went on and on, and she took as much as she gave. It was a healing, she thought as she savoured the feel of him. It was a lovely way to end her mourning.

And at some deep, primeval level she knew it was more than that. There was no thought of Ben as she kissed him, but as he pulled away at last she caught at the ragged ends of her self-control and told herself that of course this was because of Ben. She was a widow, and now she was re-emerging to the outside world. This was nothing more than a reawakening. So she sighed with absolute pleasure as he broke the contact, as he held her at arms' length and smiled down at her in the moonlight. She sighed with pleasure and tried to hold back the regret that the kiss was at an end. And she tried to think of Ben.

'You're beautiful,' he said, and she managed to smile back.

'You're not bad yourself, buster,' she whispered. 'Though I'm not sure I go for the hair oil.'

'I'm serious,' he told her.

Her smile faded and she looked up at him, wondering. 'Serious?'

'I want to ask you something.'

She didn't want to talk. She so wanted to kiss him again. She desperately wanted to kiss him again. But… She was a sensible woman. She had to move on.

'About Barret and Anna's wedding?' she asked. 'Can it wait until tomorrow? I'm really tired.'

'Jenny, I wondered if you'd be interested in marrying me.'

She stilled. The words seemed to echo over and over in the stillness. Marrying…?

He's gone mad, Jenny thought at last. The romance of tonight must have gone to his head.

'I beg your pardon?' she whispered, and he raked his fingers through his hair—then remembered the oil slick. He stared down at his oily fingers with a rueful smile.

'Urk. I've made a mess of that.'

'Of what?'

'Of my proposal.' He took a too-big handkerchief from his breast pocket and carefully wiped his fingers clean. 'I haven't had that much practice, you see. I didn't mean to do it.'

'Then why did you?' She was having trouble making her voice work. She was having trouble making *anything* work.

'I could make you safe,' he said, and she looked up at Guy's earnest face, at his mock pistols and his slicked-down hair, and suddenly, irresistibly, maybe even hysterically, she started to laugh.

'What?' he said, sounding offended, and she bit back her bubble of laughter and tried to be serious. Or tried to be light-hearted. Or something.

'I don't need a bodyguard,' she told him. 'But it was a very nice offer. Thank you.'

'I'm not offering you a bodyguard. I'm offering you a husband.'

She stilled at that, her laughter fading. It wasn't a joke, then. He was…serious?

He was asking her to marry him?

The idea was so preposterous that she almost choked.

'I'm already married,' she said, before she could stop herself, and she watched as his face changed.

'What—?'

'I'm married to Ben,' she said stupidly.

'Ben was killed two years ago.'

'Yes, but…' She took a deep breath, searching for… Searching for she didn't know what.

'I can't remember him properly,' she said inconsequentially. 'I can't remember the way he held me. I can't—'

'Jenny, it's natural.'

Was it? She felt her heart clench with a well-remembered pain. Ben was dead. Move on, people said. Her own mother-in-law… Let Ben go. And she had tonight. For the first time she had. But to have this moment become a decision about the rest of her life…

Ben, her heart screamed. Ben. I'm not ready to let you go.

'He's my husband,' she whispered. 'He's in my heart. I thought you at least would know that.'

Guy stood, gazing down at her in the silence.

'I do know that.'

'Then why…?'

'You make me feel different.'

'You make me feel different, too,' she said, and she put her hand up to his face and cupped the curve of his jaw. The feeling she had then...it was indescribable. Say yes, her heart screamed. Say yes before he changes his mind.

'I can't do it,' she whispered. 'You must see it's impossible.'

'Why is it impossible?'

'Henry...'

'Henry would come with us,' he said strongly, taking her hands in his, trying to make her see where his thoughts had taken him. 'You can't tell me he's getting optimal medical treatment here. The world's best doctors are in New York.'

She stilled. 'You'd take us both to New York?'

'Of course.'

'But our home is here.'

'I have a massive apartment in Manhattan. You can see the Statue of Liberty from—'

'Our home is here.' Her voice was flat, without inflexion, and suddenly desperately weary. 'Do you think I could leave Lorna?'

'Lorna has Jack.'

'She does. And she has me. And she has Henry. We're family, Guy.'

'You don't need family.'

'At Christmas?' she whispered. 'You're saying that two days before Christmas? That I don't need a family?'

'Hell, Jenny...'

'This is ridiculous,' she said, trying hard to be strong. 'We hardly know each other.'

'And yet you feel what I'm feeling.'

'I don't.'

'Jenny,' he said, and the hands holding her shoulders suddenly firmed. 'You're lying.'

Of course she was lying. Whatever he was feeling she was feeling, too. Multiplied by about a thousand. He drew her into him, his lips met hers, and she felt... She felt...

Heat.

The word slammed in her mind as the sensation slammed through her. Heat. A conflagration that was all-consuming, starting from her lips and flooding through the rest of her. As if she was dry tinder and a match had been held to the all-too-ready fuel.

She wanted him with every inch of her being. Her lips opened under his. She welcomed him with joy. Her hands came around his chest and tugged him closer.

Guy.

The kiss went on and on. Neither could stop it. Why should they?

Guy had asked her to marry him. This man who was holding her, who was making her feel as if life itself could start now...

Guy.

He was her employer.

The thought slammed into her mind and somehow it steadied her. The thought had her remembering that her feet were planted on Sandpiper Bay ground—and had to stay that way. Somehow she tugged back, and Guy gazed down at her in the moonlight, concerned.

'What is it, sweetheart?'

What right did he have to call her sweetheart? She loved it, she decided. But…she couldn't.

'Guy, leave it,' she demanded, and he let her take a further step back. The fact that her body was screaming to remain in his hold had to be ignored. It *must* be.

'What's wrong?'

'If you weren't my boss I'd slap your face,' she managed.

'Why?'

'For taking liberties.'

'You want to be kissed.'

'I don't.'

'You do.' He was teasing her with his eyes. He was smiling down at her. And there was such…love?

She was imagining it. Love? No.

She was married to Ben.

'I still love Ben,' she said, and tilted her chin.

'Maybe I still love Christa. But it's memories that we love, and memories make cold bedfellows.'

'You want me in bed?' She'd started to shake, and it wasn't from cold. Bed with this man… Bed with Guy…

'A man would have to be inhuman not to want you in his bed.'

She could do it, she thought. She could just step forward into this man's invitation and let her life be taken over.

She could be Guy Carver's wife.

The thought scared her witless. She steadied, trying desperately to see his invitation for what it was.

For some reason he wanted her. Well, maybe that wasn't so strange. Because she wanted him, too.

But he was a billionaire, and he lived in New York in a massive apartment. Henry would have the best doctors, and she... She...

She'd be Guy Carver's wife.

It seemed so ridiculous that she almost laughed. Almost.

'You don't even know me,' she whispered. 'You don't know Henry.'

'I know that I want you.'

'But I...' She tilted her chin again and met his gaze, knowing what had to be said and knowing she had to say it. 'Guy, I want family.'

'I'm offering—'

'Your name. Your millions. It's a fantastic offer.' She managed a rueful smile. 'There's probably thousands of women who'd jump at what you're offering. And if I was alone maybe I could make a go of it. You're saying we're sexually attracted, and we definitely are, but that's not enough to build a marriage. I'm Cinderella and you're Prince Charming, but I have a feeling that marriage for Cinders had its downside.'

'I've never heard any fairytale where they divorce,' he said, startled, but she refused to smile.

'No,' she said thoughtfully. 'But being all alone in his castle, with everyone knowing she'd come from rags to riches...she'd have to be grateful for ever. And if she'd had a son, then that little boy might feel the same and resent it.'

'You're flying off at tangents,' he said, half laughing, and she grimaced.

'I am,' she said softly. 'But I'm thinking forward. You see, I must. I have a future, but it's inextricably tied up with Henry's future, and Lorna's and Jack's and this little town.' Her chin tilted some more. 'When I first came here I was needful,' she told him. 'This little town made me happy, and I'll not walk away because you make me feel wonderful.'

'I make you feel wonderful?' he demanded, pouncing on her words, and she felt a stab of sudden anger.

'Of course,' she said scornfully. 'But you've jumped in at the deep end. You've figured for some reason that you want me, and the easiest way to have me is to install me in Manhattan and have me in the pieces of time you have left over from the rest of your life.'

'What's wrong with that?'

He couldn't see?

She had to be grown-up for the pair of them, she thought miserably. She had to be sensible. Her heart had to be ignored. She was a married woman with a son to care for. With responsibilities. With Christmas in two days and she hadn't even made her mince pies.

'If you don't know then I can't teach you,' she said. She took a deep breath, leaned forward and kissed him lightly on the lips. A feather kiss that was over before he could react. Then she stepped back and felt for the handle of her wagon door. She slid in, still looking at him.

'Thank you for the proposal,' she whispered. 'It was…magic. But you're my boss, Guy, and that's the way it has to stay. Now I'm going home. To my family. I have Christmas to organise.'

He'd made a proper hash of that.

How could he go home to sleep? He couldn't. So he made his way to the little beach where he and Jenny and Henry had swum only days before.

Family.

What was she asking him to do? Take Lorna and Jack as well as Henry back to New York with him?

No. She wasn't asking anything of him, he thought. She was simply looking at his offer in surprise and rejecting it out of hand.

It wasn't a ridiculous offer. He'd made it to no other woman but Christa.

Christa would have been happy with what he was offering Jenny, he thought. He could have provided everything she'd needed. She would have been able to do whatever she'd wanted.

Jenny wasn't Christa.

Christa had been easier. He'd known what Christa had wanted. She'd wanted what their parents wanted: prestige and money.

He had that. He was offering it to Jenny, and she'd knocked it back. What else did he have to offer her?

Nothing.

So move on, he told himself. You offered to marry her because you felt sorry for her.

Was that right?

No. It was much more. He wanted Jenny in his bed.

So it's sympathy and sex. You can find sex elsewhere. She doesn't want the sympathy. You've made your offer and it's been rejected. So move on.

Back to thinking of Jenny as an employee?

She wasn't the least like an employee.

She was just…Jenny.

CHAPTER SEVEN

THE next day was frantic. Barret and Anna and entourage arrived, and had to be taken through the arrangements. Then the arrangements had to be tweaked so bride and groom were happy, and those tweaks weren't insubstantial. Guy, who'd worked with both Barret and Anna before, did the front work while Jenny stayed in the background.

Last night might not have happened. She was briskly efficient and very, very capable.

'There's an extra bridesmaid? Get her here by two this afternoon and we'll fit her out. We have half a ton of pink tulle, and our seamstresses are enjoying themselves.'

'Anna doesn't like the wedding cake? No, that's okay. We'll soak it in brandy and call it Christmas pudding for the party afterwards. I can get a couple of ladies onto sponge cakes now. Have her draw up details of decorations.'

'Gifts for the bridesmaids? Pearls? Yes, it's too late to get seven identical necklaces locally, but I can contact a jeweller in Sydney and have them couriered.'

She reassured him every time he called her, and after every call he felt about ten years old and as if she was his schoolteacher.

That was the tone she was taking, he thought. Cool, distant and bossy.

She was also never there. Every time he found an opportunity to visit the shop she was somewhere else.

'She hasn't finished her Christmas shopping,' one of the sewing ladies told him.

The three women seemed to be having a wonderful time, sitting in the back room with a vat of coffee and half a ton of chocolate biscuits, their fingers flying. 'I think she's gone to find a present for Lorna.'

'Hush!' Guy turned to the shop's entrance to see Jack pushing Lorna's wheelchair inside. 'I don't like knowing my presents before Christmas Day,' Lorna called. 'So if you know, don't tell. Guy, I'm pleased we found you.'

'I'm busy,' he said, and then thought maybe he shouldn't be that blunt. Jenny obviously loved this woman. It was just…Lorna was part of the family thing that was threatening to engulf him.

'I won't hold you up,' Lorna replied, her voice holding a hint of reproof. 'And I'm not asking any favours, so you can stop looking like that. We just called to remind you that you're doing the Santa run in your Ferrari tomorrow. You need to be at our place at nine. Henry's really looking forward to it.'

Hell, he'd forgotten. He'd also forgotten Henry's face when he'd thought it might happen.

But…

Why not ignore a few buts here? he told himself. He could do this. It didn't mean getting emotionally involved—or any more emotionally involved than he already was.

Okay, he'd do it, and then he'd walk away. He'd moved his return flight to the day after Christmas. His escape route was organised.

How could you ask a woman to marry you and then look forward to getting back to your own life?

He was having an internal conversation, watched by Lorna and Jack and three seamstresses, but the conversation went on regardless.

Easy, he told himself. I didn't ask to join her life. I asked if she'd join mine.

No wonder she refused you.

'Fine,' he managed, and if he sounded ungracious he couldn't help himself. 'I'll be there.'

'Great,' Jack said warmly. 'We'll hang up a stocking for you.'

'A stocking?'

'Wait and see,' Lorna said. 'Our Santa does the best stockings.'

'He's still coming for Christmas dinner?'

'Of course he is. He promised. And he's coming at nine for stockings. He's cute,' Lorna told her daughter-in-law. 'He drives a wonderful car. Henry thinks he's the ant's pants.'

'Guy Carver is not the ant's pants. He is an American billionaire who happens to be my boss…'

'I'm sewing him a stocking.'

'Lorna, he *can't* have a stocking.'

'Everyone in the whole world needs a stocking. Now, what will Santa put in it?'

CHAPTER EIGHT

CHRISTMAS morning.

Guy woke, as was his custom, at five a.m. There was nothing to do.

There had to be something. One of the biggest celebrity weddings of the year was scheduled for five this afternoon.

He lay and watched the weak rays of dawn flitter across his counterpane, mentally ticking off everything that had to be done.

He'd made huge lists, and Jenny had delegated.

Every person in the town seemed to have something to do. The normal sleeping-in-front-of-television end to Christmas Day was not going to happen in Sandpiper Bay. Jenny had hauled in every local, and a few tourists as well, and she'd given everyone a job.

And the best thing was that nearly all of them were doing it for nothing.

'Barret and Anna can pay,' Guy had growled, when Jenny had told him.

'Yes, but most of the town's folk believe in Christmas.'

'So what's *that* got to do with it?'

'They believe it's wrong to work on Christmas Day. But if it's for something like aiding the tsunami effort it'll strike a chord. One of our local kids is working in the international aid effort and…'

'You're asking Barret and Anna to give a donation to *charity*?'

'No. I'm asking Barret and Anna to pay a fair price for labour and then we'll give it away.'

'It doesn't make sense.'

'Maybe for you it doesn't,' she agreed. 'But for us…it's our way.' She glared at him. 'If you want to take our profits for yourself…'

'Whoa,' he told her. And then he thought, What sort of employer/employee relationship was this? She'd just given away his profits.

But there had been no arguing, and now the whole town had jobs to do for the good of the tsunami relief effort. He could lie in bed and stare at the ceiling and think he should be back in New York.

Why should he be back in New York? Christmases back home were simply an excuse for ostentation.

He hated Christmas. Even before Christa had died he'd hated Christmas.

Five a.m. Nothing to do until nine.

He hated Christmas.

Nine. He walked up the veranda steps, carrying expensive truffles and vintage wine. The screen door slammed open and a pyjama-clad urchin catapulted through, crutches tumbling as Henry toppled forward to hug his legs.

A Labrador puppy came bouncing after him. The puppy reached Henry and Henry abandoned Guy. He sat down on the veranda and shoved his nose into the puppy's soft fur.

'This is Patsy,' he told Guy, his voice muffled by puppy. 'She was on my bed when I woke up, and she's all mine, and I have to train her.'

'That's great,' Guy said, feeling…emotional. That was the end of that resolution, then.

'And there's more.' Small boy and pup looked up at him, eyes glistening with Christmas joy. 'We've been waiting and waiting, and Santa's been, and there's stockings for everyone. But Mummy says we can't open them until you come.'

'Come on in,' Jenny said, and he raised his eyes from her son and smiled at Jenny.

She was simply dressed in clean jeans and T-shirt— a T-shirt adorned with sequins carefully sewn on to make a picture of Rudolph the Red-Nosed Reindeer.

She had two glowing Santa Clauses hanging from her ears.

She was smiling. Who needed grinning Santa Clauses when there was a smile like this?

'You're overdressed,' she told him. 'A suit at nine on Christmas morning? Pyjamas are more the go.'

'I don't wear them,' he told her, and she blushed. A great blush. It made him want to…

Keep it impersonal, he told himself harshly.

'Well, at least wear a Christmas hat,' she said, and handed him a hat. Then, when he didn't react, she took it back, reached up and placed it on his head. A red and white Santa hat.

Forget the hat. She was so close. She smelled of pine needles and mince pies and…and Jenny.

There was mistletoe over his head. He couldn't see it but he was sure of it. The desire to take her into his arms and kiss her senseless was suddenly overwhelming.

But Lorna was at the door, with Jack behind her, laughing and calling for them to come in.

'It's all very well for Henry,' Jack complained, 'he's got his puppy. But every single one of my presents is still wrapped, and if we don't get to these stockings soon I'm going to bust.'

Comparisons of this Christmas to every other Christmas he'd known were ludicrous. As a child he remembered formal Christmas mornings, drinks with business acquaintances where children were seen and not heard. A ludicrously over-the-top lunch where he was the only child—he hated the food and he hated the waiting, the waiting… Then his parents would sleep off their lunch, and some time towards evening his mother would call him in and they'd open their gifts. They weren't permitted to open them early as 'the tree looks so much better with gifts under it, and we'll keep that effect until all our guests have gone.'

Whatever his gift was, it would have been exquisitely wrapped and he'd have to admire the wrapping.

It was never anything he wanted. It was always something someone had recommended. 'Oh, we gave Guy a miniature violin—so sweet—I'm sure he's musical. He takes after my side of the family, not his father's…'

There was no violin today. This little family lived on a shoestring. The major present was the puppy. The rest of the gifts were…silly?

Some were silly, some were sensible—but it was a great mix. He watched as Henry unwrapped coloured pencils, a new collar and lead for his dog, and a vast parcel that turned out to be three months' supply of puppy food—Henry was so delighted he couldn't stop giggling, and there was a pause in the proceedings so Patsy could be photographed sitting on top of her future dinners… A rubber toy in the shape of a chook for Patsy, a game of wooden blocks that Henry received with joy…

Interspersed with these—for they took turns to open gifts—were the adult presents. Romance novels for Lorna, and a crazy device for massaging feet that Patsy took instant exception to. A new summer hat for Jack—he had to take off the reindeer antlers he was wearing, so he placed his new hat on and then propped his reindeer antlers over the top.

And for Guy…

He'd expected nothing. Of course he'd expected nothing. But there was a whole stocking stuffed with silly things. When he saw the stocking he felt his heart sink, expecting to be embarrassed that this family had spent money on his behalf, but the stocking simply made him laugh.

His very own pair of Christmas antlers—to go on top of his Santa hat. A red nose that flashed— 'Wear it now,' Henry decreed, and he did. A mango—a perfect piece of fruit, wrapped with care, a vast red ribbon around it. He stared at the mango, and Jack grinned and handed him a knife and a plate and said, 'Eat it now, mate—cos it's Christmas.' So he took off his red nose and spread mango from one ear to the other and it was the best thing he'd ever eaten.

What else? A boat made of ice lolly sticks—'I wanted to make you a Ferrari,' Henry told him, 'but you've already got one. And this floats. I've put water in the bath all ready. You want to see?' So they had to troop into the bathroom and watch Henry's boat—the *Jennifer-Patsy*—take her maiden voyage round the bath, and then they had to rescue the *Jennifer-Patsy* and haul Patsy out of the bathtub and dry her, and then dry themselves, and then watch as Guy opened his last present, which was a glitzy magazine titled *How to Plan Your Perfect Wedding*.

'Lorna's idea, mate, not ours,' Jack said hastily, and then they were all laughing, and Lorna was handing round mince pies and it was time to take the Ferrari on its Santa run.

Which was crazy all by itself.

Santa—the local police chief—was waiting at the police station. With a paper bag of mince pies at his side to keep his strength up, Guy collected Santa and his lollies. Then he followed Santa's directions and made a clean sweep of Sandpiper Bay. Santa rang his bell with such strength that Guy's ears would take months to recover. From every house came children and adults and oldies, and Santa tossed lollies indiscriminately. Even from the vast houses owned by the squillionaires came kids and dogs and men and women, all at various stages of Christmas, all smiling, all cheering as they got their lollies and then disappearing back into their homes to celebrate the festive season.

Their last stop was back at the farm. Santa had arranged for his wife to collect him from there. Santa emptied the remains of his sack onto their veranda, and then drove away in state in the town's police car.

'Now dinner,' Lorna declared, and Guy wondered how he could eat any more. But of course he did—and how could he ever have thought he couldn't? He remembered the sophisticated Christmases he'd endured as a kid. There was no comparison. He ate turkey and gravy and crispy roast potatoes and every sort of vegetable he could imagine with relish. Then Jack demanded he light the pudding—and how could he not eat pudding after that?

'Brandy sauce, brandy butter, cream or ice-cream?' Lorna asked.

Jenny grinned and said, 'He'll have all four, Mum, just like everyone else.'

And Guy looked across the table and thought, She's calling Lorna Mum and suddenly…suddenly he wanted to do exactly the same.

If he married Jenny he could…

Henry was down on the floor, subsiding into an afternoon nap with Patsy, and Guy thought, I wonder what the quarantine regulations are for taking dogs into the US.

'It's not going to happen,' Jenny said softly, and he looked across the table and saw a flash of sadness behind the laughter that had been there all morning.

It was as if she knew that what he was offering was serious—but it wasn't enough.

He couldn't leave her.

He couldn't.

'No one sleeps before the washing up,' Lorna said.

And Guy heard himself saying, 'I'll wash up. That's my Christmas gift to you.' He'd brought excellent wine and chocolates as gifts, but he knew now that they were dumb gifts. Sure, they liked them, but mangoes were better.

'I won't let you do it alone,' Jenny said, and grinned. 'Nobility is my middle name. Jack, Lorna—that means you sleep. Immediately. Henry and Patsy already are asleep. Guy, into the kitchen.'

'Aren't I the boss?' he asked, and everyone smiled.

'Not around here, mate,' Jack told him, gripping his wife's hand and holding it tight. 'The women in this family make the rules.'

So they stood in the kitchen, and he washed and she wiped, and suddenly the noisy fun gossip faded to nothing. There was a silence which should have been a contented silence, but it was…tense.

'Jenny?' he tried softly, but when he glanced at her, her smile had faded and her face was rigid with strain.

'Don't say it, Guy,' she whispered. 'This is my family. This is my place. I'm not going anywhere.'

* * *

The wedding was due to take place at five p.m. They left at three. Only Patsy opened one eye and wagged a weary tail as they departed.

They drove in Jenny's wagon as they had final supplies in the back. 'Everything's there,' Guy told Jenny. 'I ran a final check before I came to your place.'

'And I ran a final check before everyone woke up,' Jenny retorted. 'Too many cooks, Mr Carver?'

'Double-checking doesn't hurt anyone,' he replied as they drove down the magnificent eucalypt-lined driveway of Anna's mansion. There was a cluster of expensive cars parked in front, obviously belonging to in-house guests. Within two hours there'd be hundreds of cars.

'I'll check the bride; you check the groom,' Jenny told Guy, forgetting she was the employee again, but acting on a rule they both knew. The most important duty in any wedding ceremony is to make sure you have two live bodies willing to say *I do*.

They rang the bell, a butler opened the door—and here was the first discordant note of the day. A man's voice was raised in fury.

'You can't do this, you bitch. I'll ruin you. I'll see your name raked across every tabloid and it's no holds barred. If you call this off just because of some moralistic damned scruples then I'll see you in hell. Have you got any idea of what this'll do to your PR?'

Before they had time to step inside—and before the butler had time to do what he should have done in times of crisis—refuse admittance—Barret himself shoved his way past them. They stared after him as the movie star disappeared behind the house. There was the sound of a motor being gunned into life—and then the squeal of a car being turned too fast and driven too fast away.

'There's your groom, Mr Carver,' Jenny murmured, wincing. 'Now for the bride.'

Anna, surprisingly, seemed to still be in control. She was sitting on the second top step of the great staircase, as if her legs had given way, but as Jenny approached she even managed a shaky smile.

'That's two less guests for the wedding,' she murmured. 'We're minus one groom and we're minus one bridesmaid. Happy Christmas.' She sniffed. 'Oh, help.'

'Happy Christmas to you, too,' Jenny murmured, and sat down beside her while Guy looked on from below stairs. 'Um…was that what I think it was? Have you just called off the wedding?'

'You bet,' Anna whispered. 'I may live to regret it, but I don't think so.' She looked down to her butler. 'Max, I won't be needing you for a bit.'

'Should I start phoning a few people?' Max asked, sounding horrified. 'Maybe I can stop a few coming.'

'There's three hundred people coming to this wedding,' Guy said. 'They're coming from all over the world, and the wedding's less than two hours away. Our chances of stopping the crowd are negligible.'

'In that case go and have a stiff drink,' Anna told the butler. 'Or two.'

'Stay sober, Max,' Guy warned. 'We're going to need you.'

'Yes, sir,' the butler said. He looked at his mistress in concern. Then he looked from Guy to Jenny and back again. 'Fix it if you can,' he said softly. 'I don't think she's seeing what she's done.'

'I'm seeing what I've done all too clearly,' Anna retorted. 'I found him with one of my bridesmaids. In Georgia's bedroom. In Georgia's bed. *I* haven't done anything. Barret, on the other hand…'

'Can you verify this?' Guy asked the butler, and Max nodded.

'I was coming upstairs to remind Miss Anna that you were to be here at three. Miss Anna was standing at Miss Georgia's bedroom door looking…'

'Gobsmacked,' Anna said, and suddenly she giggled. It sounded dangerously close to hysterics. 'You saw them, too, didn't you, Max?'

'Yes, miss. But…'

'There are indeed buts,' Guy said gravely. 'I'd imagine Barret's heading straight back to Hollywood. Anna, if he's true to form he'll slur your name in every ear that matters. People *expect* Barret to play around. They won't feel sorry for Barret. They'll feel sorry for you.'

'I don't care,' Anna said, defiant, but Jenny saw the tremor in her fingers and knelt to sit beside her and take her hand. To her surprise, the woman gripped and held. Hard.

'Where's everyone else?' Guy was asking, and Jenny

thought, He's done this before. He's coped with disasters like this.

'We had eggnog for brunch,' Anna explained. 'Barret made it. Everyone's half-drunk already, so they're sleeping it off. Or I thought they were sleeping it off. I don't know how Barret managed…' Her voice trailed away in disgust.

Good, Jenny thought. If she was up to technical thinking then maybe other sorts of thinking were possible, too. She glanced down at Guy, their eyes locked, and she could see that he was thinking exactly what she was thinking.

Guy had agreed to do this wedding because he felt sorry for Anna. Nothing had changed. And if Anna had to be protected…

'*No one* must feel sorry for you,' she said, and Guy nodded, as if he'd just been about to say the same thing.

'What do you mean?' Anna demanded, and Guy took over.

'Anna, you've just come out of rehab. Everyone's looking at you. If I know Hollywood, they're expecting you to fail, and they're half hoping you will. Half the people coming to this wedding will be coming out of curiosity.' He hesitated, but then he went straight to the hard question. 'Did you touch the eggnog?'

'I drink soda water,' she said stiffly, and Guy nodded.

'I knew you'd say that. It's why I'm giving you a Carver Wedding. You deserve a second chance. But, the way I'm seeing it, this could be your ruin. Unless we turn it around. Unless we make this into a celebration regardless. You've ditched all the other bad habits. Barret was simply the last habit you ditched.'

'What…?' said Anna.

'Let's get this organised,' he said, striding up the stairs to join them. Anna and Jenny were still sitting on the second top stair. They shifted sideways and he sat down, too, so Anna had Jenny on one side and Guy on the other, with Max watching, stunned, from below. 'We need to move fast.'

'What…?' said Jenny.

'If people have flown from London and New York and wherever to see a celebration, and they don't see one, they're going to be disappointed,' Guy said. 'And it's Christmas Day, which makes it worse. They'll be hugely disappointed if they're turned away without food. And hungry, disappointed celebrities can get nasty. If they don't see you, they'll talk about you until the next sensation happens.'

Anna shuddered. 'Don't.'

'What should we do?' Jenny asked simply, and waited.

'We go ahead as if it was meant to happen,' he said. 'Anna, you need to act. When all your in-house guests wake and your other guests arrive, you greet them as if this is the best thing that can possibly have happened.'

'I don't know how…'

'I know how,' Guy said. 'Jenny, the time to be taken for the ceremony needs to be taken up with something else. I want a map of the way to the beach—that's about half a mile from here, isn't it? Down through the hills?

An easy walk? I thought so. As every guest arrives they're to be handed a champagne cocktail, a tube of sunscreen and a bathing costume and sarong if they don't have their own. Jenny, get onto the local store owners now. Tell them we'll pay ten times face value if they have the stuff we need here in half an hour. Oh, and the camping store. I want as many folding tables as they have, plus beach umbrellas. Same price applies. Double it if you need to. As the workers arrive—our people are due here at four— they'll start ferrying the wedding breakfast to the beach. I want people toddling over the sandhills, cocktail in hand—we'll have people along the way replenishing glasses—arriving at the beach and seeing Anna in all her glory.'

'All my glory?' Anna said, gulping and looking awed.

'You'll be floating on a sea of flowers. You'll be wearing a tiny bikini and holding a fruit cocktail—something non-alcoholic, but no one need know—something that looks truly splendid. We'll have your bridesmaids—minus one, who I trust will take herself the way of your bridegroom—floating round on air mattresses. We'll use all the wedding flowers and make them look sumptuous. And you'll be saying *Welcome to the rest of my life. This is who I am. A woman who can put on the best party in the world.* It'll make Barret look stupid and you look magnificent.'

'But…' Anna whispered. 'But…'

'But what?'

'There's still the celebrant,' she whispered. 'There's

all the pink tulle. I have editors from the top celebrity magazines flying in especially to see a wedding.'

'They *will* see a wedding,' Guy said.

'Whose?'

He took a deep breath.

'Mine.' And then he looked at Jenny. 'Ours.'

For a moment there was nothing but silence. Jenny stared at Guy. Anna stared at Guy. And then Anna turned to Jenny.

'You'd pretend to get married? But…'

'There'd be no pretend about it,' Guy said softly. 'Anna, I love this woman.'

That's me, Jenny thought dumbly. He's talking about me.

'I've already said I wouldn't,' she whispered, and Guy nodded and reached across Anna and took her hand.

'I know. I was dumb.'

'Excuse me, but you don't want me sitting in the middle here,' Anna said, sounding close to hysterics, and Guy grinned.

'I've already proposed to the woman in moonlight. It didn't work. I'm trying again. Stay where you are.'

'Harumph,' said Max from below, and Guy nodded.

'You, too. I need witnesses.'

'What…?' said Jenny, and paused.

'You mean what am I asking?' Guy said. He hesitated, then ploughed on, a man making a confession before all. 'This morning I opened my stocking and found a boat made with ice lolly sticks.'

'So what?' she whispered, and he smiled.

'Let me finish,' he said. 'I need to. Jenny, fifteen years ago I turned my back on a career in law and used my savings to buy what must have been the most battered van our side of the Mississippi. I was so proud of that van. I used to walk round and pat it. But then…'

'Then Christa was killed.'

'She was,' Guy said. 'And the shock of her death made me think…well, that her values were true. I wanted to show myself that the sacrifice was worth it, and some warped, twisted part of my brain said the way to do that was make money.'

'And you have,' Anna said. 'You're such a success.'

'Not a success if I can't have my Jenny,' he said, and his eyes were holding Jenny's and they might as well be alone. 'I met Jenny a little more than a week ago, and I love everything about her. I love her bravery and her honesty and her caring and her laughter. I love her son and her son's puppy, and her mother-in-law and her father-in-law. I love the place where she lives. I was dumb enough to think maybe I could marry part of that and cart it back to New York, set it down as a possession. But it's not like that, is it, Jenny? You refused me for all the right reasons.'

'I…'

'I'm not asking you that same question now,' Guy said softly. 'I'm asking if you'll let me share your life. If you'll let me take over where Ben left off—loving you, loving what you are and where you are, just…loving.'

'Guy…'

'I've been thinking,' he went on, as if he was nervous that she'd say no before he'd fully explained. 'After the Christmas stocking…all the way round Sandpiper Bay with Santa beside me…I thought.'

'What did you think?' Anna asked, awed, and Jenny thought she'd asked the right question. She should have asked it herself, but the words wouldn't quite come out.

'I thought I could move my base to here,' he said. 'I thought we could make Sandpiper Bay the wedding capital of the world.' He grinned. 'Though I think we'd need two sets of premises. We'll take over the haberdashery and use part of it to incorporate Bridal Fluff. For any bride who wants fluff. And we'll have a special rate for locals—kids who've lived in the district for years and can't afford normal rates.' He hesitated. 'Maybe we could extend that idea to our other smaller premises, too,' he said. 'It takes thinking about, but then I'm not going to be working so hard in the future. I'm going to be doing a lot of lying on the beach, with our son and our puppy, and I can think things through then.'

'Our son?' Jenny said, astounded, and Guy's smile became almost shamefaced.

'It's not my right to share Henry's life,' he told Jenny. 'But if you'll let me…I want to so much. You have no idea how much I want to share.'

'You love Henry?'

'Almost as much as you,' he said, still gripping her hand, still holding her eyes, while Anna sat hornswoggled in between. 'I thought I loved Christa, and my shock at her death left me thinking I didn't know what love was. But I *do* know what it is. I know who it is. It's you. My love. My Jenny.'

There was a moment's stunned silence while everyone held their breath. Jenny didn't move. It was left to Anna to respond.

'Well,' Anna said. *'Well!'*

'Well,' echoed Jenny. She shook her head, as if shaking off disbelief. 'My thoughts exactly.'

'Are you going to accept?' Anna asked. 'I only ask because…'

'Time's getting on,' Max said from below, grinning broadly. 'And I've thought of something. You can't just swap from one wedding to another. There's laws in this country. Four weeks' notice before a wedding can take place.'

'But we could make our promises today,' Jenny whispered, and the whole world held its breath.

'You mean it?' Guy asked at last, and she smiled.

'Of course I mean it. I shouldn't. I loved Ben so much. But these last few days…I've been thinking and thinking, and the more I think the more I know Ben would say to grab life with both hands.' She hesitated. 'And I've been following your logic. Does this mean you want a shonky van again and not a Ferrari?'

'It might,' Guy said, cautious, and Jenny beamed.

'Hooray,' she said. 'Then let's do it. We'll write it into the wedding vows. You get my wagon and I get the Ferrari.'

He lunged at her across Anna's knees—and Anna,

movie idol of millions, a woman who'd just been betrayed and whose wedding plans were in the dust, dissolved into helpless laughter while Guy Carver of the Carver corporation reached across her and kissed his intended bride as if there was no tomorrow.

CHAPTER NINE

GUY CARVER was a wedding planner extraordinaire. His own wedding was no exception. He would have liked to have had more than a few hours' notice but, given the circumstances, what was achieved was little short of miraculous.

Firstly he barked orders at everyone, while Jenny and Anna looked on in admiration—and with just a touch of the giggles. Then he swept Jenny into her wagon and carried her back to the farm.

'For I'm not doing this without consent,' he said. Ignoring Jenny's protest that Jack was her father-in-law, and no consent was needed, he carried her into the farmhouse as a groom carried his bride. He woke the startled Lorna and Jack and Henry and Patsy from their afternoon nap and asked with all the deference in the world whether there were any objections to his taking Jenny for his bride.

They were delighted.

'It's so lovely,' Lorna sniffed. 'We'll miss you, sweetheart, but we always knew you'd move on.'

'Then you'll be disappointed,' Guy said roundly. 'You're stuck with the lot of us for ever. Me and Jenny and Henry and Patsy and whoever else comes along. Mind, I'll have to make the odd trip overseas—but maybe we can all go. Maybe you'll even like New York.'

They were speechless—for a whole two minutes—and then Lorna started to plan.

'So you're getting married this afternoon?'

'We're having a ceremony this afternoon, to get Anna out of a hole,' Jenny told her. 'The press will indeed see a Carver Wedding. We'll repeat our vows in a month for the legalities.'

'We'll repeat our vows night and morning for the rest of our lives,' Guy said exultantly, but Lorna was concentrating on more important issues.

'You need a dress, Jenny. Not the one you wore for Ben.'

'No,' Jenny said. She grinned, delirious with happiness and ready to be silly. 'Maybe I can wear togs and thongs?'

'Togs and thongs?' Guy queried.

'Bikini and flip-flops,' Jack translated, and Guy's face brightened.

'I can cope with that.'

'You can. She can't,' Lorna said roundly. 'Jenny, dear…'

'Mmm?' Jenny was hugging Henry, who was carefully thinking about all the rides he was now going to get in a Ferrari. 'Yes?'

'I never suggested it when you married Ben—to be

honest I loved it that we made your wedding dress together. But now…I don't suppose you'd consider wearing mine?'

'Yours?' Jenny said, awed. 'Oh…'

'You're practically the same size as I was forty years ago, and the fashions have come back…' So they all trooped into the bedroom to Lorna's camphor chest, and then Lorna realised that this was serious and turned and shooed out the menfolk.

'You get back to Anna's,' she told Guy. 'You'll see Jenny at the ceremony and not before.'

'Yes, ma'am.'

But as Guy made his way out through the front door Lorna wheeled herself out of the bedroom in a hurry.

'I know it's a minor detail,' she called, 'but we need to know when and we need to know where.'

The when was eight p.m. The where was on the beach. The very loveliest time of day.

The beach was crowded with celebrities from all over the world, and almost every inhabitant of Sandpiper Bay. In their midst was Anna, bouncing around as if she had the world at her feet. Whatever mortification she was feeling, she was hiding it with brilliance.

It would be Barret who was mortified now, Guy thought, watching as Anna attracted everyone's admiration. He could even feel sorry for Barret. Anna was lovely.

She wasn't as lovely as Jenny.

Guy was standing on the shoreline, where sun-warmed sand gave way to sand made damp by the receding tide. There was a temporary altar behind him, and the celebrant was beaming before it. In truth, the celebrant was a little put out—she'd expected to marry superstars—but the fact that she was marrying Guy Carver and the wonderful Jenny, who everyone knew, almost made up for it.

There was only one attendant. Guy's best man was Henry, who held the ring—the Sandpiper Bay jeweller had been delighted to open for such a need—with the reverence it deserved. Henry had his own attendant—Patsy was right by his side—but she wasn't diverting Henry from ring-minding. His hero was at stake—a stepfather who had the marks of life upon him. He kept glancing up to Guy as if he might evaporate, and every time he did Guy looked down at him and winked.

Henry was practising winking back.

'They look like two cats with one canary,' one of the reporters said to her photographer, and the photographer sniffed her agreement.

'It's beautiful.'

'If you get that lens wet you're dead meat,' the reporter said, but she sniffed, too.

And then the bride arrived. By tractor. You couldn't get over these sand hills except by foot or all-terrain vehicle, so Lorna, dressed in her wedding best, drove a trifle erratically but with aplomb, while Jenny stood on the side and held on for dear life. The crowd—wisely—parted before them. Lorna reached her destination, flushed with success. Jack helped his daughter-in-law down and Jenny was deposited by Guy's side. To be married.

'With this ring I thee wed...'

Maybe the photographer's camera did get wet then, for there was hardly a dry eye on the beach as Jenny and Guy stood together against a backdrop of setting sun and sea and mountains and were made one.

'It's a perfect Carver Wedding,' Jenny whispered as their wedding kiss finally ended, and Guy smiled at her with a smile that said life for both of them was just beginning.

'I brought you lousy Christmas presents,' he told her. 'I had to make up somehow. Merry Christmas, Mrs Carver. With all my love.'

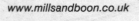

1206/055/MB066 V2

Unwrap three gorgeous men this holiday season!

For three women, the Christmas holidays bring more than just festive cheer – even as they try to escape the holiday celebrations and forget about absent partners or failed relationships.

What they don't realise is that you can't escape love, especially at Christmas time…

On sale 17th November 2006

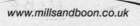 www.millsandboon.co.uk

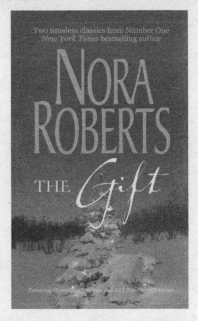